The Eye of the Storm

Tori Sunners

First paperback edition
September 2024

Book design by Gemma Cronnie

Image Credits – Woman – Photo by Filip Mroz on Unsplash. Eye- Photo by Filip Mroz on Unsplash, Clouds – Photo by Casey Horner on Unsplash.

ISBN: 978-1-0687712-0-0

To Evie and Darcey, because you are simply everything.

Chapter 1

Some days dragged more than others and this had been a particularly slow one. She loved her job she kept telling herself, she'd gone into this line of work for a reason but today for some reason she just wanted it to reach five pm.

She'd had a steady flow of women in her room that day. Some for run of the mill growth scans, others to check on the progress of their baby following concerns or complications. Nothing out of the ordinary nothing that would stick in her mind.

The couple she'd just had in had been classic new parents. Holding each other's hand during their scan, looking adoringly into each other's eyes as they marvelled at the life they had created together. A delicate tear had spilled down the mother's cheek as she heard the heartbeat of the child she had never met but already adored. All a bit vomit inducing in her opinion.

One more to go. Just one more and then she would be on her way home, she might even pick up a cheeky bottle of red to keep her warm tonight, she was looking forward to it.

She stretched her neck over to one side, lifting her arms high in the air to extend her spine allowing her back some much-needed movement from a day of sitting sedentary.

Bringing up the notes of her final patient of the day she had a brief glance over the document to familiarise herself with the task at hand. Another standard 24-week scan, this ladies last, all being well.

Opening the door, she looked down the long corridor that ended in the waiting room. She had long since stopped bothering to walk down each time to collect her patient, choosing instead to holler their name out into the ether. It was far more efficient.

'Margot Littlewood'

After a second or two she saw movement and retreated back into the room leaving the door open to allow her patient access.

She was greeted by an efficient looking, tall, slender woman in her early thirties. Having clearly come straight from work, she wore a white blouse and black pencil skirt pulled up over a petite bump. Putting her bag down on the chair she made her way over the bed, lay down and lifted up her top without needing prompting. Efficient, no nonsense, she was going to like this woman she could tell.

'Hello Mrs Littlewood'

'Miss, please if you don't mind.'

'Of course, my apologies, is it just yourself today or are we waiting for someone else to join you?'

'No just me, thank you.' She smiled as if to insinuate that there was no need for further comment on her single status.

'No problem at all, right then let's get started. As you know you're here for your final scan and blood works. All being well we won't then see you again as you'll move onto the maternity wards care. I see everything has gone smoothly for you so far, are you feeling well today?'

'Yes, perfectly fine thank you.'

'And are you up to date with your pre-natal booster vaccinations?'

'Yes, I received my third last month.'

'Great. Well, I'll start with the blood test so that it can be sent off straight away, then I'll go through the scan whilst the bloods are being processed and they should be sent back to me before we're done here.'

'OK thank you.' The lady rolled up the blouse sleeve on her right arm and offered it out to her.

Having already sized her up, she was predicting that the self-assured mother to be wouldn't be squeamish or reluctant to have her bloods taken and she was relieved to see she was correct, she hardly flinched when the needle pierced her skin and sat calmly watching as her own blood departed her arm and filled the vial. Once there was an adequate amount withdrawn, she labelled up the bloods and sent it down the chute on the wall next to her down to the lab where they would process it immediately for testing.

The scan all went smoothly. A healthy heart beat

and a nice well-behaved baby that didn't wriggle around too much as some did, making her look incompetent when she couldn't get a clear picture. This was a good way to end her day.

'Ok, that all looks fine Miss Littlewood. I've printed you off a picture that you can collect at reception on your way out. Finally, would you like to know the sex of the baby today?'

'No thank you I'd rather wait.'

'Of course, no problem at all'. She felt a thrill at the privilege of knowing what this woman was going to have when no one else did.

'I'll just bring up your blood works and then you can be on your way.'

She closed her screen to open up the secure messaging site used solely for the recording of tests and was relieved to see that there was a new result waiting for her to open. She might actually be able to get away a bit early today at this rate. Opening up the results she scanned her eyes over the numerous markers. Halfway down the page her eyes stopped moving and she did a double take at the figures in front of her, Fuck, she thought.

She took a second to consider her next steps, she had not had one of these for a long time and on the spot she couldn't think of the protocol and exactly what she was meant to say.

In a slight panic she decided that she would be best saying nothing and getting someone else in to help her. Maybe she'd read it wrong, whilst all the time knowing that she hadn't.

'I'm just going to get a colleague in to take a look

at something for me.' She mumbled before heading over to the door and making her escape, her heart pounding with nervous anticipation.

Down the corridor she asked the receptionist to page her boss. He wouldn't like being called away from sitting on his arse in his nice warm office but this was exactly what he was paid for and she was damned if she was going to deal with this shit show on her own.

After a few minutes he entered the ward, his white doctors coat billowing behind him in a supercilious manner.

'What is it?' he asked, a definite tone of impatience in his voice.

'I've had some positive markers come up on the lady in room 3, I thought it might be best for you to explain the next steps.' Boosting his ego was she decided the best way to get him on board and save her the task of doing it.

He sighed and looked down at the floor 'OK, he said, let's do this.'

Together they walked back in the direction of the room and entered. The lady had now taken a seated position on the side of the bed, her legs dangling down like a child sitting on a chair far too big for them. She still had her blouse pulled up over her bump but she didn't seem to notice or care.

Her boss walked over to the screen, unlocked it and took a second to read the markers. Glancing over his shoulder she double checked that nothing had changed, that she definitely hadn't called this one wrong.

Confirming what she already knew, he took a seat and wheeled it over to face the patient, sitting in front of her at eye level.

'Unfortunately, the tests today have revealed that the baby is showing positive markers for the X1 gene and as such is a carrier of the more commonly named Exodus Virus. Under the Public Health (Control of Diseases) Act 1984, I am therefore obliged to inform you that your baby is not viable for life and poses a direct threat to the public should it be permitted to reach full term. It is my duty to inform you that you will therefore be scheduled for an appointment tomorrow whereby this pregnancy will be terminated. Do you have any questions?'

The woman's expression never faltered once during his little speech, she was looking intently into his eyes as if trying to decide where she knew him from. She could tell that the information he was spewing from the script inside his head had reached her ears but the ramifications of what it meant had not yet seeped into her consciousness.

He turned away from the woman and looked in the direction of the sonographer who was still stationed by the door.

'Could you get an information pack for Miss Littlewood please?'

Irked by the insinuation that she was there to do his bidding she reluctantly left the room to scour the resources cupboard for the unmarked white envelopes that they fortunately didn't have to hand out that regularly now.

It took her a few minutes to locate the necessary

box of envelopes by which time she assumed she would be returning to a woman in mass hysterics having realised the enormity of the news she had just been delivered. To her surprise however the woman was still sitting in the same position, facing her boss, seemingly having engaged him in an in-depth discussion.

'I apologise to be the one to deliver this news to you today Miss' He continued 'please go home and prepare yourself for the procedure tomorrow. We recommend you bring someone with you this time.'

He politely smiled at the mother even though her gaze had now fallen to the floor. He turned towards the door and promptly exited, no doubt to return to his brandy and cigars.

The two women were alone again in the small room but were now also in the company of the heavy black cloud that had descended upon their shared space.

'Is there anyone you'd like me to call for you?' She asked in a timid voice, wary of the way the woman was so still and composed, balancing on the edge of a void where only pain and anguish lay.

'No, thank you.' The woman stood and her eyes fell to her belly that was still on show, her skin stretched taut over the new life forming, life which would no longer be forming tomorrow. She pulled her blouse down and left it un-tucked, the only sign that she was no longer the proficient, efficacious professional she was when she had walked in here a short while ago.

'If you could make your way to reception, they'll

give you the details for tomorrow.'

The woman nodded absent-mindedly whilst she gathered together her things and made towards the door.

Holding the door open for her she watched as she slowly made her way back down the corridor towards the reception desk. She wanted to go back into her room and close the door but she couldn't take her eyes off her. What was she going to do? Was she going to crack? Was she going to express any sorrow or just return home in a daze? Was she even safe to get herself home in such a catatonic state?

She watched as the mother gave her details to the receptionist and waited to be passed her letter. Instead, she was handed the scan picture that had been taken only ten minutes earlier. A scan picture that on the surface showed a healthy baby, one that she would never see alive. The woman's knees buckled slightly before finally giving way completely. As her slender frame crumpled to the floor she lifted her face to the heavens, her mouth gasping for air as her lungs constricted with agony.

The sonographer could stand it no longer and retreated to her room, closing the door behind her which did little to stifle the sound of the howling sobs which now echoed through the ward.

She would definitely be getting that bottle of wine tonight.

The Eye of the Storm

24 HOURS EARLIER

Chapter 2

Unlike most people Margot Littlewood craved Monday mornings. They were her salvation, her respite, the time when she knew with absolute certainty why she was getting up in the morning. On Monday mornings she was on her game, she was in the zone, she was going to make a difference one way or another.

There was a purpose to her step as she walked into work that day, the early September morning still harboured the happy memories of Summer with no thought yet of the cold and dark days that were soon to close in. Margot had always eagerly anticipated the changing of the seasons. Never one to stay too long in one train of thought it suited her that the world was ever changing.

She pounded the pavements in the direction towards her office. Walking was all the therapy she needed. Having never been a runner she found that being in the fresh air, with a purposeful stride to her step could cure most foul moods and she had certainly needed her fair share of fresh air therapy since the death of her parents. With no siblings she had been left devastated and alone after losing both of them in quick succession and she had thrown herself into her work as a distraction and a way of maintaining some control over her life. That was until one particularly emotional, gin fuelled night out, made her realise that suppressing how she felt so deeply was potentially not the best coping method. After this dawning realisation she had found herself a therapist and decided to offload to her instead. It was the best decision she had ever made.

Her parents had been wealthy people, they had both worked hard all their lives and had a comfortable lifestyle. When Margot had said that she wanted to follow a career in medicine they had been so proud that they had agreed to top up her salary to a more substantial one meaning that she had been able to buy herself a small house on the outskirts of the city within a close commute of her work. It was her own little piece of heaven. A few months after her parents had died, she had sold their house and the majority of their belongings. She had no use for their clutter and it wouldn't bring them back to her. The money from the sale had sat untouched ever since.

As she approached the gated compound of her work, she noticed the familiar group of protesters outside. At first, they had seemed novel, defenders of the cause who would eventually grow tired of standing out in the cold. But it had been three years now and there were still people here, every morning when she arrived, holding their pickets, bellowing their chants in her direction, judging her for the crimes they assumed she had committed. There was no differentiation between those entering through the staff entrance. No concept that Margot was there to try to find a cure, that she sympathised with their ideas and agreed that the atrocities of recent years had taken their toll on them all. They just saw someone working for the hospital that killed innocent babies. Only once had Margot stopped to try and reason with them, to try and make them see that she was trying to make the situation better but it was clear they were not there to listen. They were angry, they were hurt, most were grieving and this was their only way to express that.

Having reached the conclusion long ago that it was futile to engage with them, she kept her head down as usual and made her way towards the guarded gates. As she walked, she heard a whistle in the wind as something flew past her head grazing the tips of her hair. An egg landed on the floor by her side its yellow yolk seeping out onto the pavement.

Margot kept her head down and carried on walking. The injustice of it rose up within her, she wanted to turn to them and shout 'I'm trying to help!' but she knew it was pointless. One day she would be able to tell them she had made a difference. One day.

She held her thumb to the key pad on her right-hand side by the main entrance. Since the outbreak there had been strict rules about maintaining safe practice within built up communities. Each individual thumb scan not only registered the person as present but also logged their heart rate, core temperature and oxygen levels. The threat posed by the virus had all but diminished now thanks to the sacrifices of many and their combined efforts to do what they must to curb the spread and yet the government maintained that it was vital they continued to evidence their body stats to ensure the continued success of the population. The memories of the outbreak were still clear in people's minds. Nobody had escaped being affected by it in one way or another.

Since the country had permanently closed the borders, life had become harsher but communities had grown stronger. Many now shared allotments to grow food and crops. All men and women who were without work had been assigned jobs so that everyone could contribute to society, failure to do so meant food rations being cut. Margot's life had in many ways not altered that dramatically, she had continued to work in the lab, the intensity of her work however built with every month that passed without her having a breakthrough.

It was difficult to remember a time when she used to know what she was going to achieve from her days work. A small project here, developing a sample there. Now she faced each day with complete uncertainty of which direction to go in and what new idea she could come up with to try and tackle the problem. The department she worked in was a large one, understandably. There were other research fields across the country, but theirs was the flagship, the one that painted the illusion of paving the way towards a healthier future. The reality was in quite stark contrast. Within her department she led a small research team of only a handful of scientists whom she had known since the beginning of her career. These men and women did not shout from the rooftops about their work, they did not get emotional when something went wrong and they did not allow themselves to hope too enthusiastically when something looked promising. They went about their work methodically, calmly, productively and allowed the science to do the talking.

The thumb pad buzzed and flashed up her profile picture of 12 months ago. She snorted at the naivety of her younger self. If only she'd known what was awaiting her, she wouldn't perhaps be smiling so widely. The gates swung open to grant her access to the forbearing grey concrete building. A hospital in its former life the building now housed many government bodies from policing, to medical experimentation. Margot had worked in Pathology for eleven years, with the past three focused solely on the Exodus virus.

As she entered through the double doors she turned right towards her office and headed down the long corridor which stretched out ahead, her shoes tapping on the pale green linoleum floor. The flooring here had not been altered since the buildings hospital days and there was still the unmistakable smell of disinfectant in the air. The maze-like corridors could easily confuse people and it was not uncommon for Margot to find visitors to the building staring aimlessly at the maps that were located around the building trying desperately to find their relevant department. For Margot however it was like a second home. She knew the shortcuts and where to go on her breaks to make sure she caught some of the midday sunshine.

Arriving at the door to her office she once again scanned her thumb print on the door pad. It took a few seconds to bring up her details and then turned green underneath her skin. Simultaneously she heard the thick metal door in front of her click open. She used both hands to push the door forward and entered the cosy office that housed her and her colleagues.

Margot had always felt like the only slightly exuberant one of the group, often trying to engage her colleagues in discussions around music or what meal she had enjoyed the night before but whilst most had the capacity to reply so as not to appear rude, the reality was that they were happiest when left alone with their own thoughts without interruptions. She had learnt to moderate her natural enthusiasm for life whilst she was around them, but considering they were the people she spent the most amount of time with she couldn't help occasionally trying to drum up some enthusiasm from them. None more so than her colleague Nick who had worked next to her and put up with her irritations for far too long.

Nick was quite possibly, she imagined, the one person who relished Monday morning's more than she did. Always the first to arrive she couldn't imagine a place where he could be more at home than at his desk, head down, reading through a recent study which had been published relating to a field of work he had been working on for the past few months. Everything at his desk was not only in order but in perpendicular angles to one another. He had a place for everything and meticulously tidied up throughout the day. In quite stark contrast to Margot's desk which required her to move week's worth of reports out of the way in order to find a spot for her to place her bag down on whilst she removed her coat. It wasn't that Margot was messy, it was just that her brain worked on a number of things all at the same time. She liked to cross reference articles and flit between thoughts so her brain wouldn't get bogged down by the details. She knew where everything was and whilst it may look like chaos, she knew there was a frenetic organisation to it all somehow.

'Morning Nick' she chirped. Well aware that this was how their daily routine started every morning. He unfailingly trying to ignore her arrival, her demanding that these pleasantries remain.

'Morning' he muttered without raising his head.

She knew better than to take offence. There were emotions in there deep down she knew, they were just shielded by the impenetrable armour of a scientist. A tall man with intensely receding hair, he had always been uncomfortable with small talk. Quite happy to sit at his desk in silence for days at a time Margot had spent years trying to get him to open up more. She had been feeling recently that he might be starting to warm to her. He had recently taken the decision to shave off what little hair he had left and Margot felt it had been a vast improvement.

As she turned on her laptop a calendar reminder flagged up immediately. She normally resisted scheduling any meetings in before 9.00am to allow herself time for at least two morning coffee's so it was unusual to see something ping up at her so early.

Opening it to see in more detail her heart sank.

'Oh damn'

Ordinarily a compassionate colleague might have questioned what was wrong but Nick either out of disinterest or a desire not to appear nosy didn't even raise his head. As always, she decided to share her woes with him anyway so he wouldn't feel left out.

'I've got a new student in today for shadowing.'

Margot despised medical students, they were by and large a pain in the proverbial, with their questions and irritating necessity to try and impress. However, as they were a teaching laboratory, there was a requirement for them to offer a small number of students the opportunity to shadow them occasionally in order for them to better understand the field.

Right on cue the telephone rang and Margot answered.

'There's a Miss Price at reception for you Margot'

'Thank you, I'll be right over.'

With a sigh Margot dragged herself out of her chair and walked back in the direction she had just come from. This, she thought, was exactly the reason she wore comfortable shoes.

Her worst fears were realised when she finally made it to the reception area to find Miss Price eagerly awaiting her arrival, practically bouncing on the pads of her feet, keen to make a good first impression.

'Hello Miss Price, I'm…'

'Ooh call me Amy please I'm so pleased to meet you; I've been begging my course leader to let me come here on placement for like a year! But, you have to wait until you're in your third year before they'll allow it, so as soon as I started back, I put my name down on the list but they said it was picked at random so I couldn't believe my luck when my name was picked first! I think it's probably a good thing I'm in my third year though because I've been able to spend some time elsewhere and learn even more about the field so I think I'll be in a stronger position now, don't you?'

The noise and enthusiasm coming off this petite, energetic young human was almost offensive so early in the morning. Why did she always get lumbered with them? And on a Monday too.

She managed to rearrange her expression to one of mild interest and started to walk back in the direction of the office with Amy tottering along beside her. For every one of Margot's long strides

Amy's short legs had to take about three but she seemed the type to move everywhere at speed so it didn't occur to Margot to try and slow down.

'I've always been interested in science but obviously since the outbreak I just feel like I need to do more, you know what I mean? I mean no one saw the last few years coming did they, and we've all got to play our part haven't we, so I just figure what better place to do that than here, right?

Margot wasn't sure her young student had yet drawn breath since she had arrived in the building. She wondered if she needed to just wait for her to pass out in order to get a break in the conversation. They turned the corner off the entrance hallway to walk down the main building corridor.

'Wow it's big isn't it! Much bigger than it seems when you're just walking past outside. I only live around the corner so I walk past here a lot, but it is a lot bigger than you'd think. Have you worked here long? I always imagine that people end up working in these places all their lives, I mean I can't imagine why you'd want to work anywhere else, and I imagine there's lots of opportunities for progression once you work in an organisation like this one so it just makes sense to climb the ladder once you're here I suppose doesn't it.'

Margot struggled to grasp if there had been a question in amongst the ramblings. Amy didn't seem to be waiting for any answers though so Margot settled into her role of silent observer. It suited her just fine.

Finally with Amy still chattering away to herself

they reached the office door and Margot scanned her thumb print to gain them entry. Amy's eyes never left her, taking it all in, she was like a puppy on Christmas morning unable to contain her excitement.

Margot took a small amount of pleasure from the fact that the one person who would struggle with this new recruit more than she did was Nick. She wondered how he would react to someone so exuberant invading his personal space. As they entered however, she was disappointed to see he had already left his desk, no doubt to continue some research in the lab. She toyed with the idea of taking Amy straight down there and leaving her with him for a few hours, but she wasn't sure her conscience would allow it. As she walked Amy over to her desk, she noticed the papers had been shuffled to one side to create a small square of free space in which stood a steaming hot mug of coffee waiting for her. She smiled to herself; he did care really.

Now in her own domain she decided to take more control of the situation. She wheeled a chair over for Amy to sit at and they both took a seat, unable to pull up close to the desk for fear of dislodging piles of research paperwork. The intensity of the small room seemed to have had a calming effect on the young student, the volume had definitely diminished and she was taking slower steadier breaths.

'So, Amy, is there a particular field you're interested in or wanted to ask more questions about or are you happy to follow me around what I would call a typical day in life of a research scientist?'

'I want to see as much as possible! I'd love to see the lab but I've been told that most can't go in there. I'm fascinated by your research and how that's going and I'd love to be able to help out in any way I can.

Finally, Margot seemed to have been given the opportunity to have a voice

'Well as you'll know the only line of defense we've had in stemming the flow of the virus has been through prenatal testing. Whilst a cure still eludes us the only way we can prevent another outbreak is to test unborn babies DNA to check if they're a carrier. If the baby tests positive, then we terminate the pregnancy, thereby preventing additional outbreaks. Obviously, the work we do here is based on trying to find a cure for those that do test positive, allowing the birth of healthy babies but it's a long process'

'Do you know yet why some are carriers and others aren't?'

'Not yet, there doesn't seem to be any genetic link, some babies are just born as carriers. The alarming thing is when we've tested the babies they've shown different strains of the virus, so it's mutating somehow even though we're not allowing it to become airborne.'

'My Aunty had to have a termination last year. They'd been trying for 6 years to get pregnant. She's still not got over it. Do you ever think about all the babies you've killed?'

Margot had become used to such abruptness and disapproval at their methods, more usually wrapped up in a bit more of a sensitive way but the question was still the same.

'We don't kill babies Amy, we test them for a disease that would kill them, before they would be viable for life and if necessary, we prevent them from coming to full term in order to avoid another epidemic. We want to get to a point where that's not necessary but for now it's what has kept us all alive. Sometimes we have to make difficult choices for the right reasons.'

'Do you think you'd still agree with it if it were your baby?'

'If a baby tests positive it would not be viable for life anyway. It's the kindest thing to do for everyone.'

Keen to cut this topic of conversation off before it had time to grow into a full-scale moral debate Margot handed her some research to have a read through and excused herself to visit the ladies.

As she locked the door of the cubicle, she rested her forehead against the cool tiled wall. Ethical discussions on a Monday morning should be outlawed in her opinion. She breathed deeply, basking in the silence for a minute as she gathered her thoughts. The countless women whose lives had been affected because of her inability to discover a cure were rarely out of her thoughts, but she stood by their work and the decisions the Government had made in order to keep them all safe.

Now, more than ever though, it seemed all a bit too close to home. Would she still agree with the decision if it was her own body that was affected?

She let her hands come to rest on her tummy

where the hint of a bump was beginning to show.

She would find out all too soon.

Chapter 3

Her relationship with Ben had been such a cliche that she cringed now looking back on it. The frisson of tension had been there from the very first time they had laid eyes on each other when he had been interviewing her for a Senior Research Management position. Sitting opposite one another across the table he had been asking her about her capability for the role whilst she had been mentally undressing him with her eyes. He was relaxed without being cocky, well-spoken but not aloof. She could tell through the contours of his arms underneath his shirt that he worked out but not excessively. He was speckled with flecks of grey hair, which only added to his allure.

He was however the ultimate professional throughout the interview until it came time to shake hands at the end. He had held onto her hand for just a fraction of a second too long and gave her such an intense gaze that she felt heat rise in her cheeks.

She knew she was hooked when she found herself

waiting for his call, not to hear whether or not she had been successful in the role but to get the chance to speak to him again.

She had been disappointed when the voice at the other end of the phone had belonged to a woman. A very friendly lady informing her that Mr Sykes had been very impressed with her and that they looked forward to welcoming her to the team. She had gladly accepted before immediately going out and buying herself a new work wardrobe consisting of skirts considerably shorter than what she would have previously worn.

Over the next six months the two of them shared flirty glances which led to a hand casually resting on her shoulder every now and again until one afternoon she accepted an invitation for after work drinks. When she walked into the pub, she could sense he was there before she had even seen him. Sitting casually at a table in the corner with her other colleagues she sauntered over and took a seat on the stool next to him.

'What can I get you to drink?' he had asked

'I'll have a beer please' she replied trying to remain calm about the fact that his hand had come to rest on her thigh. He held her gaze as his hand slid higher underneath the table. One drink became seven and they stumbled back to her apartment barely making it through the door before they were tearing each other's clothes off.

The next morning, she woke to find he had already left. Alone and with a sizeable hangover she spent the next day wondering what to make of it all.

They hadn't even swapped numbers so she didn't have a way of contacting him, she would have to wait until Monday morning.

It was a friend who eventually put her out of her misery on the Sunday evening. She had noticed the chemistry between them on the Friday night and told her to be careful as rumour had it that his wife was not a woman to be messed with. Margot had felt like such a fool. Why had she not asked if he was with someone? More to the point why had he never mentioned it? He didn't wear a ring and there was nothing else to suggest that he was taken. What an idiot she had been.

She managed to avoid him for a few days at work until he cornered her in the hallway one day and tried to turn on the charm. She'd told him that she was no home wrecker and that it would not be happening again. She had planned to throw herself into work to forget about the whole unfortunate situation and then she'd missed her period.

She wasn't sure at what stage she had decided to keep the baby but similarly she had never truly considered the option of not. She had created life. She had no control over what this person would look like or speak like and yet she alone was responsible for its entire future and simultaneously in control of nothing at all. She tried to maintain a level of calm over her growing fears of what was to come. Having children had never been in her life plan. She had always been so focused on her work that she didn't pine for anything that was going to take her away from that.

She knew raising a child alone was not going to be an easy task but despite her never having been a person of faith she felt strongly that life had been created in her for a reason. Who knew if she would ever get this opportunity again. All she had to do now was focus on the future.

*

Having exhausted the amount of time she could hide in the toilet, Margot returned to the lab and decided to change her mindset with regards to her enthusiastic student. She herself had once been fresh faced and wide eyed and it was thanks to her tutors and her parents' endless patience and encouragement that she had been able to develop her skills. Now it was her turn, and perhaps soon enough it would be her own son or daughter following in her footsteps so she may as well start perfecting her skills.

Amy was sat at her desk engrossed in their latest monthly newsletter outlining their work. Margot returned to sit next to her and make a plan for their day.

Amy immediately burst into dialogue.

'Some guy just came in looking for you, he said that they were starting soon in the observation room and he didn't want you to miss it?

Margot racked her brain unable to think what else had been scheduled in for today that she'd forgotten about. Suddenly she realised that he was talking about the post-mortem which had been slotted into the calendar at the last minute on Friday.

A pregnant mother had passed away in a Road Traffic Accident and the bodies had been approved for organ donation. The mother had already saved three other people's lives with her organs but the baby at only 23 weeks gestation was too young and so was being donated to them for research.

Margot had previously struggled with these kinds of procedures on any one let alone a young baby but as she had progressed in her career and experienced first-hand the importance of what their research did she was now able to compartmentalise her feelings and focus on the scientific realities. Granted this was somewhat harder whilst carrying her own child but she had long since come to terms with the hardships of this world and made a conscious decision to do the best with it. These two lives had come to an end all too soon but that was out of her control, what she could do now was learn something from it and help others with her discoveries.

'Amy, I forgot this had been scheduled for this morning sorry, there's an abundance of paperwork and research that you can be reading through and I should be back in a couple of hours.'

'Oh, can't I come? I promise I won't make a scene!'

Margot had been expecting this from her overly enthusiastic scholar and whilst every fibre of her being told her that this was not a good idea, she also appreciated that students wanted to fully submerge themselves in this experience whilst they had the chance.

'It's not for the faint-hearted Amy, and I can't be holding your hand if you get squeamish. I need to focus on what's happening on the operating table. Are you sure you want to be there?

'Yes, absolutely, oh my goodness wait until I tell my tutor about this.'

'There's no shame in needing a break so if you need to leave to get some fresh air please do so, OK?'

'Uh huh, yes I promise' she mumbled distractedly as she frantically pulled out her pink notebook and fluffy pen from her handbag.

Turning away Margot began to gather her things together. She grabbed her laptop and wandered out of the office towards the east wing, Amy's excited footsteps not far behind her.

Whilst most people she knew hated hospitals she had always felt a thrill from being inside them. Anywhere that was open 24/7 had always intrigued and excited her. During the frequent nights where sleep eluded her, she found great comfort knowing that the hospital was still a hive of activity.

At this time of day there were multiple appointments taking place, people starting to wander in for their scans and x-rays and consultations. So many conversations happening, emotions flowing and thoughts churning. Margot felt like she could channel all of them at the same time. She often felt like this in crowded places, like she couldn't filter out what was happening to all those around her and instead she soaked it all up to the point where it became overwhelming. Her mother had often described her as a deeply feeling child, one who was prone to feeling overcome with emotion, unable to separate herself from others plights. Far from this being described with any negative connotations her mother had always instilled in Margot that this was to be considered a strength. One which she should be aware of at times in order to protect herself but one still which would enable her ultimately to help others.

Margot's difficulty was filtering out the information that landed in her brain to focus on just the few things that were in her control. Recently she'd had to stop watching the news and turn off alerts on her phone. She couldn't deal with all of the world's problems right now but what she could do was try to make a small change here in this hospital.

Arriving at the examination room, she found Nick sitting on the front row of the observation area with a seat saved next to him. The room was elevated above the operating theatre with a large glass wall and tiered seating to allow it's occupants a clear view of the room below. In her early years Margot had been caught out by the multiple doctors that exceeded six foot in height sitting in front of her and completely obscuring her view and so now always aimed for an early arrival to bag a front row seat. Unsurprisingly, therefore, they were some of the first ones there and she was relieved to have a seat with a perfect view. It was a rare occurrence to be able to observe a procedure like this and one which she wanted to make the most of. Much to her relief the seat next to the one Nick had reserved for her had been taken so Amy was directed to one further down the row. Margot was relieved to be separated from her to avoid the distraction. She would be amazed if Amy managed to stay silent throughout the whole thing.

Opening her laptop, she used the time to catch up on emails which had come through over the weekend. The hospital welcomed flexible working in order to accommodate a work life balance which Margot appreciated but she still couldn't contemplate how some people found the time to send emails at 4am.

Slowly others started to filter in, no doubt expecting that they too would be the first to arrive but caught out by Nick's forward planning. She was relieved that most hadn't witnessed Nick reserving a seat for her though, she didn't want anyone to think they were treating this like a trip to the cinema. Eventually the room became more and more crowded as all the seats were taken and people began to shuffle into the sides crouching down at the font to allow as many people as possible to have a view. With so many people crowded into such a small space the temperature of the room began to creep up. She now wished she'd brought some water with her but there was no time for that now. She closed her laptop, eagerly anticipating the start of the procedure.

She noticed that Nick kept giving her furtive glances and then looking away, obviously tempted to say something but not finding the words. She wondered if he wanted to ask about the procedure or what they would be most keen to observe but she decided not to interrupt his thoughts. He would find the words in his own time.

Eventually she sensed him take an intake of breath before opening his mouth to speak

'Are you sure you're happy to observe this? I'm happy to take notes if you'd rather skip this one.'

Touched by his unexpected thoughtfulness Margot was a little taken aback initially.

'I'll be fine, thank you Nick'

She had never explicitly told Nick that she was pregnant, but working so closely with someone every day allowed you a unique insight into their lives. Certainly, in the first few weeks there had been multiple dashes to the toilet to hurl up what little breakfast she had been able to eat. Returning to her desk with a sweaty pallor she had then spent many an afternoon tentatively sipping peppermint tea to help ease the quease. She had also caught herself unsuspectingly placing a hand on her tummy whilst she was reading a paper or stretching her legs in between meetings. She was certainly never going to be able to keep it a secret forever but once she realised that Nick knew she felt comforted by the fact that someone was looking out for her. Especially someone who wasn't interested in gossip and had no friends to gossip too even if he'd wanted to.

They retreated back to their comfortable silence for another few minutes until the doors opposite them opened and the staff began to fill the room.

After a brief spell of setting up, the young infant

was wheeled through and laid down on the operating theatre table. Perfect and tiny he looked to be in a peaceful sleep. Margot steadied her breath as she reminded herself to detach from the emotions that had cause to rise up within her. At 24 weeks pregnant herself her own baby would look almost identical to that of the one lying in front of her. She was determined however not to be that woman. She had worked too hard to prove herself and climb the metaphorical ladder. This was to be a test of her professionalism and composure and she intended to see it through.

The surgeon leading the procedure performed his final checks and made a note of the time before stating for the records that he was about to begin. The room around Margot fell silent and everyone simultaneously leaned forward to get a better vantage point.

As he lowered his scalpel to the infant's chest, Margot noticed him pause. There were only a few millimeters of space between his blade and the young child's skin. Margot initially thought he was gaining his composure but as he stayed immobile, she noticed the faintest crease of a frown form on his forehead above his mask.

Margot leaned forward further to better see what the delay was. Squinting her eyes together as if that would improve her vision, she focused on where the scalpel lay poised and observed the chest of the baby rise an infinitesimal amount so that it came up to touch the tip of the blade before slowly falling away again.

The surgeon with his other hand felt under the baby's jawline, the look of confusion now appearing on the faces of those nearest him.

Margot inadvertently reached a hand out towards Nick resting it on his forearm.

'Is that baby….' She paused waiting further confirmation unable to put into words what her brain was witnessing.

'Breathing' Nick finished for her. He too sat transfixed on the events taking place below them.

As the surgeon began to disbelievingly utter words about heart beat and active signs of life, the tiny being laid out beneath him slowly blinked his eyes open.

Margot felt an icy chill flood her body from head to toe. How could this be happening? They had been about to perform a post-mortem on a living child. The people behind her in the observation room were now on their feet, confused questions were escaping from everyone's lips with no one able to provide an answer. An urgency grew in the room below them too as they realised that action was required and suddenly staff began to move about the room grasping for equipment and additional support.

Margot felt her legs go weak, she couldn't bear the thought of what had been about to happen and despite her earlier protestations about her ability to compartmentalize, she now struggled not to imagine her own child lying on that table surrounded by the frantic energy of people trying to make right their error.

Unable to peel her eyes away from the helpless child she noticed its tiny fingers spread wide reaching out into the void around him for something, someone.

To her left she heard a thud as Amy promptly fainted and fell to the floor. Not one person in the observation room turned to assess her however, their attention held all too attentively on what was happening in front of them.

The infant was now surrounded by doctors and nurses. One holding a small oxygen mask over its face another listening to his chest and putting in requests for medication.

The crowd of people around her were becoming more agitated. She felt someone's hand rest on her shoulder as they tried to surge forward in an attempt to better see what was going on.

This was not what Margot had signed up for this morning and she suddenly realised she didn't have the capacity to view any more.

'I have to leave' she muttered, quietly, to no one in particular peeling her eyes away from the scene she no longer wished to witness.

Leaving her belongings on the floor she stood up and attempted to move along in between the glass pane and the front row of people who were now all on their feet.

She slowly squeezed through, one hand outstretched in an attempt to part the crowds the other protecting her bump from the people who were surging forwards. She uttered apologies and polite requests for them to move but no one took any notice. No one had the capacity to take anything in other than what was unfolding beneath them. Eventually she began to just force her way through, her claustrophobia building as her heart beat increased, the sweat beginning to drip from her forehead. Stepping over Amy's unconscious heap on the floor she reached for the door desperate for fresh air and space.

Already her mind was a flood of incomprehensible questions. How could that have just happened? The baby had been pronounced dead over 48 hours ago. Would they be able to save it? It was so tiny and helpless how had anyone missed this?

Bursting out through the fire exit doors closest to the morgue she took deep rasping breaths of cool air. As she felt her lungs fill, she allowed the breaths to seep through her body calming her nerves and steadying her heart rate.

She attempted to slow down her thoughts at the same time, thoughts that were rapidly spinning out of control. She focused in on her own bump, her own healthy child still cocooned within her. The movements within her had become so familiar now that she often didn't feel them as she was going about her day but as she forced herself to focus in on her inner self, she noticed the familiar fluttering of small kicks and shuffles. Her baby was fine, she was fine, the two of them were not connected to what she had just witnessed.

She stood outside the door for a while calming

her breaths and trying to make sense of it all. Already the creeping sense of shame was settling in on her for leaving. She was the consummate professional, this was not what she did. She consoled herself slightly with the fact that if people hadn't even noticed Amy collapsing they certainly wouldn't have noticed her leaving the room. She needed to get her things though and her laptop but couldn't face going back into that observation room. Fortunately, her phone was rarely away from her person and she pulled it out of her inside pocket.

Unable to face phoning anyone she resorted to texting Nick

'Can you please take my laptop back to the office? I just need to get some air.'

Once sent she realised she probably shouldn't bail on her student so she sent another message:

'Could you also please wait for Amy to come round and take her back with you?'

Not her most maternal response but it was all she could muster at this stage. She realised she had no idea how Nick had been affected by what he'd just seen. He too may be on the verge of a mental breakdown outside a fire escape gasping for breath. But somehow that image didn't fit with the man she had worked alongside all these years. After a short wait she received a brief response.

'Yes, of course. Take your time.'

She couldn't even engage her brain enough to be able to contemplate going for a walk so she slumped down onto the floor with her back against the wall, allowing the silence to calm her mind whilst the questions kept repeating themselves on a loop inside her head.

What had allowed that baby to seemingly survive unaided for two days whilst presumed dead? How had no one noticed that there were signs of life until the last minute? What if this had happened to her?

She needed to get a grip of herself. From a medical perspective there was a lot to learn from this and she needed to make sure she was considered fit and well to be a part of that research.

After a further ten minutes she gathered herself together and was steeling herself to go back inside when the doors opened and Nick stepped out.

'I thought you might want your bag out here' he said and handed it over to her.

'Thank you' she took it from him and laid it down at her side.

Without invitation he came and sat next to her against the wall, he too gathering his thoughts no doubt.

'What just happened Nick?'

'I don't know, they tried to give him oxygen but he passed away a few minutes later'

Margot closed her eyes; it was no surprise being so tiny and after such a long period with no life support but still it was desperately sad.

'How could nobody have noticed the baby was still alive?'

'I don't know, there'll be an enquiry I'm sure.'

'But the way that he opened his eyes. I just don't understand, that poor child… and that poor mother.'

Mortified but unable to stop herself she felt shuddering sobs course through her as uncontrollable tears slipped down her cheeks.

'I think you should go home, get some rest' Nick offered. He was calmer than she thought he'd be faced with an emotional woman. Most men she knew acted like you had a contagious disease the moment the tears began to flow but Nick sat resolutely next to her, not seemingly fazed or uncomfortable.

Margot composed herself and unceremoniously sniffed her runny nose away.

'Thank you but I'd rather stay. I feel more at home here than I do in my own home most of the time. Plus, I've got my scan tomorrow which will take me away from the lab for a while and there's a lot I want to get done before then.'

'OK, if you're sure.'

'Has Amy come round yet?' she sniffed determined to pull herself together before she returned to the office.

'Oh yes, she's doing just fine. She'll be regaling that story with a flourish by the time she's back in class tomorrow.'

Margot managed a half smile at the thought, no doubt that he was right.

'We'd best get back in then' he said peeling himself off the wall and holding the door open for her 'Cup of tea and a biscuit and we'll be right as rain.'

She smiled through her tears, unable to put into words how much it meant to have a colleague looking out for her. She had never considered that she would be able to build a connection with someone who was so drastically different to her but in this environment, dealing with the things they were dealing with she realised she might actually have been fortunate enough to have also found herself a friend.

Chapter 5

Returning to the warmth of the lab Margot took a seat at her desk. A few people turned to look at her, no doubt news of the post mortem had spread and people were wondering how she was going to deal with it. She decided it was best addressing everyone early to avoid the rumour spreading.

'Can everyone listen up please?' she announced.

'No doubt, it's already been made public that there was quite a traumatic event in theatre earlier. I can't give any of you answers right now as to how or why this happened but needless to say that there will be a thorough investigation and if I hear anything further, I will let you know. If anyone feels particularly affected by what happened please do come and speak to me, regardless of if you were in the room at the time or not and please continue to support one another, it's fortunately very rare that these occurrences happen but when they do it's more important than ever that we pull together.

You all know where I am if you need anything,

but unless anyone has any questions can I ask that we all get on with our work please?'

There followed a silence, some had their heads bowed others looked still shocked by the news of what had happened but one by one they filed back to their desks and got their heads down.

Margot walked over to Amy who was sat nursing a mug of warm water and lemon.

'How are you feeling Amy?'

'I just can't believe it, I've never fainted before. One minute I was there and then the next that baby started breathing and I was like 'what is going on?' and then it all went black and I think I banged my head. Have I got a bruise? I've got a date tomorrow and I can't have a black eye!'

'You look just fine to me Amy, but I think you should go home and get some rest. Is there anyone that can come and pick you up?'

'Yes, my mum can, I'll phone her.'

She pulled her mobile out of her bag and attempted to dial in the numbers.

'Your phone won't work in here; all the signal has been blocked so that it doesn't interfere with the machinery. Do you feel well enough to make your way back to reception? Someone there will be able to call her for you.'

Amy nodded and put her things back in her bag it had certainly not been the day she'd expected but Margot felt confident that she'd be fine once she'd got over the shock.

Once Amy had left the lab Margot returned to her desk. She felt better now that she had no one she needed to be looking out for, she'd dealt with the team and their concerns, now she could sit quietly and regain her composure. As usual she found that the best way of calming her mind was to read. She read historical notes on previous post-mortems trying to find some mention of something similar happening but came up with nothing. She followed up some lab results she was waiting for but was told they were still outstanding, she trawled through her emails finding something to distract herself with but eventually had to come to accept that her mind would not be calmed.

The events of the day had forced her to contemplate the vulnerabilities of her own child's existence. She had been looking forward to her scan the following day, naively going about her business under the assumption that everything was going to be ok, but what if it wasn't? What if she tested positive tomorrow? What if she and her child only had one more day left together? The prospect of that being the case was impossible for her to comprehend and yet her anxiety about it happening was now building.

Slowly but surely the room began to empty, some taking their time to tidy their desks, set their things straight, clean their mugs before wrapping up to head outside. Others simply flicked the switch for work mode to off and departed with an abruptness that insinuated they'd been waiting to do it all day.

Herself and Nick were usually the last two standing and more often than not she left Nick alone to finish off his day in peace. Today however she was in no rush to return home. She felt comforted being in this environment, here there were the promise of answers, here there was the possibility of progress. Home was quiet, home was lonely and thoughtful. She didn't need any of those things tonight.

Nick was one of those who took his time to bring his day to a close. All of the items on his desk were returned to their rightful place, his keyboard and mouse placed neatly underneath his screen, research papers put away, chair tucked neatly under his desk.

'Anything I can do for you Margot?'

'No thank you Nick, you get yourself off, thank you for your support today.'

'No problem. I'll see you tomorrow'

'Goodnight Nick'

As he walked out of the room closing the door gently behind him, she exhaled slowly releasing the tension from the day. Sitting back in her chair she allowed herself a moment of reflection.

The image of the baby taking that breath, the look of shock on the doctors' faces, she felt the events of the day would be imprinted on her brain forever. Having always been one step removed from the reality of what was happening to women all over the country she felt today's events had brought it well and truly onto her radar. There was so much happening in the world right now, so much uncertainty, she needed to be able to fully embrace her pregnancy, to know that her own baby was going to be OK.

Something that she had been considering for a

while now came back into the forefront of her mind. She knew it was morally wrong, in fairness it was more than that, it was outright forbidden to undergo testing on yourself but she felt like she had earned the right to know what was going on in her own body. No one would ever know; she had the whole lab to herself for the night and she was only carrying out a test which was going to be re-done in a few hours anyway.

If she was going to raise a child alone, she was going to have to make decisions that she felt was in the best interest for the two of them and right now she needed reassurances that they had a future together.

Going through into the laboratory next door she pulled together all of the items she would need before taking a seat at one of the testing stations. Pulling off her jacket she cleaned her hands before putting on some gloves and cleaned the crease in her arm where she would be taking the sample. It was trickier doing it on yourself than it was on someone else but she managed to attach the tourniquet before picking up the needle and pulling off the plastic cover. Steadying herself she could see the vein swelling underneath the skin allowing her a clear line of sight for where to draw the blood, without hesitation she forced the needle under the skin and watched as her blood began to seep out. Releasing the tourniquet, she waited for few seconds whilst the tube filled before removing the needle and applying pressure to her arm.

As she waited, she noticed the small tingle of self-doubt start to creep in. What if this came back as positive. She knew what she would have to do and she would do it if it came to that. She had seen the reality of those that had been born unable to survive and she would not do that to her own child. She still found it mind boggling that to some people the worst thing in the world was death. She had seen all too often the reality of a fate worse than death and the responsibility that we all have to our loved ones to ensure they meet their death with as much dignity and as little pain as possible. In spite of this however she couldn't imagine the pain that awaited her should it turn out that she had to terminate her pregnancy. The risk of losing her child brought home to her just how much she was now invested in her new role of motherhood. At the very least finding out she was positive now would give her a night to comprehend the news before she was told publicly at the scan.

She delicately placed her test tube sample into the centrifuge machine and set it running for five minutes. She waited in silence; her brain too distracted to contemplate moving onto an additional task. She let her eyes close and focused in on the whirr of the centrifuge machine as it spun around, forcing her cells down to the bottom of the sample leaving her serum at the top ready to be analysed. She felt like she herself was being spun around in a whirl with no time to steady herself. At least after this she would have her answer, she would be able to start to plan her future in whatever form that may take.

Once the five minutes were up, she was able to transfer the sample to the immunoassay analyser which was permanently set up for this particular prenatal screening. They had no need for the many other functions that this machine could test for, these days they only had an interest in one result.

Setting the machine off left her with another 10 minutes of waiting. She was starting to feel on edge now, if someone were to come in and see her testing unsupervised it would mean an instant dismissal. Maybe this wasn't such a good idea after all. Her foot started its impatient tapping as she kept one eye on the door willing the handle not to turn. She just needed to hold her nerve, just a few more minutes and she would know.

After the longest wait she heard the beep of the machine and she turned to the screen to read the results. Working her way through the different markers she allowed herself to believe this was really happening. All looked normal, all looked healthy. Before she allowed herself to smile, she focused in again, making absolutely sure there was nothing she had missed. No, she was certain, the baby wasn't a carrier, she was growing a healthy human, there were no shocks awaiting her tomorrow, she could relax.

With a lightness that she hadn't felt in months she moved around the lab discarding the evidence of her test and deleting the results from the screen. Only she knew the outcome of the tests but tomorrow it would be public news and she could delight in the rest of her pregnancy journey.

She gathered up her things, wrapping herself

snugly in her coat before turning off her screens and locking up the office with a flourish.

Tomorrow was going to be a good day.

Chapter 6

The following morning Margot was feeling better equipped to return to normality. After a long soak in the bath the night before she had rationalised with herself that whilst the events in theatre yesterday had been surprising, these things must happen from time to time. She would be interested to take a read of the incident report when it was published to see exactly how far gone the baby was and what exactly seemed to have gone wrong, but it was, she decided, not something for her to fixate on. She was looking forward to her scan and hearing the heartbeat. She had been kept up the night before by stronger movements and what seemed to feel like hiccups from her unborn child so she knew it was quite happy in there. It would be nice to see her progress and then get back to her work. She couldn't imagine that Nick was one to gossip and so felt fairly certain that her wobble yesterday wouldn't be the talk of the office.

She was relieved to see when she arrived at the office that this appeared to be true. Whilst there were the occasional mentions from her staff of earlier events, she was grateful that most were happy to get on with their work. She once again felt grateful for her fortune at working with such an honest and reliable group of people.

Whilst she had been planning to get her scan done first thing that morning, she took a call almost as soon as she had entered the office to inform her that due to an emergency they were going to have to push her scan back to the last one of the day. This suited Margot better, she was in no rush to get the results that she already knew and also gave her a chance to catch up on the work she'd let slip following yesterdays events.

With no students to distract her today and no dramatic trips to theatre planned, Margot found she was able to sit quietly and catch up on her workload. By half past four her inbox was in order, her head space was clear and she felt like her old self again. She gathered her things together and glanced over at Nick to say goodbye.

'Good luck' he muttered with an awkward side smile.

She was half tempted to tell him that she didn't need it but thanked him anyway and said she'd see him tomorrow.

Punctual as ever Margot arrived in plenty of time for her appointment in the vain hope that she would be called forward early and be able to get home at a suitable time, but the receptionist informed her that they were running slightly behind schedule and that there would be a short wait.

She didn't mind however, on the contrary she found it quite soothing to be around other pregnant woman. Having not had the time nor the inclination to join any new parent groups she had not had the opportunity to be around others with a shared experience. She made a mental note to look into prenatal groups near her in the next few weeks. It would be good for her to meet other new mothers and bond over their impending new arrivals.

Eventually she heard her name being called a little further down the hallway and she gathered her things and headed in that direction. There was a young woman with dark hair leaning out of a doorway, seemingly too busy to wander down the corridor to personally collect each patient.

After the initial formalities were out of the way Margot was invited to sit down on the chair in order for them to take her blood sample. She offered the opposite arm to the one she had used yesterday, keen for no one to see the evidence of her self-inflicted puncture wound.

Relieved that she had an efficient medical professional taking her bloods, the process went smoothly.

Once her bloods were taken and sent off to be analysed, she lay herself down on the bed, she was keen now to hear the heartbeat and get confirmation of all being well with the scan so that she could relax once and for all. Lying on the bed Margot lifted her

blouse to reveal her swollen belly.
'Right let's have a look at baby shall we?' The sonographer spoke in a monotone voice as if repeating words from a script she had read too often.

Placing the scanner on her skin Margot waited for the picture to fill the screen.

'There we are, nice strong heartbeat'

Margot exhaled, unaware that she had been holding her breath. The repetitive beating sounds of her child's heartbeat filled the room and she relaxed, closing her eyes to focus in on it.

'You just lie still for me now and I'll do some checks, then all being well you can be on your way.

Resting her head back against the pillow Margot let the sounds of the heartbeat fill her head. Trying to picture what the child associated to it would be doing inside her. She had never before been able to understand why people cooed over scan photos. The blurry form of an alien like being bearing no reflection to her of a human child. But now that it was her own alien, she could spend hours smoothing out the blurred lines of the photograph imagining what her offspring would look like.

The sonographer worked in silence absorbed by her tasks, slowly moving the device over her bump and then pausing as she carried out a number of clicks on her computer screen. Margot didn't like the sensation of the probe being pushed into her; she had become so accustomed to protecting her bump it felt unusual to allow someone to put pressure onto it. She waited patiently for the tests to be completed as the probe came to rest in one position and stayed still for another second.

Much to her relief the scan came to a satisfactory conclusion and she stayed on the bed whilst the professional had a glance through the results of the blood works that Margot had illegally run herself the day before.

As she lay there, in the silence, she became acutely aware that something in the room had changed. She opened her eyes and looked around her, nothing had moved, the sonographer still sat in her chair and continued to look at her computer screen but there was a weight in the air which hadn't been there before. The clicks of the mouse had stopped and the woman was starting with an intensity at the screen in front of her. A small knot of tension formed in the pit of Margot's stomach as she tried to assess what her sixth sense was picking up on.

Without making eye contact the sonographer put down her instrument, stood and began to walk towards the door.

'I just need a colleague to take a look at something for me, I'll be two minutes' and she left leaving the door open.

Margot sat up and pulled the computer screen round to face her. To her frustration the screen had been locked so she couldn't view what it was that required a second opinion.

Determined to keep her emotions under control she returned the screen to its original position and perched on the side of the bed unable to allow her body to relax back into a horizontal position. Her foot began to tap on the bars of the bed, a frantic rhythm of unknown origin created from the worn-out heel of her shoes, she'd been meaning to get to them repaired for weeks.

Moments passed which felt like hours until the sonographer reappeared accompanied by a short man with olive skin wearing a white lab coat. He fleetingly looked in Margot's direction and gave an impulsive half smile before moving over to the screen. Placing his hand on the mouse and bending over to better see the screen he performed a series of clicks and swipes before standing upright and exhaling. He looked Margot in the eye and moved the chair over so that he was sat in front of her.

'I'm sorry to have to be the one to tell you this but the blood tests today have confirmed that your baby has shown positive signs for the X1 gene.'

Margot raised her eyebrows as he continued to speak, words which she couldn't focus in on as she processed the unexpected news that he was giving her. Despite his short stature this was a man who clearly thought very highly of himself. He had delivered this speech before and he would deliver it again. He wasn't unsympathetic, but he was also clearly not going to lose any sleep over this interaction either

A strange buzzing filled Margot's head temporarily drowning out the rest of the words coming out of his mouth. She knew that he was wrong but she couldn't tell him that, she was also mentally preparing herself for the formal complaint that she would be putting in regarding the incompetencies of staff and their ability to read basic blood work.

'Once again I apologise' he said as he came to the end of his speech.

She hadn't noticed the female member of staff leaving but was aware now that it was just the two of them in the room.

'I'm sorry but you're mistaken' she responded with a degree of pity. She was all too aware that her baby was not a carrier she just couldn't explain this to him.

'I'm sorry, but I'm definitely not. The markers leave no room for ambiguity and the baby is definitely a carrier.'

'Show me.' Margot replied with indignation. This incompetent fool obviously had no idea what he was dealing with.

He tensed slightly at her demands but nevertheless pressed a few buttons on the screen and whirred the printer into life. A page of results slowly emerged from the printer and they waited in silence for it to finish its run. The Doctor pulled the page away and handed it to her with an air of finality. He was used to women being in denial during this process. As Margot worked her way through the various markers, she was struck by the fact that they were all noticeably different from yesterday. Not just slightly elevated, she was looking at a completely different set of results. These markers, as he had said, clearly showed a child who was a carrier.

With her mouth open Margot simply stared at the

figures willing them to provide her with an explanation. She turned back to him but couldn't think of how else to explain her knowledge that this wasn't right. Staring into the face of this stranger, aware that she would never be able to forget his features. His bushy eyebrows that branched off in a hundred directions on his forehead. His teeth, perfect apart from the two at the bottom which slightly overlapped. This man she had never met before, who knew nothing about her circumstances or the journey she had taken to be here and yet who would potentially be the one to deliver her the news which would change her entire existence.

A numbness filled her head followed in quick succession by a white noise which grew louder and louder in her brain. She couldn't process what was happening and yet there was a silence in the room which she felt she was expected to fill. She opened her mouth hoping that words would appear but they did not so she simply closed it again.

The door reopened and the female handed her a sealed plain white envelope.

'There is some additional information in here which you can read through once you've been able to digest the news, please go home and prepare yourself for the procedure tomorrow. We recommend you bring someone with you this time. Thanks Joanna' he nodded in the direction of the Sonographer as he walked out closing the door quietly behind him leaving Margot and Joanna alone.

Joanna's face had now softened slightly in the light of the situation she was faced with. She may perform these scans multiple times a day but these circumstances were now fortunately quite rare. Margot stood and realised her top was still lifted above her bump, her skin stretched around her new life form. She pulled down her blouse and placed her hands protectively over her bump willing it to move, willing it to kick, willing it to show some sign of fight and defiance but there was nothing, only stillness. The stillness of a child cocooned safely inside its mother, safely nestled against harm and unaware of the fate that now awaited it.

Margot had it on the tip of her tongue to confess that she had carried out her own blood test yesterday and it had been negative but she had crossed a line in doing that, the rules were clear but very strict and testing your own child was definitely against the rules. If she confessed now all that she would achieve would be criminal charges and the end of her illustrious career. Was her test correct or was theirs? She knew what she was doing, she'd been working in the field for nearly twenty years she'd taken the test correctly and it had been negative, how had theirs come back with such a different result?

There was very little to say once the man had left and whilst Margot knew she had questions she couldn't quite find the ability to put them into words so after an uncomfortable few minutes gathering her things she began to head back towards the reception.

She still felt completely disconnected from herself and what was happening but knew that she had been told to go to the desk to get information about her termination that had now been scheduled for the following morning. Her termination? She couldn't wrap her head around those words. Words that had the ability to cause acid burning bile to rise at the back of her throat.

Their results, which at this moment in time, in this ward, were the only ones that mattered showed that her baby was a threat to the wider population. Their results, so drastically different from hers, meant her baby was going to be murdered in a matter of a few short hours.

Her heart rate quickened and her palms started to sweat, she felt sheer panic start to rise in her chest as everything closed in on her, her worst fears now realised that she might lose her baby.

The receptionist handed her something which she took absentmindedly but it was not the coarse folded material of a paper letter she was expecting but a silkier smoother texture. Looking down she saw the perfect outline of her child. Its legs bent up towards its torso, an arm up by its face, safe and warm and protected.

She had been preparing herself for the eventual birth of the baby, the agony that would no doubt be felt as their bodies tore themselves apart from one another, delivering her a healthy, warm blooded child with air in its lungs that would fill the room with its emerging cries.

But tomorrow a cold, silent lifeless being would emerge from her. The end of their story together.

She couldn't remember when she had last taken a

breath and her lungs suddenly burnt with a fire that needed to be doused with oxygen. As she gasped, she felt her legs give way underneath her, and an aching sob emerged from her mouth as she slid to the floor.

Chapter 7

Some time later Margot wandered down the bustling corridors in a daze. Since the day she had found out she was pregnant she had known that this was the path that her life had been meant to take. In the relatively short time that she had been growing this child inside her she had planned for an entire lifetime together.

She felt as if she was going to lose a limb. She mourned for a part of her body which she didn't want to be parted from. She had been told at the reception to go straight home and prepare herself for the morning, as if any form of preparation would be possible.

She considered turning back and demanding further tests. They must have got it wrong. What if she followed their advice and went in tomorrow and terminated a perfectly healthy baby all because of an error? The image of the baby on the cold operating table yesterday came flooding back to her. People make mistakes, this must be a mistake. She stopped in her tracks unable to walk any further forwards. There was no way out of this for her now, she was trapped any which way she turned. She looked ahead in her mind's eye to a picture she had created at some unknown time over the past six months. She was walking along a beach in the late afternoon sunshine. Her child, a boy, was running along beside her splashing in and out of the waves. She could feel the cool salt spray refreshing on her skin as she looked down into his olive-green eyes. He stood beaming with adoration in his face as he tried to impress his mother, his protector, his best friend, his whole world.

She tried to erase the image from her mind. A false reality she had created for herself, one which she now doubted would ever come to life. She had less than 24 hours before that image would be taken from her forever.

She couldn't face walking any further, the ability to walk and process such strong emotions felt like too much to contend with so she slumped down onto some chairs nearby and sat staring out of the window.

Unable to think about the prospect of the following day Margot tried to focus her attention on the next hour and what she needed to do. Little steps she told herself, one thing at a time. All she wanted to do was go home, cradle her bump and cry into the void of the uncertainty she was now faced with.

*

Arriving back at home only a few short hours after she had left it, she was struck by how different home now felt.

Foolishly she had allowed herself to begin to imagine it being a home for herself and her child. There were only a few new items dotted throughout the house but it had been a change of perception that she hadn't fully acknowledged was happening. The spare room had begun to be cleared out in anticipation of new furniture being bought. She had allowed herself to buy one outfit the previous week, a simple white baby grow with two birds mid-flight on the chest. It had been hung up on her bedroom door ever since she had purchased it as a reminder that this was real, this was happening. To allow herself the possibility to enjoy the process and not focus on the fear that threatened to engulf her when she thought about what she was tackling on her own.

How foolish she had been. She should have known that it was too soon to get excited. Especially considering the field she worked in, she knew how often it went wrong. People didn't like to talk about it but it still happened with fairly common regularity she should have known to get this scan over and done with first before buying into her new future.

Had she been a drinker she would have been tempted to pour herself something large and strong but even the thought of that whilst she had life growing inside her was too much to bear. She had done everything right! She'd slept well, she'd eaten properly, she'd taken light exercise each day keeping herself fit and active. Why her? Why now?

She wandered through to the room that she had planned to use as the nursery still wearing her coat, she perched on the end of the chest of drawers unable to slow her brain down to allow herself to relax. Her mind wandered to the image yesterday again of that young baby fighting for life. Her child unaware of its fate trusting her to keep it safe from harm.

She longed for companionship and reassurance someone that she could trust to blurt all this out to just to know she wasn't dealing with this alone, comfort only her mother would be able to provide in this type of situation. The pain of losing her own parents rose up in her again. A physical ache in her chest when she thought of how much she still longed for them both and for their guidance as she navigated her way through life. Despite being a grown adult when her parents had died she had still relied on them both a lot in her everyday life and despite most people's thoughts about their parents she had genuinely enjoyed being in their company. Losing them had forced her to grow up quicker than she had planned and over the years she had grown accustomed to facing life's trials and tribulations on her own two feet. This however felt like it was too much for anyone to process on their own.

She had replaced all of her feelings of loss with a burning desire to find a cure. Never did she imagine that she would be required to murder her own child for the greater good.

Her brains coping mechanism turned to practical details that she could control in order to try and allay her fears. She had nursery furniture arriving next week, should she try and cancel it?

No she decided practical thoughts had no place right now she needed just to pace this one out. She decided to make herself a strong cup of tea and try to calm her nerves.

As she walked back through her flat towards the front door, she noticed a note had been pushed underneath it and was resting on the floor at an awkward angle. All her post was usually delivered to the post box outside of her house.

Bending down to pick it up she turned the note over to reveal handwriting she didn't recognise:

'Don't trust what they tell you, find a way to get out.'

She stared at it for a long time her hand gently shaking with the adrenaline that came with knowing something wasn't right. She cautiously went to the door and opened it to look outside. There was no one there, no hint of anything being disturbed just her simple front garden with the apple trees on the other side of the road gently swaying in the breeze.

Nobody knew what she had been told this afternoon she hadn't had the opportunity to tell anyone so how could this note relate to what had happened to her today?

The more she thought however the more she realised that people did know. The hospital staff knew. The sonographer, the doctor who had delivered the news. It would be written up in her notes by now and accessible to a number of people.

Could this be genuine or just someone's idea of a sick joke?

If it was meant for her then there was no ambiguity about what it meant but could she trust it?

She had a background in medical science, she had seen first-hand the horrors that this disease had brought to the innocent young children who were born with it. She knew that every pregnancy carried a risk and she had never doubted her integrity that if she were to find herself in this position she would do the right thing, the honourable thing, for herself and her child and the wider community.

Was her resolve failing her? Was she just looking for a way out because the reality of any other option was too difficult to process? But the baby yesterday was still alive, and her own test was definitely clear and now this note. Perhaps if she could just have more time to make a decision, to do more research or to try and find the author of this note to get more information.

But the reality was she had no more time. Tomorrow morning would be here before she knew it and there would be no going back then, her child would be gone, she would no longer be a mother and her opportunity to get more answers would be gone.

How could she legitimately buy herself some more time to figure this out? Just to establish more facts to come to an informed decision, to know that she had done everything she possibly could before taking her fate into her own hands.

She knew that if she failed to attend the appointment tomorrow they would send people for her. She would be arrested, sedated, the termination would happen anyway whilst she was unconscious and she would face imprisonment for her crimes. The question really was if she was willing to accept those repercussions in order to establish the truth of what was happening.

A plan began to formulate in her mind. A crazy one but a plan all the same. She had money that was easily accessible but what she would need was time to get away. She would need help to do it, and someone who had access to the hospital.

She could pack a bag and be gone within the hour which was tempting but it only bought her until tomorrow morning. As soon as she didn't show for her appointment the next day they would know that she'd run and begin the search for her and she knew she wouldn't be able to elude them for long.

She pulled out the printed sheet that she had been given at the scan to take another look at her results desperate to find something that would explain this to her. Her attention had been so focused on the results of the markers that she hadn't even considered looking too closely at the other details on the page. Her name and address were correct these were definitely her test results and everything else looked to be in order.

Then her gaze came to rest on the time the sheet had been generated. She frowned and gripped the paper tighter in her palm. None of this made any sense, she needed more answers.

If she took a bit of time now and put her plan into action, she could buy herself some time to get more of the facts. Once she began to go down this route though there was no turning back. She placed her hands on her belly and looked down imagining her child. This really was all the resolve she needed, whilst there was a chance that her baby was healthy she would do whatever it took to protect them both. She took a deep breath walked towards her front door and walked out onto the street.

The cold air brought her to her senses a bit. She felt like she may be losing her mind, what was she even thinking, considering such a ridiculous notion? She'd just keep walking and see if any other solution came to mind. If another plan came to her before she arrived at her destination then she didn't have to go ahead with what she was currently planning.

But the more she walked the more she felt certain that as extreme as it was, this was her only way forward. She owed it to herself and her baby to leave no stone unturned before going ahead with the termination. Her test had been negative, she kept repeating to herself over and over again. She was not being selfish, she was not being irresponsible, her test had definitely been negative.

Pounding the pavements helped her settle into a beat of self-assurance, with every step she reiterated the mantra to herself.

'This is just to buy me some time, I can't kill my child without knowing for sure, my test was negative, the note, that baby in the morgue.'

Images flooded her mind; her own life would not

be worth living if she ever found out she had killed her baby unnecessarily.

Eventually she reached the road she had been heading towards. The sky was turning darker shades of mauve and crimson as the sun began to settle over the horizon. The final hours of her last day of life as she knew it. Once she stepped into this house, she had no idea of the path her life would take.

She had only been to this house once before when she had needed to collect a file for work, she hoped she could remember which one was his. As she walked along the streets, she began to pick up her pace. The smallest second of doubt in her mind now would make her turn around, she needed to stay strong. Nobody was going to get hurt, except perhaps her and it was her only chance to give this baby an opportunity of a life it deserved.

She arrived at the end of the road and looked down it. A row of terraced houses on the left-hand side and larger semi-detached properties on the right. At the very end was a corner shop with a small flat above. She walked down careful not to allow her pace to turn into a jog, so eager was she to get there and get her plan into motion. Round the side of the shop was a red door with a worn-out intercom to the left-hand side. She pressed the button and frowned at the high-pitched squeal which emitted from it and echoed down the road.

What felt like an eternity of time passed and she was just about to press it again when an irritated voice came through

'Yes?'

'It's Margot' she paused knowing that this would confuse him 'from work, can I have a word please?'

She suddenly felt incredibly foolish, stood outside his home with no prior warning. Did she have time to think of another reason for her being here. Could she do this without his help after all? No, she had to stick to the plan it was her only chance.

She heard footsteps coming down the stairs on the other side of the door then a few clicks of the lock before it opened a fraction and he appeared peering through.

'Hi Nick, sorry to bother you.'

'What is it?' He gazed at her with an intensity that she wasn't expecting, obviously aware that something must have happened for her to be behaving in such an unusual way.'

'Can I come in please? It's a bit sensitive' She could tell that she had caught him off guard but putting him on the spot in such a way gave him little choice but to allow her entry. The sweet aroma of marijuana hung in the air. She had often amused herself imagining what her colleagues got up to outside of the office, Nick typically spending most of his evenings playing video games in his underwear. The addition of a spliff in hand at the same time seemed quite fitting and she almost smirked.

The flat itself was surprisingly tidy. A few plates and cups in the sink but nothing offensive. He gestured his arm towards the beige sofa in the corner of the living room and she took a seat.

'What can I do for you?'

Margot was aware of the normal pleasantries that would pass between two people initially but she really didn't have the time and she knew that Nick would want this visit to be over with as quickly as possible so she got straight down to business.

'I need your help Nick, I had some bad news today. Some really bad news. The baby's tested positive, I've been scheduled for a termination tomorrow.'

Her eyes filled with tears but she bit down on her lip and stopped them. Now was not the time for an emotional outburst. She needed to stay strong.

His brow furrowed in concern but he didn't immediately offer any platitudes or words of comfort, waiting perhaps for her to explain why this news had brought her specifically to his door.

'I can't do it Nick, I just can't. Not with the things we've noticed over the past few weeks. That baby yesterday really threw me, I've been reading up since then and there's never been a case of a baby at that stage of development surviving that long unaided.' She knew this alone wasn't enough to convince him, she needed to be completely honest with him but this was her biggest risk. Would he turn her in? Would he convince her that she was wrong or just force her to go to the appointment tomorrow?

She had no choice but to put all her trust in him.

'I tested myself yesterday Nick, I know I shouldn't have but after the post mortem I just needed to know everything was going to be OK. It was negative. And I don't just mean slightly below the threshold but 100% negative. The markers they showed me today were completely different, they can't have been right.'

'Can you show me yours Margot so I can take a look?'

She'd been worried about this. Knowing how it sounded and how it looked

'I deleted the test results, I knew how much trouble I'd be in and I was just doing it for my own peace of mind, but I have nothing to be able to prove it to you. There is this though'

She reached into her pocket and pulled out the scan results they'd given her along with her photograph, she handed them over to Nick to read through.

'The markers are definitely positive Margot' he said, sorrow in his eyes as he acknowledged how hurt she must be feeling.

'Not the markers Nick, look at the time.'

She jabbed at the page with urgency willing him to see what she was seeing

'The time of the test reads 9:08, my scan was moved from the first appointment of the day to the last. How could blood works supposedly completed during my appointment have been generated 8 hours earlier?'

He continued to stare at her intently, taking in every word, processing her state of mind no doubt and deciding how best to get her to come to her senses.

'And then, when I got home today, I had this note put underneath my door.'

She pulled out the note from her bag and passed

it over to him

'It can't be a coincidence, Nick. I know every mother must feel like this when they've been told what I've been told but I genuinely feel like this can't be right, they've got something wrong but I can't tell them why I think that. I feel healthy, the baby feels healthy, people make mistakes! What if this is a mistake? I know how to do those tests Nick, God knows you've seen how many I've done over the years and it was negative, I promise you it was negative.'

She was starting to sound shrill now and she knew she must look like she was losing her mind but she needed him to believe her. She was worried that he was going to tell her to leave and do the right thing.

'I need time Nick to go through all of this and process it. That's all I need just some time. I can't get back into the lab now this evening to take another test and it would raise suspicions if I even tried now that I've had the scan but I need to give this baby the best opportunity I can. I need to disappear for a while and I've come here to ask you to help me.'

He continued to stare at her, the silence thick in the air as she waited for his response. She had no other words to try and convince him to come to her aid.

Eventually he spoke.

'What did you have in mind?'

His calmness and apparent willingness to help her threw her off guard, she had been mentally preparing for the next round of hysterical pleas. She tentatively took a step towards him knowing that if he really was willing to help her to do this, he needed to understand the severity of what she was asking of him.

'Nick, I need to die.'

Chapter 8

'And how do you plan to do that?'

Nick was the type of man to want to get all of the information in front of him before making a decision.

Aware that this could also be a ruse to get her to divulge all her plans before alerting the authorities she wanted to be cautious but she really couldn't do this without him so she may as well trust him and accept the consequences.

'The mother of the baby from the autopsy yesterday, I need to know if she's still in the morgue. If she is I need her body bringing to my house. I can't be seen anywhere near work right now; I'm supposed to be at home preparing for a termination and you're the only other person I trust that has access to that building.'

'Do I dare ask what you want to do with a dead body once you've stolen her from the morgue?'

'It's probably best that you don't know too much. I don't want to incriminate you more than I already have and if it doesn't go to plan I won't mention that you played any part in it. I just need you to move her file to the archives and bring her to my house in your van. If anybody notices her missing in the morning, they can check her file which will show that she was incinerated during the night.'

Nick maintained his cool stare, he glanced down at the floor seemingly weighing up his options.

'It'll be best if I go this evening. The night shift starts at ten and they might have already destroyed the body if I go any later. Give me the key to your place and I'll leave her there. You go somewhere public, make sure that you're seen so that you've got yourself an alibi. She'll be there for you when you get back.'

Margot didn't know what to say, she was suddenly seeing him in a new light. Why was he so willing to help her? He was risking so much to come to her aid.

'Nick I'm asking something of you that no one should ever have to do, are you sure you're willing to do this for me?'

He looked down at his feet, nervously pulling together the words that he had been wanting to say for years.

'I'd do anything for you Margot.'

As her eyes filled once more, he coughed and looked away from her unsure how to move on. Neither of them quite knew what to say next. Margot crossed the room and handed out the spare key to her house she had picked up before she had left, placing it in his palm before resting her hands on his shoulders and gently kissing his cheek.

'If this goes to plan it could very well be the last time I see you. Please know how grateful we are' she said resting her hand on her belly.

'Take care Margot.'

She walked slowly down the stairs and back out into the weak afternoon sunshine. Everything had shifted now. There was no going back.

With the knowledge that she couldn't return home for a while she decided to walk to try and gather her thoughts. She needed to process what she had just decided to do and make plans for the next few days.

She walked the two miles to a local park she used to come to as a child. Her memories of this place were filled with warm sunny afternoons spent with her mother, the two of them on the swings, daring each other to try and touch the clouds. Making daisy chains with her father whilst her mother had a doze, her face obscured by her straw hat which was doubled up as a sun visor.

Today the landscape was in clear contrast to her memories. Cold and damp there were still a few children running around, wrapped up in thick coats and boots, their cheeks red from exertion, their parents no doubt desperate to get them out of the house for a few hours to run off some steam.

Had she known all those years ago what her own future had in store would she have cherished those days even more? Would she ever get the opportunity to push her own child on the swings? Even if this crazy plan did work out what kind of lifestyle would she be able to provide for them both? Her plan was in no way fool proof and if they spent any amount of time investigating what had happened, they would no doubt quickly find that something was amiss.

If she could just safely deliver her child, she would be able to prove to the authorities that their tests were wrong, that the outcomes weren't always inevitable. They would be living proof that mistakes were made and that she had done the right thing. They would be free to live out their lives in peace. She couldn't simply give up.

She decided to leave a paper trail of where she had visited just in case they decided to trace her steps from her last night on earth. She walked through the park and around the small lake to a cafe on the other side. Being sure to pay using her card she ordered a small sandwich and a tea; she didn't feel like eating but even in her mild state of panic at her future plans she acknowledged that after tonight she wasn't sure where her next meal would come from and that it was probably best to eat now whilst she could.

She got full very quickly these days with the baby taking up more and more space inside her so by the time she'd finished her sandwich she felt suitably stuffed. With another good few hours to kill she pondered how she might be best spending them. Nick had told her to make sure she was seen but who could she meet up with now? She was meant to be beside herself with grief at the prospect of losing her child. She tried to imagine exactly what she would be doing had she accepted the decision earlier today; she could very well be out getting fresh air and she would want to reach out to somebody to share her grief. The only other person who might need to be aware she supposed was the father. Her mind wandered to Ben, she pictured him sitting at home with his beautiful wife, no doubt sitting around the dinner table basking in their life's successes.

Whichever way the next few days and weeks worked out she would probably never see him again. She knew that he would not be willing to throw away his marriage for a one-night stand but she realised now that she had been harbouring some weak belief that he may someday come around to the idea and be the father that she needed him to be.

She decided that he deserved to know partially what was going on. She would never be able to trust him with the truth but a modified version of it would do no harm and would in fact give her the perfect alibi for the evening. If she was truthful with herself, she also felt a thrill at the opportunity to speak to him again. She wanted for some part of him to know the pain he had brought into her life. She knew he wasn't worthy of her but like so many men it was the ones that were completely unavailable that you wanted the most.

She trawled through emails on her phone to bring up one from him sent to the whole department, as she had hoped at the bottom of his email signature was his work number. She decided to send him a message and break the news not wanting to disrupt him by calling if he was at home. The idea of her phone being found the next day and his secret being found out also gave her quite the thrill.

'Hi. It's Margot. I realise this will come as a shock to you but I'm 24 weeks pregnant with your child. I had my scan today and the baby has tested positive. Termination scheduled for tomorrow. Just figured you should know. M x'

She knew she was antagonising him but she was so frustrated at the injustice of his ability to screw over so many people and be completely oblivious to the carnage it had caused. She wanted him to at least feel some sense of responsibility for what she was going through, although the reality was probably that he would just feel relief. She hit send quickly before she had time to calm down and re-word it. She'd been careful with her wording so as not to lie to him but at least he knew now what he's put her through.

As she went to put her phone back in her bag she felt it vibrate with an incoming message. It couldn't be him; six months of radio silence had made it very clear he wanted nothing to do with her.

'I'll call you in five minutes.'

She was shocked, she had never assumed he would acknowledge her message let alone call her back. Now she was going to speak to him? She felt her heart leap with nervous anticipation. It would be harder to maintain the lie over the phone, she would have to be cautious what she said.

She wandered outside of the cafe wrapping herself up in her coat and scarf whilst she waited for him to call. She walked around the lake twice whilst she waited, repeatedly checking her phone in case she had somehow missed her. Everything with this man was a power struggle, she thought she'd had the upper hand sending him the message but here she was hanging off his every word, desperately waiting for him to call. She was just about to leave the park when her crisp clear ring tone rang out from her hand. She took a breath not wanting to appear overly eager to answer

'Hi Ben'

'Margot I don't know what to say, I just wanted to offer my condolences'

His professional manner of speaking almost made her want to laugh, did he think he was coming across as sincere?

'I just thought you had the right to know, I realise it won't be the worst news in the world for you.'

'I never wished you any ill Margot, but you must realise this was never in my plan. You meant a lot to me but I can't jeopardize what I've got here.'

She picked up on the past tense of meant. Granted it had been months since they had been together but it was clear whatever feelings there had been were now no longer.

'It was never in my plan either Ben but I own my life choices, I don't run away from them. Either way the decisions been taken out of our hands now, I won't be a nuisance to you anymore.'

'If there's anything I can do Margot'

'It's fine, there's no going back now, I don't think I'll be able to see you for a while.'

'Take as much time off as you need, I'll clear it with Head Office… Margot I really am very sorry for your loss.'

Hearing her name run off his tongue made her heart ache, how desperately she'd wished to hear him say her name recently. The ghosting from him had been insufferable making her constantly doubt what they'd had together and what it had meant to her. She heard a female voice laughing distantly in the background of his phone and she sensed his hasty need to end the conversation.

'Go back to your life Ben, I'll see you around.'

She ended the call before he could say another word, a very small sense of achievement at having the last word. She felt the heartache that she had suppressed for months rise up in her again. She was embarrassed to even admit to herself how much she had pined after him. Why didn't he love her? Why had she meant so little to him?

She had hoped that contacting him would give her a sense of closure but all it had done was bring back to life her aching need to be loved by him again. Now she really was on her own. Tomorrow she would have to start a new chapter of her life, she knew she would find the strength from somewhere when the time came but for now, she sat down on a bench head in hands and contemplated how it had all gone so wrong.

Chapter 9

Returning home later, with a shaking hand, Margot placed her key in the lock and turned. Although she was prepared for what she was going to find she still felt a nervous anticipation of how the situation would present itself. Where would Nick have left the body? Would she be covered up or laid bare? She turned on the hallway light and paused looking down the length of the corridor. On the hall table to her right she noticed her spare key had been placed down next to her potted orchid plant. This must mean that he had been able to carry out the task. There was no note or message on her phone from him but that was a good thing, she didn't want this to come back in any way on him.

If he had been able to carry out the job then it meant that somewhere here was a dead body which she had to get rid of. She had gone too far down the path now to change her mind, she had to see this through so she had better just get on with it.

Clenching her hands into fists she felt her nails

digging into the palms of her hands as she began to walk forwards towards her living room. She decided to turn on all the lights as she went along the hallway to banish away some of the demons created by the darkness. Wasn't that always the frustration in the horror movies that no one ever turned on the lights! Well not her, she was going about this sensibly.

She pushed open the door into her small open plan living room and kitchen and flicked on the switch. Everything was just as she had left it, her mug from that morning rested on the draining board, her newspaper still open on the island in the kitchen showing the sombre faces of the prime minister trying to control the ever growing tensions of a population in crisis.

She turned to face her living room area where two cream sofas sat at a 90-degree angle towards her patio doors. The view from her patio door windows had been one of the first things she had fallen in love with when she bought the house. She adored sitting in the dark at night time with the curtains open looking out into the garden. Her favourite weeping willow tree stood a few meters down the garden path and she had decorated it with warm white fairy lights wrapped around its gnarly twisted trunk. In fact, her curtains were rarely closed due to her secluded spot giving her ample privacy. Today however they were tightly pulled together which must have been Nick's doing.

The oak coffee table which normally stood pride of place in the middle of the living room had been pushed towards the window to create extra floor space in the middle which gave her good reason to suspect that this would be where she would find her body double.

As she walked forward towards the sofa, she was able to get a better line of sight of the floor space. She began to see the edge of a black body bag laid out flat on the floor. She steadied her breathing with each step until she was stood at the foot of the bag covering the body. The gravity of her situation began to sink in. This was actual insanity. She had become so far removed from the person she thought she was, she felt that if she looked at herself in the mirror now she wouldn't recognise the person staring back. But whether she liked it or not this was her reality, her path, she had made her bed and by goodness had she got to lie in it. There was no time to ponder, delay or procrastinate this was her fate. Like ripping off a plaster she needed to do this and it needed to be done now.

She placed her hand on the zip and with a purposeful grip moved it down the length of the bag and across the top. She parted the two sections open and exposed the naked body of the woman who until that evening had lain in the morgue. She could feel the cold emanating from her body and involuntarily shivered. It was important for her to remove the body bag and take it with her, she didn't know how well it would burn and it would raise immediate suspicion should it be found.

She wasn't however going to be able to take the body bag away without touching the body which had been something she had desperately wanted to try and avoid. Somehow touching the cold lifeless skin made her feel more like a criminal than ever before.

She rested her hand on the woman's far shoulder. She was of a slim build and her bones jutted out of her frame in obscure ways. Pulling the shoulder towards her Margot levered the body up onto its side coming to rest on her hip. With her free hand Margot pulled the black body bag out from underneath the body before slowly laying her down to rest again on her back.

A wave of nausea swam over Margot with the effort and repulsiveness of what she was doing. She needed to get away from the body for a second, to breathe in fresh air without the stench of death. Bundling the bag up into a ball she took it away and placed it by the front door so she wouldn't accidentally forget to take it with her. She decided to pack some of the essentials that she would need to take her mind briefly off what she had just done. She knew she couldn't take too much with her but a few items wouldn't cause suspicion. Going into her bedroom she opened up her wardrobe and reached up to take out her rucksack. It was a decent enough size to hold the majority of her money along with a handful of clothes to see her through the next few days or weeks. Where she would end up after that she had no idea.

Above her head hung one of her favourite paintings of all time, Monet's impression, Sunrise depicted a hazy morning of a French port. It symbolised to Margot the dawn of a new day and had served as a constant reminder that every morning held the potential for change. It also served a dual purpose as being the perfect size to cover up the opening to her personal safe.

She removed the print from its hanging and entered her code into the electric key pad. She had not looked at this money since her parents had passed away. She lived a frugal existence and had not needed any extra cash other than what she earned each month, until now that was. Now she was relieved that it remained untouched. She was also more than thankful for her father's forward planning. When he had foreseen the country going into such decline, he had withdrawn all his savings and passed them onto Margot as some sort of obscenely large rainy-day fund. She dreaded to think what he would make of the circumstances in which she would now be spending it. She only prayed he would have given her his blessing to fight for his grandchild.

She began to pack the money into the bag, calmly at first in neatly piled bundles but as time drew on, she began to get more and more anxious to leave the house. Before long she was throwing fistfuls of money into the bag in a mild panic before grabbing a handful of clothes forcing them on top of the money and zipping it closed. The bag was now surprisingly heavy and she worried that she might struggle to carry it to the train station. Dragging it to the front door she laid it to rest in the hallway. There were plenty of other things she would have liked to have taken with her but she could only afford to take the essentials.

She went into the bathroom and tied her long brown hair up into a bun before pulling a black beanie over her head. She would need a more dramatic makeover in the next few days but there wasn't time for that now. She went to her closet and pulled out her long green mackintosh coat which she put on and pulled up the collar. Now all she had to do was disappear.

She picked up the petrol can she had left in the hallway and walked it into the living room. She kept her eyes averted now from the body of the naked woman on the floor and began to pour the fuel all over her home. She splashed it up the curtains, over the cushions and the rugs. The smell was so pungent it made her nostrils burn. Well aware that the house would go up quickly once the petrol caught aflame, she needed to give herself time to get away from the house before the flames took over so she went to the kitchen cupboard and took out one of her large pillar candles. She balanced it precariously on the floor next to a puddle of fuel and took out her lighter. With one last glance back at the door to check she had everything ready she bent down and lit the candle. She had no idea how long the candle would stay standing for and nor did she want to wait to find out. With a purposeful stride to her step, she picked up her belongings and walked out of the front door, never to return again.

*

Just at the moment when she feared that she would

lose control of her emotions everything came into very clear focus. She knew what she had to do and it was vital that she stay composed. As she walked down the road towards the train station, she kept her pace steady and her head down. It was as if all her life had been leading up to this moment. She didn't even feel fear anymore. This was what she was meant to do. She was creating an opportunity for her child, one which a few hours ago had seemed unobtainable. She almost had to stifle a grin. It must be the nerves she told herself, she had to be careful she could imagine herself getting hysterical if she wasn't careful. Just get on the train she told herself, once she'd made it to the train she'd feel like she'd really begun her escape.

Her bag was heavy and her coat thick. She tried to slow her pace down to make her walk easier but was torn between catching her breath and arriving at her destination as quickly as possible. She had been considering her options regarding where to travel to throughout the afternoon. She figured the more remote the better and had decided to go North.

It took her ten minutes to arrive at the train station, it's large brick archways a welcome respite from the night air. She had anticipated it being quiet but had forgotten just how well used public transport was these day. Families crowded around the giant TV screens depicting the departures and arrival for the next two hours. Workers still on their late commute home. She suddenly started to panic that she might struggle to get a seat on a train but reminded herself that the world was her oyster. She could travel wherever she needed to and if that didn't turn out to be right, she could move on. Suddenly with a feeling of elation and a lightness she had not felt in years she headed over to one of the nearby ticket booths to begin her search.

She knew that she couldn't use her card again and the self-service booths didn't take cash but she didn't want to raise suspicion by going over to the desk and being unsure of where she wanted to travel to. She decided to scout out her options and then once she'd made a decision she would head over to the desk.

Fortunately, the large screens hanging down from the ceiling in the main atrium were awash with information and were visible to all. Scanning today's list of imminent departures she looked down the list of possible destinations. There were four destinations listed as departing in the next twenty minutes which were heading North. The first to Birmingham, then Manchester, Liverpool and Newcastle. Whilst she knew that distance alone wouldn't keep the authorities at bay, she felt there was an added comfort in being as far away as possible and so settled on Newcastle. It was one of the most expensive tickets for that very reason but she justified that she would have to spend some money initially to get herself set up. At the very least it would make her rucksack slightly lighter.

After purchasing her tickets, she found herself with fifteen minutes spare. Just enough time to grab herself some food for on the train and get herself to the platform. It was a blessing not to have too much thinking time. She needed to stay active until she got onto the train. Her mind began to wander to the house and what state it would be in now but she quickly pushed the thought to the back of her mind, it would do her no good to focus on what was now her former life.

She found a small kiosk selling sandwiches and purchased herself some dinner, then following the guidance of the large atrium screens she navigated her way to the correct platform.

She was relieved to see the train already there waiting for departure. Her feet and back were now aching with the exertion of the walk along with the heavy load and she craved a seat to take the weight off.

As she stepped up into the carriage, she could see that half of the seats were already occupied but as she walked along the centre aisle towards her numbered seat, she was relieved to see that her seat and the one next to it were currently empty. One man sat alone on the opposite side of the table facing her, engrossed in his newspaper. Relieved that she would have some space to spread out a bit she took her seat and placed her bag on the seat next to her. Even though it would technically fit in the overhead cabin the thought of it not being within touching distance made her feel anxious.

She opened up the cool bottle of water that she had purchased and eagerly gulped it down. It was the first time she had appreciated any kind of sustenance since she had been given the news at the scan. She felt the cool liquid flow down her throat all the way into her stomach relishing each mouthful. Draining the bottle, she let out an audible sigh as she placed the bottle down onto the table followed immediately by an involuntary burp. Instinctively she placed her hand over her mouth to stifle the sound but the gesture was futile.

She noticed the newspaper lower slightly opposite her to reveal the warm brown eyes of the gentleman sat opposite her. He caught her gaze and raised one eyebrow in mock surprise. She could tell that masked by his paper his mouth had formed the faintest hint of a smile.

'Excuse me' she mumbled, feeling the warm heat of mild embarrassment rise up her face.

She turned away from him pretending to be interested in something at the far end of the carriage to save her embarrassment and was relieved to see in her peripheral vision that he had lowered his gaze and returned to his paper.

Content now that she had found her seat and was relatively safe for the next 3 hours, she took the time to relax into her chair, attempt to slow her breathing and her heart rate and watch the remaining passengers take their seats.

The usual hum drum of activity provided her with a good distraction from her thoughts as people struggled with their luggage and wandered up and down shouting out seat numbers to their travelling companions.

A musical tone overhead announced that they would soon be departing and listed off the stations that they would be passing through on their way.

With a hiss she heard the doors slide to a close and after a few minutes the train slowly began to pull away from the platform. She watched as the walkway outside of her window disappeared to reveal the exterior of the train station and then out into the city of London, past the high-rise flats and office blocks of the surrounding areas.

She hadn't been outside of London for years, too consumed with her life and her research to consider having a break. She wondered when if ever she would return and under what circumstances they might be. She laid her head back on the head rest and let her eyes close, safe in the knowledge that for now at least she had successfully escaped.

Chapter 10

As the concrete labyrinth of houses merged into rolling green fields Margot felt more and more relieved to be out of the city. It wasn't just the last six months she was distancing herself from it was the past five years, hell the past 34 years for that matter.

Leaving London meant leaving behind everything that had ever weighed her down and constricted her into becoming the woman she had. Even as a young child she had never done anything reckless. Always too afraid of retribution or disappointing those closest to her. Whilst she knew she was incredibly lucky to have had the childhood she'd had with such loving and supportive parents she had also felt that her path had been laid out for her from her very infancy. She was always going to be an academic, she was always going to go into the field of science and medicine. Every time she achieved something impressive in her life it was always met with a lack of surprise because that was what had always been expected of her.

Until that was, she became pregnant.

She was sure that her parents would have supported her with the pregnancy had they been alive but it would have been the first time that she had truly taken them by surprise. The first time they would have potentially been disappointed in her. Would they have shown it? Margot was sure it would have taken them a short while to come around to the idea but surely becoming grandparents would be considered a blessing. Maybe the joy is tainted when you also have the benefit of experience of knowing how difficult the road ahead was going to be for their one and only daughter. As joyful as children can be they certainly bring with them their challenges especially when raising them alone.

Margot's thoughts wandered as the landscape outside became less industrial, interspersed with wide open spaces as they powered North. It dawned on her how big the country was, how much opportunity it gave her, how much potential.

She felt the baby turn inside her and a limb of some sorts pushed out of her side in a stretch. She felt the now familiar feeling of her bladder being squashed, not helped by all of the water she had guzzled down and she started to consider the best way of making a visit to the toilet.

She shuffled sideways into the aisle of the carriage and reached back over to drag her rucksack towards her. The gentleman sitting opposite once again lowered his paper to view her struggle.

'I can watch your bag for you if you'd like?' he

said

Her eyes rested on his full face for the first time and she felt a further flutter of embarrassment as she remembered her burp earlier.

His chocolate brown eyes twinkled with a youthfulness that made him instantly endearing. His jet-black hair was lightly tousled in the nonchalant way which some men could pull of impeccably. He wore a grey t-shirt and black jeans showing off a toned physique but his manner was one of ease and self-assurance.

Margot's initial response was to thank him for the offer but insist she was fine, but common sense prevailed. She was in the middle of a train carriage with at least 30 minutes to go until they stopped at the next station. Even if he did steal her bag there was no where he could go with it and it would be so much easier to pop to the toilet without it for two minutes.

'That would be great, thank you' she replied with a smile and navigated her way to the intersection of the carriages where the toilet cubicle was located.

It was occupied when she made it there so she waited patiently to enter. She could never understand what took people so long in public toilets. Surely the aim was to be in and out as quickly as humanly possible. Eventually the light on the door turned to green and an elderly lady vacated allowing her to enter.

Her unexpected wait had made her anxious as she considered the length of time she'd left her bag unattended. She couldn't return to collect it now though as that would look suspicious so she did her business as quickly as she could before heading back.

She needn't have worried though as upon her return she saw that both her bag and her attractive travelling partner were both exactly where she had left them.

He, having now discarded with his paper, sat gazing out of the window and looked up with a smile when she returned.

'All done?' he questioned as she returned to her seat.

She looked at him with a puzzled expression unsure how to respond to such a question

'Sorry, I've got no idea why I just said that' he said with a grimace 'that's embarrassing'

Margot inwardly smiled

'Well, I guess we're even now then' she smiled and he laughed a warm laugh.

'I never was any good at conversation starters' he confessed with a boyish grin

'I tend to find just a simple hi works best most of the time'

He chuckled to himself 'Well, in that case Hi, I'm Sy, nice to meet you'

'I'm Margot' she replied returning his smile.

There followed an awkward silence, neither of them quite sure whether or not to continue the conversation or leave it at that. Whichever they chose they would have to maintain for the remainder of the journey of which there was still quite a long way to go.

It also occurred to Margot that maybe she should have given a false name. She was new to this whole fugitive lifestyle and hadn't considered yet what new personality she was going to give herself.

She remembered seeing once in some crime drama that she'd been hooked on that the best method was to create an alias which had similarities to your real life to make it easier to remember when you were put on the spot. She decided to stick with Margot moving forwards and to create a new false surname for when the time required.

'Are you heading up to Newcastle?' he asked her.

She wondered if he'd had the same internal dilemma about whether or not to continue the conversation and she was secretly pleased that he'd decided to.

'Yes, it's my first time. Any recommendations?'

'Ah, you'll love it, it's got everything you need. A great city, lovely coastline, the countryside and the nicest people you could ever come across.'

Despite speaking about the area so passionately his lack of a Geordie accent implied that he didn't originate from there. He spoke with a soft and gentle, well-educated tone. He paced out his words implying a thoughtfulness behind them and Margot found herself wanting to hear more of it.

She was also suddenly conscious of her disheveled appearance, having not had the time or energy to warrant looking in the mirror for the past few days.

She was amazed at herself for even having these thoughts. One attractive man seemed to be all it took to take her mind off task, but it wasn't very often that you just happened to strike up a conversation in this way. At the very least it was nice to just pretend she was like all the other people on the train for a little while without a care in the world.

'Have you spent a lot of time there then?' she queried

'I've got family there so I try to come up when I get a break from work. It's nice to escape London every now and again'.

'I agree, it feels more peaceful already'.

She partially stood up to remove her coat showing off her petite bump for the first time. His eyes came to rest on her expanded waistline and she expected to see his face drop and his attention waiver. Instead, he smiled warmly.

'How far gone?' He asked

'24 weeks, or six months in normal terminology. I never used to understand why everyone talked about in weeks but then you get sucked into it when it's happening to you.'

'I know that feeling, I work in that kind of terminology all day long so I'm used to the jargon.'

'Are you a doctor?'

'A surgeon, I'm based in Cambridge'

'Ah I see' she was tempted to add 'attractive and successful, where do I sign?' but that would be a new flirting low even by her standards.

'How about you?' he asked

This was slightly more dangerous territory for her. There were a limited number of people working in her field and confessing what she truly did would be a bit too close to the bone. She decided to stick with what she knew best outside of her own career.

'I'm a science teacher' she said, the lie rolling off her tongue with surprising ease. It had been her mother's profession for over thirty years so she knew enough about it to hold down a conversation and technically she did teach a science of sorts in her lab so it was only a little white lie.

'Ah I see, haven't the schools just gone back?'

She hadn't even made the connection to it being the start of a new academic year but with relief she realised that her bump gave her the perfect alibi.

'I've taken a bit of a sabbatical before my maternity leave kicks in just to extend it a bit.'

'Sounds great, I'm envious. I only get a long weekend before I'm back to it'.

'Yes, it's a nice opportunity to get away and visit somewhere new' and whether it was the unexpected connection she'd just made with this new man or the sense of adventure that her pseudonym had created but she suddenly felt like there was some small chink of hope for her and the new life she was starting.

They continued their conversation for the next hour, the topics flowing freely as they discovered more about each other. He spoke openly about his upbringing and the difficulties of balancing the traditional views of his family whilst being a single man in the city. They both laughed at some of their dating failures over the years as Margot confided that she had never envisaged being single and pregnant by the age of thirty-four.

'You seem like an extremely capable woman, I'm sure you're going to be an incredible mother' he told her and she felt a flicker of pride at the unexpected compliment.

All too soon they found themselves pulling away from Darlington train station with Newcastle announced as the next stop. People began milling around collecting their bags and wrapping up in their coats and scarves ready to leave the train.

Margot found she didn't want the journey to end. What a joyful little pocket of fresh air she'd found herself in. A window of time where she didn't need to be looking over her shoulder every five minutes or questioning her every move.

Sy, who was travelling much lighter than Margot, discarded his newspaper in the bin between the seats and picked up his designer Barbour holdall. He reached over to lift her bag across the seats for her.

'I'll carry this to the door for you' he said

'No!' She practically shouted with an unnecessary sense of urgency. She'd warmed to him that was true but she certainly wasn't going to allow him to carry her whole life in his hands.

'Thank you, but honestly I'll be fine'

He looked slightly taken back by her outburst but didn't force the issue, no doubt putting it down to a stubborn independent streak.

As the train pulled into Newcastle she led the way down the carriage and off the train. The ticket barriers were directly ahead of them leading out onto the street. As they exited through the beautiful arched building, she was shocked to feel the bitter chill in the air. The temperature was drastically cooler than it had been in London.

'Well, I'm this way' Sy said pointing to his right down the high street.

Not knowing which way she was going but not wanting to show it she decided to go in the opposite direction.

'It was nice meeting you Sy, thank you for keeping me company' she said

'The pleasure was all mine' he smiled and for a brief second she felt like reaching out and taking his hand. Absurd since she'd only known him for a grand total of three hours but this was the only person she knew in this unfamiliar city and she wanted desperately to hold onto him.

Instead, they shared an awkward smile, one which seemed to say everything they'd left unsaid.

'Bye' she waved in an upbeat tone masking her rising sense of anxiety and they simultaneously turned and walked away from one another.

'Don't look back' she said to herself, 'don't be that woman!' But despite her best efforts she couldn't resist one more peek. She glanced round behind her only to find with disappointment that he had already been swallowed up into the crowd.

Chapter 11

Quite what her next steps were to be she wasn't too sure. Had she not become distracted by her travelling companion she may have had some time to make a plan but the journey had gone all too quickly and she now found herself in an unfamiliar city, late in the evening, with nowhere to sleep.

She knew she couldn't stand around waiting for a solution to miraculously appear to her and so she walked into the cold evening air with her jacket pulled closely around her to keep herself warm. She rationalised that there would be lots of hotels in the middle of a city and surely there must be ample rooms available, it being a random Tuesday in September. She did however need to be conscious of her finances and so a night anywhere swanky was definitely out of the question. Her head ached with the developments of the day. It was astonishing to think that only a matter of hours ago she'd been going about her business without a care in the world. How was this the same day that had started so normally?

She let her instincts direct her as she headed towards what felt like the centre of the city.

The streets were mainly lined with students at this late hour, some already worse for wear, enjoying the freedom of mid-week drinking that only university life provides. She could ask someone for directions she realised but she didn't want to draw any attention to herself unnecessarily.

Just as she was starting to consider finding herself a cafe to get warm and consider her next steps she saw at the end of the road a familiar logo for a travel lodge. The marketing department should be proud she thought, just a brief glimpse of a colour and a sliver of their signage told her exactly which company it was and it was universally accepted as a cheap but clean place to stay for the night.

She decided it would do for the evening, she could rest up for the night and in the morning consider her next steps.

Walking into the foyer she felt anxious at being somewhere so public. Could the authorities have followed her here? Was there any way they could have traced her movements yet and tracked her down?

The young man behind the reception desk looked like he wished to be anywhere other than at work on this cold dark evening. After establishing from his mono syllabic grunts that it was a decent price for one evening, Margot handed over her money, gave a false name of an old family friend and was given her key for the evening.

The rickety lift was out of order so although it was the last thing she felt like doing after such an arduous day she resigned herself to climbing the three flights of stairs to find her room.

Unlocking her door and walking into her home for the evening she peeled her bag off her back and methodically removed her layers and her shoes. Stretching out her toes into the worn carpet she allowed herself a moment to enjoy the cool air touching her skin. She was hot, sticky, physically exhausted but mentally wired. Part of her wanted to collapse in a heap on the bed and sleep for the next three days straight. Another part of her desperately wanted a shower, to wash away her sins in an attempt to cleanse her soul.

Stripping off entirely she double and triple checked the lock on the door before stepping into the steaming shower.

She stood for five minutes under the stream of water, allowing it to pour onto her face and down her body waiting for it to soak through and make her feel clean again. Images from the day flashed in front of her closed eyes. The scan, the doctors face, those markers so different from the ones she knew to be true, the corpse, her house. What state would her house be in now? She hardly dared to think about it, so frightening a concept it was to consider what she had done. So far removed had she become in such a short space of time from the woman she thought she was.

Her body cleansed but no less absolved she dried herself off and went back into the bedroom. Sitting on the end of the bed she cast a furtive glance at the door every few minutes. Every sound she heard she queried. Every silence she listened out for she wondered if they were tiptoeing down the corridor ready to break in to her room.

She had never felt so alone. What was she doing? Up until now in the rush of it all and with the adrenaline running hot in her blood she had embraced her sense of adventure and gone with it. She had felt like a vigilante, taking the law into her own hands, doing what needed to be done to protect her helpless child.

Now, in the stillness, with only her thoughts, in an unfamiliar city, she felt like a criminal on the run. Frightened and shocked by her own actions and what she had so quickly turned into. In a couple of hours she would not arrive for her appointment and if news hadn't already spread about her house fire they would soon be aware that she was not going to be arriving for her termination.

She wondered how Nick was feeling tonight, the reality of what she had asked of him sitting like a dead weight in the pit of her stomach.

She knew why she had made the choices that she had but that didn't mean she felt any better about them. With low energy and an even lower mood she got herself into bed and pulled the covers up to her chin attempting to find some comfort and solace in their unfamiliarity.

She had discovered long ago that tiredness went hand in hand with anxiety and despair and it stood to reason that this was not the time for her to be making any major decisions about her future whilst she feeling so melancholy.

For now, she had to sit with the uncomfortable emotions, keep breathing, attempt sleep and see what tomorrow would bring.

*

Sleep, fortunately, was granted to her and Margot blinked open her eyes to the morning light filtering through her curtains. Her body in the exact same position she had lain down in, she didn't appear to have moved all night. Perhaps the criminal life was becoming to her. She remained still for a while, savouring the feeling of being well rested before she needed to start her day, before more decisions were thrust upon her. Would this perhaps be the day her journey ended? Would they catch up with her that quickly or by some twist of fate might she be given more time to figure things out.

She felt the baby stretch inside her, pushing a limb of sorts down into the mattress. 'It's OK sweetheart' she thought 'mum's got this.'

Getting herself up and dressed she decided to get an early start, though quite what her rush was now she wasn't sure. Her life was one long list of things to do normally, she always got up and started her day with enthusiasm, perhaps her new lifestyle would have to accommodate being slightly more leisurely.

Her first priority was to organise somewhere more long term to stay. Somewhere she could legitimately call home until the baby was born along with being somewhere that would be suitable to give birth in.

Taking one last cold shower to wake her up she dressed in the clothes from the day before, re-applied all of her many layers and hauled her bag once again onto her back. Her muscles and feet protested immediately at being put back to use so quickly after such an exerting day yesterday. They would have to get used to it, she couldn't imagine the next few weeks and months were going to be any more relaxing.

Traipsing back down the stairs to reception it appeared that the moody teenager had finished his shift and there was somebody new on reception. She had been planning on asking about somewhere she could stay locally more long term but it felt like leaving a trail of breadcrumbs for whoever may be looking for her, so instead she thanked the lady for a restful nights sleep and wandered out into the weak morning sunshine.

With nowhere particular to be she took a little time to simply familiarise herself with her surroundings. The city felt welcoming, her walk from the train station the night before hadn't felt intimidating despite the lateness of the hour and she realised now that it had taken her almost from one side of the city to the other. Far smaller than other cities she had been too this felt more compact and easier to navigate. The modern shop fronts masked the more traditional aspects of the buildings and the obvious history of the City was a comforting backdrop.

Treating herself to a coffee and a croissant from a bakery she enquired as to where she might find a library and was relieved to be told it was only around the corner. She had always found libraries a huge comfort and in the absence of a mobile phone and internet access this was going to be the next best thing. Following the easy directions she turned off the main high street and walked towards the large glassed building of the city library. Walking through the doors she felt a hush descend on her mind. The juxtaposition of being cocooned in a room of silence in the middle of a bustling city was like a hot water bottle for the soul. Coupled with the fact that she was surrounded by academia and the words of the greatest minds in history and she was quite frankly in her element. If there was the option to move in here she thought she may have found her utopia.

She had always found the people that worked in a library to also be genuinely nice people. She couldn't imagine anyone impatient or abrasive working in such a blissful environment.

Despite longing to sit and immerse herself in a research paper she kept her mind on the task of getting herself somewhere to stay. As expected the delightful elderly lady behind the desk informed her that for a matter of pennies she could use the internet on their computers for 3 hours and she plonked herself down in a corner and set about her task.

As she had expected there were no end of available places for her to stay but somewhere that would be available long term and within her budget was proving to be trickier. The further out of the city she looked the more the price dropped, understandably, but she had to balance this against the life she wanted to have for the next three months. If she wanted to be able to try to continue her research she would need to be frequenting the library regularly and it didn't make sense to be paying for transport every day.

On top of that she still wanted to be within a reasonable distance of the hospital should there be an emergency. She knew how risky childbirth could be at the best of times and ultimately if something went wrong she had to prepare herself for the worst. She was doing this to try and save her child, she needed to make sure she didn't die trying.

After an hour of googling and a page of scribbled notes she headed out to the payphone to make her enquiries. The first two she phoned were unable to provide accommodation for such a prolonged period of time without a contract and proof of ID. She kept her tone light informing them that that wouldn't be a problem and that she had a few more calls to make before making a decision. It wouldn't be wise to let anyone know how much she needed to go under the radar right now.

The third establishment she called marketed itself as a B and B with rooms available for more than two weeks at a discount. The phone rang out initially which didn't bode well but on the second attempt eventually someone picked up. There was the sound of a dog intermittently barking in the background which made it hard to establish what was said.

Margot pressed a finger into her other ear to hear better.

'Hello?'

'Yep, how can I help?'

''Hi, I'm looking for a room for a month or two, do you have anything available?'

'Aye, when from?'

'Well tonight if possible.'

'Name?' The noise in the background was constant so she imagined it was hard for them to hear her too.

'Sam'

'It's two hundred a week with two weeks cash up front'

'Yes, okay that's no problem.'

'Booked' and with that the line went dead.

Dubious but relieved she at least had something to get her started she replaced the retriever in the holder. At that rate she could stay until the baby was born, still have enough cash for food and drink and a bit left over to see her through afterwards before she moved on. She knew it wasn't going to be the ritz but she couldn't be fussy right now. She could slum it, she reassured herself, it's not like she was going to be camping. She would have a roof over her head and somewhere warm to sleep at night, what more was there to life?

Upon arrival however she realised that in fact there was a lot more to life. Having walked thirty minutes out of town to the outskirts of the city she had noticed her surroundings getting far less salubrious. Looking up at her new address she was not filled with relief at having acquired a home. Paint was peeling off the front wall and there were smashed bottles on the pavement leading up to the door. A group of teenagers stood around, some of them on bikes, having a discussion and blocking the entrance. As she walked towards them they stopped their conversation and looked her up and down. Holding her head high, she knew not to show them she was intimidated as they parted slightly forcing her to squeeze through the middle of their group.

She didn't have to stay she consoled herself. She could go in, ask to see the room and then say she would come back later if it was truly terrible. The trouble was, she realised, that the day was already starting to get away from her, the library would only be open for a few more hours and after eliminating those that she couldn't afford this really had been her last hope.

The entrance hallway was dark and smelt of damp. A patterned red carpet underfoot had become threadbare in the middle section over the many years of people following the same route. She dreaded to think what stains were hidden underneath that pattern. She walked towards a small hatch on the right hand side which had a bell on the ledge. Establishing that there was no one around she cautiously rang the bell and waited for someone to appear. No one did. She could hear the teenagers again outside the front door, jostling and teasing one another. She was sure it was just friendly banter, they were just kids after all.

Not wanting to appear impatient she waited a

while in silence, not daring to ring the bell again. She realised eventually however that she had to take action one way or another. Her two options were return to the city and stay another night in a hotel, eating into her money once again and enduring another 30 minute walk or push on. It might not be as bad here once she'd settled in.

With more confidence than she felt she rang the bell again this time with more pressure and it rang out louder into the rooms beyond.

'There's someone at reception!' shouted a male voice from not too far away.

Once again she waited until she heard the shuffling steps of someone heading in her direction.

An older lady came into view in what appeared to be her dressing gown and slippers. With a cigarette in one hand she slowly made her way to the hatch and raised her eyebrows expectantly at Margot as if questioning what on earth someone like her would want from a place like this.

'Hi, I phoned earlier about a room for a couple of weeks.'

'Name?'

'Sam.'

'Two weeks, four hundred cash.' The woman drawled. She looked as if she expected Margot to try and barter her down but she was not in the mood for trying to strike a deal with these people.

Feeling pressurised by the situation and longing to just have a space she could call her own she made the decision to sign herself up for two weeks.

Relieved that she had had the foresight to count

out her money and put it in her inner pocket before she had left the city she pulled out the exact amount and handed it over.

The woman took a second to count out the notes, obviously dubious about anyone that would hand over that kind of money so easily.

Satisfied that she had it all she reached behind her, took a key off the hook and handed it over.

'Number 32, best room in the house.' She smiled and showcased a shocking set of yellowing crooked teeth. Drawing on her cigarette still she remained where she was, watched Margot pick up the key and head up the stairs.

'Mind how you go' she shouted after her. Margot couldn't tell from her tone if it was meant to be reassuring or threatening but something inside told her it was only her money that was welcome here.

Chapter 12

The room was not what she would have pictured living in, let alone giving birth in. Years worth of wallpaper were peeling off the walls, each layer unveiling a past time and long forgotten era. The booming bass of her upstairs neighbours music made her walls shake with each beat and there was a distinct smell of mould emanating from the building. She sat on her single bed leaning her back against the wall feeling dejected. Could she really stay here until she gave birth? She felt a shiver run through down her spine as she thought of the previous occupants of her room, and the different activities they may have been up to in there.

Giving herself a shake she reminded herself that it was not forever. If this was the worst thing that she needed to endure to protect the two of them for the remainder of her pregnancy then she would need to suck it up and get on with it. She would buy some cheap cleaning products and give everything a good scrub, then at least she may be able to relax a bit more in her surroundings. Homely it was not, but nevertheless it was a space she could go unnoticed in for a while.

And so she settled into a new routine. Her room became her new office, the amount of newspaper clippings she trawled through and stuck up on the wall grew by the day as did her waistline.

The local library had some of the older research papers available on their ancient PC's which were dotted around the vast room and Margot spent endless hours staring at the screen, piecing together microscopic bits of detail which may point her in the direction of some answers or the next place to look.

Some of what she came across was well documented evidence, a lot of which she had already read and used in her work in the lab.

Other research however, often much more difficult and rare to come across shone new light on the possible mutations of the gene. Documents from scientists who implied that their funding had been cut just as they were coming close to a breakthrough.

Margot recognised the dangers of the rabbit hole she was falling into. Once you started even with the merest hint of interest in conspiracy theories it became difficult to separate the myth from reality. Nowadays too there were so many people with opinions and with the internet there was no shortage of a platform for them to shout their ideas from.

A few of the articles she read though did sound plausible. They appeared to be written by legitimate individuals who at least sounded like they had a background in an appropriate field. Could it be that progress had been made elsewhere but was being thwarted? Covered up before it could become public knowledge? If so, why? Why would anybody not want to stop the disease from spreading?

She pulled out her dog eared notebook from her bag and began to jot down names and dates of things she may find useful in the future. If she could track down any of these people and have a conversation with them she felt sure she would be able to quickly establish if any of what they said had any substance.

One name in particular she noticed kept appearing, a Doctor Marsha Fenwick who came up in her searches more due in part to the fact that she happened to be based in the North East. Conspiracy theorists on multiple sites made reference to her work over the years and an interview she had done on the local radio regarding the mutations of the gene and where she imagined the research taking them in the future.

Margot had scoured You Tube and Google for a recording of the interview but it didn't seem to be available anywhere.

How she missed her laptop, with her files and folders. There was a romanticism to doing it old style but life was much easier with electronics.

When she wasn't whiling away her days in the library Margot had done as good a job as possible making her squalid flat a bit more homely. The local charity shops were a hive of cheap finds and she'd been able to source new bedding and a few new born baby items from her frequent trawls of their rails.

She was well aware that her due date loomed ever closer, only a few precious weeks lay between now and when she would meet her child. A small collection of bags lay at the end of the room by the window. They contained the basic essentials for what she felt she would need in the first few weeks of the babies life. A handful of vests and baby grows, two packs of newborn nappies and wipes, some toiletries and a dummy. Beyond this she hadn't the faintest idea what to expect. She hoped that maternal knowledge would flood her body once the baby entered the world and she would instinctively know what to do but this was a distant and far flung hope.

Sustenance in her new residence had been one of her biggest concerns. Having always maintained a balanced diet she knew that she would have to be a bit more imaginative with her limited means of cooking, which consisted of a kettle and a microwave. Fortunately, the city had plenty to offer at a very reasonable price if you knew where to look and when to get it. It had taken her a few weeks to get her bearings but she was now familiar with all the local market traders who set up stall daily off the main high street and would always call in on them shortly before they closed when they were happy to sell off things they hadn't sold that day at a much cheaper price.

That being said it wasn't a guarantee and she'd lost count of the amount of evenings she'd sat glumly on the end of her bed nursing microwaved noodles and a banana for her main meal.

She was now noticing a distinct waddle to her walk as her belly continued to expand daily and sleep was becoming more elusive as she struggled to get herself comfortable each evening. The springs of her mattress felt as if they were about a centimeter from the surface and she had to shuffle herself around to find positions where she wasn't leaning directly on top of one. Normally just as she'd found a comfortable position she'd have to get up again to pee and the process started all over.

Fortunately, it wasn't as if she had anything she had to get up for these days and so she allowed herself to rest longer and longer into the mornings each day. If her past self could see her now she wouldn't recognise her. What had happened to the enthusiastic woman who squeezed in a run before work, took pride in her appearance and didn't take any bullshit from anyone. She was ashamed of herself, hiding out in what felt like a jail cell, becoming more and more reclusive as time went on.

She knew she would be starting to draw attention to herself visiting the library as often as she did. Who else visited daily, practically camping there from morning till night? But it was her only solace. If she stopped herself from going there she was gravely concerned about the dark places her mind would take her to.

Having had a particularly restless sleep the night before, Margot, having seen the weak sunlight seeping around the edges of her curtains that morning, had allowed herself to roll over and get another couple of hours rest. It was the latest she had slept in since she had arrived at her new home and despite the fact she was ashamed of herself for being so lackadaisical she must admit that she felt she had benefited from the extra rest.

Getting up and looking at herself in the tiny rectangular mirror which hung above her bed she was dismayed to see the tired bedraggled face that stared back at her. There really was no excuse for letting herself go to this extent. Should she be captured tomorrow she should at least look respectable whilst they dragged her off to her fate.

She took herself off for a hot shower and decided she would treat herself today to a clothes wash. She was running out of underwear and the few items of outer clothing she had brought with her were definitely a little worse for wear. Everything could do with a freshen up and she had seen a launderette the other day which seemed very reasonable. For the little it would cost her she imagined it would do her mood no end of good to remind herself a little of who she really was.

Stepping out into the weak sunshine she felt lighter than she had done for a while. Maybe it was the extra sleep, maybe it was just that she was starting to become more familiar with her surroundings but she felt today that she could cope with what life threw at her. Preferably no more huge surprises but in theory six weeks from now she could find herself with a healthy baby, showing the world that they'd made a mistake. Six weeks from now this may all be over. She might be able to go back home.

The alternative was too horrendous to contemplate, an infected child who would immediately infect Margot. The two of them wouldn't be able to leave their room, their fate sealed with only one another for company until the end. She had already decided that she would phone the police in those circumstances and inform them of where she was and that there had been an outbreak. If she stayed contained in her room they should be able to restrict the spread but her and her child wouldn't be long for this world.

The fork in the road of her life was racing towards her ever closer but the ways in which her life could unfold were so starkly different. What she would give for a crystal ball right now. Just to see if she was still here a year from now, if she was alive and if her child was alive she could cope with anything else.

Her only option was to focus on the route she hoped her life would take. Her testing had been accurate, that she knew with absolute certainty, and her testing had shown her baby was negative. She had to believe it was all going to work out.

Having dropped her clothing at the launderette she wandered the now familiar path to the library. She wasn't making any progress with her research with the limited means that were available to her and she wanted to make some headway. On the plethora of chat groups she had searched she noticed many using notice boards to pin questions or start up topics of conversation. Maybe, if she worded it carefully, that might be a way for her to reach out to the research scientist she had found mentioned so often.

She knew it was a risk but she was feeling like more of a risk taker today and wanted to grab life by the horns whilst she still could. She used the rest of her walk to formulate how she might word her request.

By the time she arrived at the library and took her familiar seat at the computers she had formed her post in her head. She hoped it struck the right balance or professional to give her credibility without giving away too much about who or more importantly where she was.

She typed in the website and found the page that she was looking for. Opening up a new feed she carefully typed out her pre formed text before reading it back to herself, trying to look at it from the perspective of someone else.

Former renowned research scientist, looking to track down Dr Marsha Fenwick. Unable to divulge name or location but we have a shared interest in a specific field of study and I think you would be interested to hear my story. Please respond through this channel if you want to discuss further.

Having gone over it in her head multiple times she didn't want to allow herself too long to talk herself out of it. Feeling somewhat reckless no doubt due to an uneventful few weeks she checked it briefly for typos before hitting post and it instantly transported itself up to the top of the feed. That was it, it was out there in the world now in the lap of the Gods.

She knew it was a risk and she knew she would probably just get a hundred weirdos responding to give her their multitude of opinions but at least she was doing something. The idea of getting her story out into the world was something that she had been mulling over for a while. How her story ended may well still be up in the air but regardless there had been a clinical error one way or another. Either her test was wrong or theirs was and she was convinced that she had taken hers correctly. She may have six weeks before she would find out their fate but she also felt like if these were her last six weeks on earth then she should perhaps leave a legacy so that her story could be re-told. Lessons could be learnt and future lives protected.

On the one hand there was the possibility that this was a medical error which could have resulted in the termination of a healthy baby. Was she the only person this had happened to or could there be more who needn't have suffered such unimaginable pain? At the other end of the spectrum though, something that Margot didn't want to believe but had been forced to acknowledge during her restless nights, was the possibility that there was something more to this, more stories to uncover, more truths to find. What if hers was only the tip of the iceberg, and she only had a limited amount of time to tell the tale?

Chapter 13

After posting on the forum Margot felt better having achieved something, it was the first time since she had arrived in the north east that she had actively done something other than just survive. She wanted to throw caution to the wind but knew she was very limited on what she could actually do. This small act of defiance though had had quite the effect on her. She felt more like her usual self. Never having been adverse to sanding up for herself this felt like putting two fingers up at those that were trying to hunt her down. Albeit whilst hiding behind the protective shield of the internet.

She walked out of the library with more of a bounce to her step, her head lifted for the first time in a long time. She felt able to take in her surroundings, noticing the people around her, feeling the weak sun on her face.

That afternoon after collecting her newly laundered clothes she allowed herself to purchase a full priced punnet of strawberries and some earl grey tea bags. Smiling to herself she realised that by her standards this was positively wild.

Returning to her flat she unpacked her clothes and laid them out in the three drawers that she had use of. For all she mocked herself for her outlandishly extravagant purchases of the day it did get her mind wandering to her finances.

Her rucksack of money had remained untouched underneath her bed for over a month now. She had carefully calculated how much she needed to spend on food and rent on a weekly basis and had pulled this much out at the beginning of the month. Far better she figured to regularly handle a smaller amount of cash than to keep digging into her big stash. If there was one thing she knew how to do well it was budget. She had managed to stretch her money even more than she'd originally anticipated over the past few weeks and was only now needing to consider making another withdrawal.

Whilst her mind was on her finances she decided to take out another lump sum for the next few weeks. She got down on all fours and reached underneath the bed pulling out her rucksack. As she lifted up the bag to rest it on the bed she felt a muscle twinge in her back. Reflexively she twisted to one side to protect herself and as she did so she felt her stomach muscles spasm and a warm fluid leak slowly down her leg. Initially she closed her eyes in despair at the thought that she had reached the stage in her pregnancy where she was involuntarily wetting herself but as the leaking continued and her mind gained some clarity she realised with a rising terror that in fact her waters had broken.

Shit. Was this it? She wasn't ready. She'd been planning for this event for what felt like an eternity but she most definitely wasn't ready.

Just at that moment she was snapped out of her terror by an enormous banging on her front door. She stared wide eyed across the room at the door wondering what to do. Another insistent banging followed, insinuating that they knew she was there and they weren't going to go away.

Her black trousers hid her leaking waters well enough so she figured she could get away with a short conversation with whoever was at the door in order to get them to leave her alone. She walked tentatively across the room, aware that she was leaking more with every step. Resting her hand lightly on the door handle she gave herself a second to compose herself before opening it up.

It was a face she vaguely recognised from downstairs. She had seen him inside the landlords flat on the first floor on the few occasions she'd had reason to pop in. His eyes were slightly glazed over and the strong odour of stale beer hit her straight in the face. He looked her up and down with a lazy glance, his mouth hanging half open.

'Rents due' he murmured as he leaned forwards and rested his hand on the top of the door frame.

'Sorry who are you?' she muttered

'Rent boy' he smiled a wide smile showing discoloured uneven teeth whilst further plunging her into his stench.

'I normally pay at reception, I'd feel better giving it directly to them there'

'They've sent me, you can give it to me'. He took a step closer to her as if to make his way into her flat.

With a surge of dread Margot realised that she had left the bag of money on the top of the bed. She couldn't remember if the money was visible and had no way of looking back to check without drawing his attention to it.

She decided it was best all round if she got him to leave her alone as quickly as possible and the best way to do that was to pay him. She just had to hope that it would make its way downstairs as promised.

Without moving from her position she lent across the shelf to the left of the door where she kept the envelope of rent money ready to be collected. It wasn't technically due until tomorrow but fortunately she was organised and she wasn't in a position to argue.

'OK, fine here you go' she said as she handed over the bundle.

He slowly reached out and took it, seemingly in no particular rush to leave her in peace as he roughly jammed it into his inner pocket. She couldn't be sure but she thought for a second that his eyes flickered over the top of her shoulder gazing into the flat. She held his gaze, desperate to close the door on him but not wanting to antagonise him further.

'Anything else?' she asked

'Not for now' he replied in what she hoped wasn't a veiled threat and with one last glance down her body her turned and walked down the corridor towards the stairs.

Margot closed the door and pushed across her chain. Turning towards her bed she looked at the rucksack which was open at the top. The very corner of one pile of notes poked out but she doubted he could have seen that from his vantage point. She consoled herself with the thought that he appeared too inebriated to notice much of anything and allowed herself to breathe a bit more freely.

She had bigger things to consider however. If her waters had broken that surely meant the baby wasn't far behind. She wasn't in any pain right now but she should definitely start to get things ready. Except she wasn't ready. She hadn't bought half of the things that she was planning on buying. Fortunately, she had picked up a good haul of second hand towels in the charity shop just the other day which she assumed would come in useful but what about everything else? In the films all they seemed to talk about was bowls of water and towels. Well, she had that at least.

How long might this stage take? If it was another few days before the baby arrived she would need supplies. She been taking each day as it came up until now but she would need to stock up if she wasn't going to leave the room for a while. The realisation that she might never leave this room again came crashing down upon her with a wave of despair. 'Oh God' she thought 'this could be it'. The weight of this possibility almost took her breath away. 'I am not ready' she kept repeating over and over again in her head. Not ready for labour, not ready to become a mother, not ready to die.

If this baby was coming then she really didn't have much choice in the matter, she was going to have to figure this out. She didn't know how but like with everything else in her life at the minute she would just have to take it one step at a time. She was going to sit down, rationally go through her options and decide her next steps.

At that moment and with the most resounding crash her front door exploded open, the chain ripping apart and the wood pulled from its hinges. Margot placed her hands up over her ears to protect her head from what felt like an explosion. Multiple bodies swarmed into the flat, flooding her senses so that she was unable to take in any of the finer details of the situation before she was roughly grabbed and thrown down onto the bed. A thick black hood was pulled down over her head engulfing her in darkness whilst her arms were held behind her back. There was a lot of shouting and movement and her heart pounded in her ears making it almost impossible to figure out what was going on. She desperately tried to protect her bump aware that she was lying on her front and putting pressure on the baby. She attempted to twist her body to one side to ease the pressure off her child but she was held firmly and restricted from moving.

Whoever was holding her hands behind her back tightened their grip and she startled as a voice manifested itself only inches from her face.

'Don't fucking move, you hear me?' It was loud and aggressive and it terrified her. Had her knickers not already been drenched with her leaking waters she would have noticed the warm heat of fluid trickle down her leg as she wet herself.

She could hear footsteps of multiple people moving around the room seemingly trying to find something. Her legs were moved roughly to one side as someone moved her out of the way to reach underneath the bed. She could picture the scene as they pulled out the rucksack and opened up the top realising that they had hit the jackpot. Despite her not being able to see anything through the black hood she lay there, wide eyed, desperately straining to take in any glimmer of what was going on.

She tried to remember to breathe, to just survive this situation. She was under no illusion, she was going to lose all her money but she didn't care right now, she just wished they'd take it and leave. The concept of screaming for help didn't even occur to her she was in such a state of petrified silence and she had simply lost the ability to put up a fight.

'Please don't hurt the baby, I'm having a baby' she sobbed, unable to articulate effectively that she was having a baby at this very point in time. Wracked with fear her whole body shook as she waited for them to do whatever it was that they were going to do to her.

'Let this be over', she silently pleaded to herself. 'Let this be done'.

Her wish was granted. She felt an almighty force make contact with the side of her face and then everything faded away.

Sometime later, unsure exactly how much time had

passed, Margot's eyes flickered open. She lay on her side, half spread on her bed, with her legs resting on the floor. She took a second to breathe and let her mind gain some clarity. She remembered what had happened and she instantly felt the searing hot pain in the side of her face. All was quiet and all was black. She sensed that wherever she was she was alone. Reaching up she felt the soft material of her hood and slowly pulled it up over her head. Light flooded her eyes and she blinked back the brightness allowing her eyes to adjust. She was still in her flat, she was alone and it had been trashed. Drawers had been pulled out and tipped upside down, her bags of baby clothes had been strewn all over the floor and the picture of her parents lay shattered on the floor.

She knew the rucksack had been taken and with it all of her money. Her body was drained of emotion and she felt completely numbed by the reality of her situation. She had to leave, of that she was certain but what her next move would be she had no idea. She simply gazed around the room taking in the destruction. She cast her mind back to the men breaking in and was positive that one of them had been her not so friendly rent boy. He must have spotted her haul and decided to waste no time in taking it for himself.

There was no way she could call the police she was meant to be a dead woman. She suspected that most people who stayed in such squalid conditions wanted to live a life away from the authorities and for this reason her attackers probably knew there was little chance of repercussion.

She turned to cross the room and looked into the mirror which still hung on the wall but now only held half the amount of glass. It's jagged shattered pieces depicted an abstract reflection of her decimated room. As she moved in line with her reflection she gasped at her appearance. Dried blood leaked out of her nose and her right eye was already swollen and shiny. It would no doubt be turning an impressive shade of blue over the next few hours.

The logical part of her brain knew that there was no reason for her attackers to return but she felt too terrified to stay there. As she turned to collect some of her belongings she felt a tightening in her back which travelled all the way around to the front of her belly. She placed a hand on the wall as she attempted to breathe her way through it as the pain built. Just as it grew in strength it then began to recede and she exhaled. Her first contraction.

She had time, she consoled herself, it was her first baby and everyone knew that labour took time, sometimes days. She would get through this one way or another, she would have to. She felt like she had been left for dead, the side of her head throbbed with such intensity that she struggled to gather her thoughts, she had nowhere to go but every fibre of her body told her that where she was now was not safe. What if they decided that she'd seen them and was a risk of going to the police, what if they thought that she might have more to give her. What if she gave birth and her child was infected? There were too many scenarios to play out, all of them an unknown.

Right now she had to deal with the facts which were that she needed to leave this building, she needed to get somewhere safe, she needed to be alone and it looked like she needed to prepare herself for the imminent arrival of her child.

Chapter 14

As Margot walked away from the block of flats the intensity of the pain and their frequency were building. She now had to stop walking as each one built and rest her head against a wall as the pain grew inside her hot, strong and fierce. With her eyes shut tight and her fingernails clawing into the brick work she forced herself to breathe. Slowly she felt the wave of pain recede, ebbing away from her body allowing her a blissful reprieve until the next one.

As her eyelids parted she focused her vision on the brickwork she was resting her head against. Its texture rough and cool from the autumnal wind. She thanked its welcome support as she continued to breathe away the latest contraction aware that the next one would not be far away. She needed to find shelter and soon. She couldn't afford to ask for help from anybody this was something she would have to do alone. Nobody could be trusted, she wouldn't allow anybody to get close to the child.

As she began to walk away down the cobbled

street she felt her stomach muscles tighten and another wave of pain beginning to build. Panic started to rise up in her throat. This was too quick, she hadn't anticipated them building so quickly. She didn't think she could now even manage to get back to the flat but she couldn't risk being found and taken to the hospital. At this rate she was going to end up delivering her baby in an alley way.

Tears welled up in her eyes, never had she felt so afraid and so alone. The impossible nature of what she had to do suddenly hit her. How would she be able to keep a child alive if she couldn't even bring it into the world safely? She felt herself losing control of her emotions, resigning herself to the fact that she was a failure. How did she think she would ever be able to get away with this? She wanted to erase the last 9 months, for that fateful night to have never happened and for her to have never wound up here. But whether she wanted it to happen now or not there was a baby exiting her body and she was going to have to go with it.

She allowed herself 30 seconds to fully acknowledge the fear that had been growing inside her for months. That there was no physical way that she could open wide enough to push a child out. That she would die here today in the street alone with only herself to blame. Unable to stand any longer she lowered herself down to the floor, the pain blurring her vision and stabbing at her insides like hot knives. The cold concrete exacerbated her feelings of despair and hopelessness. The last of the sun's weak glow disappearing behind the city skyline.

Was this her last day? Was this how it ended for her? She clutched her belly and began to whisper a silent prayer to herself willing herself to find the courage to carry on when all hope was lost. Praying to all the gods that they would help her now when she was so desperately in need.

At that moment she felt a hand come to rest on her shoulder. She wasn't able to acknowledge the unknown person for another minute or two whilst she remained trapped in the shackles of pain but it remained there steadfast and reassuring.

As the latest contraction began to fade she was finally able to acknowledge the stranger. Looking up from her seated position she was able to identify that he was an older gentleman but the late afternoon sun shone directly behind his face and she couldn't make out his features. He offered her his hand which she shied away from initially, however she soon realised that her current predicament really couldn't get any worse and one way or another she needed to get to her feet. She placed her hand in his and with surprising strength he lifted her up.

As she came face to face with him she saw he had a tanned face with wrinkles around his eyes. He creased his white eyebrows as he looked at her and with a worried expression held out his other arm to steady her.

'Come on love, it looks like we need to get you some help doesn't it.

Something about this man finding her now when she was devoid of hope seemed to Margot to be a sign that she couldn't ignore. She decided with nothing to lose she would trust her instinct and risk putting her trust in this man. Far too aware that her window of opportunity for speaking would not be around for long.

'Please' she gasped 'I can't go in to them, they'll take my baby.'

She gripped his hand tightly imploring him to see the desperation in her eyes. She had neither the strength or the time to get away from him so whatever he chose to do now she was at his mercy.

'Please' she sobbed again, tears now falling freely down her cheeks ' They'll kill us'

He turned to stand by her side and placed his arm around her back and under her arms. Her legs weak with exhaustion she allowed him to take her full weight and with strong arms he supported her and began to walk back down the street where she had came from.

'My cars at the end of the road' he said gruffly 'Lets get you there for starters'.

Unable to put up any resistance she followed his lead, stopping at the bottom of the road as a new wave of pain consumed her body. Unable to control herself she clenched her teeth together and felt her throat constrict as the pain reached its peak and transformed itself into a pressure she could not ignore. As every part of her body responded to the weight of the pressure inside her as she felt a groan escape from her mouth. She pushed down away from the pain. She realised now there was no escaping this, her body was doing things that she could not prevent and this baby was coming out of her.

She managed to focus back on her immediate surroundings. The man's arms still supported her, patiently waiting for her to be able to walk again. Fortunately, the streets were all but deserted and they had a clear path ahead to where she hoped his car would be parked near by.

'Looks like we don't have a lot of time miss, lets get you back to my Barb she'll know what to do.'

As they reached the bend at the bottom of the road she saw a blue Volvo parked up. The lights blinked at her as he unlocked it remotely in anticipation of their arrival.

He opened the back door for her and helped her lower herself in before moving round to the drivers seat and sitting down. Unable to sit properly herself Margot leaned forward on the chair clinging onto the headrest in front of her. They had been driving for all of 30 seconds when the next contraction began. She had no experience of child birth but was able to make an educated guess that with the ferocity of the pain and the uncontrollable need to push, this baby wasn't going to be far away. She prayed that wherever they were going wouldn't be far away but she had no available breath to ask. With only a minute between each contraction she barely had time to recover from one before the next one began. Fortunately, they had been driving for no longer than 10 minutes before she felt the car turning left and slowing down. There was the unmistakable sound of gravel underneath the tyres as they rolled along what she could only imagine was a very long driveway. As the car came to a stop she couldn't raise her head to inspect her destination. A few seconds passed and then she felt the door open and a welcome breeze on her forehead which was now dripping with sweat.

'Barbara!' the man shouted into the air 'You're needed'

She heard light footsteps crunch across the gravel floor followed by a gasp.

'Oh John! You only popped out for milk! Bring her into the kitchen, I'll grab some towels'

John had seemingly now decided that asking her to walk into the house would be futile and so lifted her weight completely in his arms and carried her from the car towards the house and across the threshold into the kitchen. He stood her up inside and pulled out a chair for her but primal instinct took over and she lowered herself down onto all fours on the floor as she began to push with every bit of strength she had left.

'Okay deary' Barbara muttered 'I need to see what's going on down here so let's take these trousers off.'

Unable to move an inch from where she was, Margot allowed Barbara to remove the clothes from her bottom half.

'Well it looks like you've done most of the work already' said Barbara in a calm soothing tone 'You keep doing what you're doing, poetry in motion my sweetheart.'

Stretched open more than she believed possible she pushed with everything she had. Feeling the head of her child slowly emerging from her body. She gritted her teeth through the stinging sensation and focused on the fact that it must now surely soon be over.

With one final contraction she pushed new life out of her body and heard a gargled scream from somewhere behind her.

'Well look at you, aren't you a picture! Put your hands down lovey and I'll pass your baby through to you.'

With shaking hands she felt between her legs and pulled up a wet and bloodied child. With open eyes mother and baby simply stared at one another. One person split into two, still attached by the placenta which ran inside Margot yet to be delivered. The same piercing blue eyes stared back at one another as Margot realised that the world had inexplicably shifted. She had not desired this life or this child but she could not now imagine how she could have ever had such feelings. Her whole world now centred around this tiny human being in front of her. Any plans she previously had for her own life were obsolete. Her only role in this world now was to protect and love this tiny child.

She had a daughter.

Chapter 15

Margot continued to catch her breath on the floor of the kitchen unable to take her eyes off her new daughter. Her initial thought had been to check the child thoroughly for signs of infection, to scream at the unwitting couple to protect themselves from the hell that she had unleashed onto them all. But it was immediately apparent that there was no need. Her daughter was the epitome of health. Ten fingers, ten toes, pink unblemished skin and thick dark hair, she was incredible.

Margot couldn't believe how quickly the pain disappeared. Understandably she was sore but she also felt like she had conquered the world. She had transformed into a warrior, a burst of endorphins were surging through her veins. If she thought she had been protective of her child before hand it was nothing to how she felt now. She would have literally moved heaven and earth to protect this little girl. She turned to look at the woman who had helped deliver her baby for the first time.

'I don't know how to thank you'.

'No need pet, I've spent 35 years of my life bringing babies into this world, although I must admit it's the first time I've done it in my own kitchen!' Barbara had a warmth about her smile which resonated across her face. Her rosy cheeks and wavy hair added to her gentle manner. She made Margot feel instantly at ease under her care. Looking around her she discovered she was on the floor of a traditional farmhouse kitchen at one end of a wooden table and chairs which dominated the space in the middle. Fresh flowers sat on the windowsill and a pot of something warm and hearty sat bubbling on the aga. Despite Margot's desperate situation she felt immensely guilty for barging into their idyllic lifestyle in such dramatic fashion.

Barbara helped Margot up off the floor and spent the next half an hour delivering the after birth, getting her cleaned up and checking her over. Fortunately, she had escaped needing any stitches and Barbara reassured her that she should heal relatively quickly. Clinging onto her daughter, who was now wrapped in a clean warm towel they both went through to an adjacent sitting room where two soft cushioned sofas sat facing one another. Margot gingerly lowered herself down onto one where she was enveloped by the soft cushions.

John who appeared to have made himself scarce during the all the action poked his head round a door at the other end of the living room.

'Is it safe to come in?'

'Yes dear, I think we could all do with a sweet tea

if you wouldn't mind'

Looking relieved to have something to do he wandered through to the kitchen and could soon be heard pottering around gently humming a tune which Margot recognised from a previous life but couldn't place.

Barbara sat down opposite them and gazed lovingly at the baby.

'Now dear everything looks fine to me down below but you really should go to the hospital to get you both checked over. You look like you've been through the wars and I think someone needs to take a look at that eye of yours.'

Margot looked up at her with tired eyes. She wasn't sure how much to divulge about her situation or what she'd been through in the last 24 hours. She was so grateful to them both for their support but she knew how dangerous it was to trust anybody.

'I can't go to the hospital right now, it isn't safe for either of us. I realise how much I'm asking of you but if you could find it in your heart to keep this to yourself it really would save our lives. I'll catch my breath and we'll be out of your hair very soon if that's OK with you both?'

Barbara looked at them both intently. Despite her softened appearance she had an intensity about her gaze which made you feel like she was seeing right into your soul. This was not a woman who suffered fools gladly.

'Well now, there's time for all that yet. Let's get your strength up first shall we and the same for this little lady. Do we have a name yet?'

Margot paused and looked down at her daughter. Lying in her arms she seemed completely at ease with her new surroundings.

'I was thinking of Iris. It was my mothers' name.'

'Iris' Barbara repeated 'That's a beautiful name, she's a little treasure that's for sure. But she'll be needing some clothes and a feed soon. Did you have anything prepared?'

'I had a bag with me when John found me. It had a few clothes in ready for her but I don't know how to feed her' Feeling self-conscious and a little foolish at being so unprepared she bit her lip and fell silent. The magnitude of what lay ahead for her was starting to settle in.

Picking up on her naivety Barbara took the lead.

'Well now why don't we see if she's hungry. You've got everything you need to feed her right here.'

With Barbara's help Margot positioned Iris across her chest.

'Just support her neck there and she'll do the rest' Barbara reassured her as Iris nuzzled her way across her breast searching out her nipple. As if she'd been doing it for years the tiny infant latched onto Margot's breast and began to suck. After a few moments Margot allowed herself to ease into the unfamiliarity of the strange sensation and felt herself begin to relax. Closing her eyes she couldn't believe how much had happened in the past twenty four hours and the good fortune that she had found this amazing couple. The realisation that she had successfully survived the labour and both her and her daughter were alive and well came crashing down on her and she felt overwhelmed with relief.

John returned to the room with a tray, on which rested a teapot and three china cups. Margot couldn't remember the last time she'd experienced such pleasantries. A life time ago it seemed, in a different world, when she was a different person.

'Thank you John for everything you've done for us both and for getting us safely to your incredible wife. I really don't know what would have happened to us both if it weren't for you.'

John simply smiled and rested his hand on his wife's shoulder. Barbara simultaneously lifted her hand to rest on top of his in a gesture so familiar to them both it was obvious how their years together had bonded them as one. Both looked adoringly at Iris who having satisfied herself with her immediate need for sustenance was closing her eyes once again on Margot's chest.

'She looks content enough that's for sure' John said pouring out the tea 'First time you've delivered a baby in a few years ey Barb!'

'Like riding a bike' she chuckled

'Do you miss it?' Margot enquired

'There's nothing quite like the buzz of bringing new life into the world but I don't think I'd have the energy to go back to it now. I feel fair done in!'

Suddenly the full extent of recent events washed over her and she felt heavy with exhaustion. Unable to hold up the weight of her eyelids any longer she allowed her eyes to close. Craving the numbness of sleep she allowed herself to fall into the abyss.

She felt her baby being lifted from her chest and threw her eyes open, her body reacting immediately to the threat.

'There now dear' whispered Barb 'You need your rest. I'll sit right over here with the little miss. She'll be safe with me while you sleep'.

Margot watched Barbara sit down on the opposite sofa and begin to hum a quiet lullaby. Unable to fight the weight of tiredness any longer she lay down along the length of the sofa and allowed her eyes to close. John carefully placed a blanket over her body but she did not notice it's comforting warmth as she had already drifted off into a dreamless sleep.

Chapter 16

When she awoke it was to find Barbara sitting in the same place directly opposite her, rocking Iris back and forth humming a tune. Iris was swaddled snugly in one of the thick woollen blankets Margot had bought in anticipation of her arrival and seemed to be in a peaceful slumber. The early morning sunlight broke through the window as Margot realised with surprise that Barbara must have been awake all night cradling the infant for her, never leaving her side.

For a few minutes Margot simply lay still and took in her surroundings. Content to be able to lie in silence gazing at her new daughter and process the events of the past few days. She took stock of her own body and tried to assess the extent of the damage from both the labour and the brutal robbery. Her face still throbbed and felt swollen, she had no idea how the bruising had developed over the past few hours but she could bet that she wouldn't be looking her best. The rest of her body felt weak and she ached in places she hadn't previously known existed. She had a new found respect for women, literal warriors tearing their bodies in two bringing new life into the world.

Despite her earlier feelings of elation immediately following the birth, she now felt an overwhelming, unexplainable sadness right to her core which she couldn't quite explain. Watching her beautiful daughter sleeping on the other side of the room in the arms of a stranger, she felt like she was a million miles away, that she had in some way lost her. She missed her being inside her body, like the baby had given her an internal strength but now she was out of her she was all alone and it was terrifying. Not to mention how scared she felt for Iris being out in the world unprotected and vulnerable. It had been hard enough to protect her inside her own womb, how was she supposed to do it now she was a living breathing human being all of her own? What chance did she have when all the odds were stacked against her and how beautifully innocent she was. She needed to be strong now and she should be making plans but she was just so tired that the thought of moving or even thinking about moving made her want to weep. Tears slid silently down her cheeks. They were not noisy sobs but merely her body cleansing itself of her emotions which were too overwhelming to contain inside her body and it felt good to allow them to be released. With each tear that fell down her face and pooled on the pillow beneath her head she felt lighter and calmer.

Barbara lifted her gaze and looked concerned at Margot's appearance

'I don't know why' Margot croaked, her throat constricted with the emotion.

'You'll feel a bit wobbly for a few days deary, but give it time, you'll be back to your old self in no time, you'll see'

Margot just nodded, hoping that Barbara was right. She didn't have the luxury of being able to break down now, not after everything she'd been through.

It was reassuring to know though that her behaviour wasn't out of the ordinary. Had she delivered Iris alone like she had planned she would have worried for her mental state. Tired, hormonal, battered and bruised how were women expected to then devote themselves 24 hours a day to a helpless infant? Only now she'd had the baby did she realise the importance of having good people around you to support you, quite how she'd been fortunate enough to come across these two people she would never know.

Now that she had properly awoken from her sleep Margot was able to take in her surroundings a bit more. A traditional farmers cottage, the living room where she was situated was cosy and well lived in. There were pictures on the walls of extended family old and young, traditional wooden furniture, plump soft sofas and a comforting fire. Everything about the ambience in the room made Margot feel homely and safe.

'You looked like you could do with a couple of those' Barbara said nodding towards the table to the side of the sofa.

Margot looked across to see that Barbara had left her some paracetamol and a glass of water for her.

'I don't know how to thank you.'

'Why don't you tell me a little bit about how you came to be here, and how you got yourself in such a pickle come to that?'

Margot had decided long before this point that she was going to actively choose to trust these people. There had been ample opportunity for them to turn her away or tell her to leave and yet they hadn't done so, despite it being obvious that she was running from something. So, for the first time she spoke freely and without reservation to Barbara about everything that had happened right from the beginning, from the death of her parents to her working at the lab and her pregnancy. When it came to re-telling the news that she had been delivered at the scan she took a breath and paused, there was no going back once she had confessed this. If John and Barbara felt that they had been put at risk they had every right to get angry with her and tell her to leave but at this stage Margot felt she had no choice. There was no other explanation for why she was running from the authorities and they must have assumed some version of her truth by now.

So, she went on to explain what the sonographer had said and how she had then gone on the run, choosing at this stage not to go into the finer points of how that feat had been achieved and to leave out the graphic details of her fake death. Which then led her on to her trip North and her getting the flat and then the robbery and the desperate situation she had found herself in when John had come to her rescue.

It was quite the saga when it was retold to someone out loud and Margot herself found it quite overwhelming to have to re-live it all.

'But I can't say that I regret any of it, especially knowing what I know now' Margot finished with 'I know it was immoral and especially given all that I know about the virus and the dangers and I should have accepted my obligation to do the right thing, but look at her! She's perfect. They must have got it wrong.' Realisation dawned on Margot that her saga might now be over. She'd been through so much but it had been so worth it and she'd successfully brought her daughter into the world. 'So now I can come out of hiding. I can show them that she's not a threat, it'll all be over and they'll leave us alone.'

Barbara's face did not share the same sense of relief.

'She is perfect deary, but shouting about it from the rooftops right now would not be a good idea. Can you imagine the upheaval it would cause if people thought even for a second that their precious little ones might have died for no reason?' Her eyes filled with tears and she placed a hand on her chest as if to steady her beating heart.

Margot felt the sting of guilt once more as she realised the ramifications of what she was saying. This would affect thousands if not hundreds of thousands of people and if she was right the authorities wouldn't want her to start shouting about it, moreover they wouldn't want living breathing proof of a healthy baby that shouldn't have ever been born.

Margot had fooled herself into believing that once Iris had been delivered all her worries would be over but the stark truth now hit her full force that if Barbara's train of thought was correct then the two of them had potentially never been in more danger.

'Well, there's nothing for it but for you to stay with us until this all blows over.' John calmly announced from behind them. Margot didn't know how long he'd been standing there for but he spoke with a finality to his tone which implied his mind was already made up.

Barbara still looked contemplative taking it all in but nodded along as if in agreement.

'I don't want to put you out any more than I already have.' Margot said. It was a weak argument and the truth was that she had already fallen in love with being here with these two people who made her feel more safe than she had done in a long while. Whilst it was true that she hated the thought of being a burden to anyone, the past few days had taught her maybe this wasn't something she could do on her own.

'Well, we could do with a young pair of legs around here to keep on top of this place, so how about when you get yourself back on your feet you give me a hand? In return we'll offer you board and lodgings and your body weight in Earl Grey tea.' John said with a wry smile.

She could tell that he was mocking to a certain extent but was relieved to hear there might be some way of her paying her debt of gratitude back to them.

'You've got yourself a deal.' She said with a grin.

Chapter 17

That morning Margot was shown up to her room where she would be staying. The room was painted a delicate shade of pastel pink, the bottom half of which was decorated in pale floral wallpaper. An ageing dado rail ran the length of the room and divided the wallpaper from the magnolia above. There were nondescript pictures on the top half of the wall, a seascape and a still image of three doves mid flight further along. Nothing about the room was particularly personal other than the fact that it had obviously remained this way for a few decades or more. The outdated decor only reiterated the feeling of warmth and familiarity for Margot, welcoming her into its nostalgic bubble of a more simple time.

After successfully feeding Iris, Margot dressed her in one of the few baby grows which she had bought in advance of her birth. It was a pale yellow, made of soft towelling material with two sunflowers leaning towards the sunshine on the front. It had made Margot smile the first time she'd seen it with sunflowers being her favourite flower. it was surreal now seeing it on her daughter after all these months of picturing what it would look like on her. She put one hand under Iris' head and another under her soft cushioned, nappy covered behind and lifted her to her chest. She got a rush of endorphins as she brought her up to her neck and nuzzled her in close, breathing in her beautiful scent it made her heart ache. How could something so new smell so good?

Barbara offered to watch Iris whilst she had a wash so after being handed a plush fluffy pink bath towel she headed off to the bathroom to allow herself 10 minutes of a hot shower.

Looking in the bathroom mirror she almost didn't recognise herself. Her face was painfully swollen, her lip had cracked open again at some point and blood had once again dried thick and dark. The shades of blue and purple around her eye would have been impressive had they not been extremely painful.

Her whole body it seemed physically ached, she was still bleeding, her throat hurt from all her screaming and her brain buzzed from tiredness even after her few hours on the sofa and yet she felt so at peace in this strange house where she had found herself quite unexpectedly.

Over the past few months Margot had pictured all kinds of horrendous images following her delivery. Would the baby have breathing difficulties, would she have been in obvious pain, would there have been physical deformities or brain damage? She had imagined every possible scenario knowing that she was going to love that child without question or hesitation regardless of the outcome. What she couldn't bear though was the prospect of her child being in pain and it being her fault, because of the decision that she had made and her cowardice not to make a hard decision at the time that would have been for all the right reasons.

What she had never allowed herself to imagine however was this beautifully healthy baby girl she now shared a life with. That had been a dream she hadn't dared herself to have until now.

The shower was one of the best she had ever had in her life. Gingerly she washed away the cuts and scrapes on her body and soothed her aching muscles as she allowed the jet stream to pour down her back.

The woman that emerged ten minutes later was noticeably in a better head space. Holding her head up high with a renewed sense of purpose she felt she could at least take on the day now.

Wide awake now and surprisingly thirsty Margot dressed and put on the fluffy beige slippers that had been left for her at the end of the bed. As she wandered downstairs through to the farmhouse kitchen she found Barbara sitting at the wooden table cradling Iris with a pot of tea brewing and a rack of toast waiting to be devoured.

She looked up at her new house guest and smiled a knowing smile.

'It looks like that did you the world of good.'

'It really did, thank you.' She wandered over to Barbara who offered Iris back to her without hesitation.

'People often under estimate the benefits of a wash!'

She pulled out the chair next to her and gestured for Margot to take a seat.

'You help yourself to some breakfast, you need to keep your strength up. I took the liberty of asking John to bring a few of our old things down from the attic for little miss. No point in them going to waste up there now there's a lovely young lady in need of them.'

Margot turned back to look through the door into the living room to see John bending over a Moses basket and stand partially made up. He didn't look in the least bit put out by his new task in fact he looked quite at peace with himself as he hummed away gently focusing on the task in hand.

'I'm just freshening up some sheets for the cot and then it'll be right as rain.' Barbara stood and began to potter around the kitchen, topping up the tea pot and putting a fresh round of bread in the toaster.

'Why are you being so nice to me?' Margot asked, unable to think of a way of asking it any less bluntly. Going off the past few months she couldn't for the life of her fathom this unexpected show of generosity. She knew in her heart that she didn't need to be wary of these two. That there was no malice or threat of manipulation to them and yet she couldn't figure out why they would be willing to put themselves at risk and to go to so much trouble for a complete stranger and a fugitive stranger at that.

Barbara gazed out of the window for a second seemingly lost in her own thoughts.

'There's no one left to help these days. If we don't who will?'

A thoughtfulness descended on the kitchen broken only by the intermittent gurgles from Iris and the occasional murmur from John as he attempted to re-erect the nursery furniture.

By the afternoon Margot had drunk more cups of tea than she had in the last six months combined. John had successfully finished building the moses basket and along with the freshly laundered sheets it stood pride of place in the middle of the living room with Iris snugly asleep inside. Barbara had even pulled out some of her own hand made crocheted blankets as an extra layer of warmth for the infant. The three of them stood around the sleeping babe watching her for a minute, united by the pleasure of seeing new life so at peace in the world.

'How old are your children?' Margot inquired without taking her gaze from her precious bundle.

There followed the merest hint of a pause which caused her to look up at the couple.

Both John and Barbara continued to look down at the infant but a heaviness had descended upon their shoulders. John rested his hand on Barbara's shoulder and gave it a squeeze.

'God didn't grace us with our own sadly. When me and John found out we weren't going to be able to have children of our own I decided to help as many other women to do it instead. It was a form of torture for me in one sense and therapy in another. We came close a couple of times but it wasn't to be. Never did have the heart to throw all this away though did we?' She looked up at her husband and they shared a knowing smile, each the supporter of the others grief.

'I'm sorry' Margot replied, all other platitudes seemingly insignificant against the obvious weight of their sorrow.

John made his excuses and left the room on the pretence of needing to attend to some jobs but his discomfort discussing the topic was palpable.

Whilst Margot empathised with the couple it also went some way to helping her rationalise why they were going so out of their way to help her. It was a clear source of joy for the two of them to be able to experience even vicariously the life they so desperately had wanted for themselves.

'John doesn't like to talk about it too much. There's not much that he's not been able to fix for me in our long years of marriage but I think he's always felt he let me down when it came to us not having a child.'

'I can tell he loves you very much.' Margot smiled, it gave her such joy to see them together 'It gives me hope that a love like yours exists'

Barbara chuckled 'Oh don't get me wrong dear there are days I could hit him over the head with my rolling pin, but yes on the whole I couldn't have asked for more.'

A contented silence fell on the room as the two women already comfortable in one another's company pondered their conversation.

It was interrupted by a stifled yawn from Margot. All the tea in the world couldn't keep her tiredness from the last few days at bay.

'Go on up and have a rest lovey.' Barbara demanded. You're welcome to leave Iris down here or lift the basket upstairs if you'd rather have her close. Rest when the baby rests, that's the best bit of advice you can ever have, and you can only do it with your first because when there's more of them running around you don't ever get a moments peace.'

Margot couldn't help but balk at the idea that she might at some point have more children.

'If all pregnancies are like this one then I think I can safely say I'm done! I think you're right though, if you don't mind it would be good to get a bit of rest whilst she's asleep.'

'Of course, I'm making a pie for dinner but if you're not up for it I'll leave you a portion in the aga for later.'

Margot felt like she was being waited on hand and foot, nothing could have prepared her for falling on her feet in this way when everything had been looking so bleak only a day earlier.

Barbara had her back turned to Margot now, sprinkling flour onto her work top in preparation for her afternoon of cooking.

'Barbara, I'm going to make this up to you one day, I promise'

Barbara didn't turn back but just continued with her task

'Go along now pet, go get some rest.'

Chapter 18

The first few days following the birth were a blur. After the most exhausting day of her life bringing her new daughter into the world she then moved immediately into a relentless routine of feeding, changing, burping and rocking on a three hourly cycle day and night. Margot had never before given too much thought to what women have to adjust to in those first few weeks of parenting, impossible to imagine what it will be like until you experience it first hand.

She had been worried about not having enough of the essentials for Iris and had wanted to go down to the local foodbank on the first day to collect some nappies and babygrows but John wouldn't hear of it and had made her write down all the things the two of them needed and had gone out to get them for her.

Day three hit her hard with every decision feeling overwhelming, the outside world seeming more dangerous than ever before and left Margot doubting her ability to parent more than usual.

After sharing these doubts one morning with Barbara she told her that it was perfectly normal especially on day three and four and to just sit with the feelings and wait for them to pass. This she did and by the end of that week she felt considerably brighter.

She'd also started to get to know her daughter a bit more and was becoming more astute at picking up on Iris' cues for what she might need. On the whole if she was clean, well fed and had slept enough then she was content. Margot realised that as a general rule of thumb this was also a good mantra for her own happiness moving forwards too.

She hadn't left the house once in the last five days and even within the confines of the house Iris rarely left her side. During the day they would both sit in the living room in front of the fire. Margot had one of her baby books for guidance which she had picked up in a charity shop a few months ago but more and more these days her frame of reference was Barbara.

Barbara was midwife, mother, grandmother, doula, chef, housekeeper and friend all rolled into one. Margot didn't know how anyone could take on motherhood for the first time without someone like her by their side. If they could bottle her up and sell her they would make a fortune.

She didn't smother Margot for which she was very grateful as someone who had always needed her personal space but she was always on hand to offer a comforting word at the right time. Between the two women Iris was barely out of their arms, even John had been caught cooing over her picking her up to comfort her when she became restless. It seemed that in a short period of time the young child had managed to get everyone wrapped around her little finger.

Despite her initial worries that she was going to be a terrible mother she did feel a certain sense of pride that so far she had managed to keep her daughter nourished and clean and warm. She figured that for the next few weeks and months at least so long as she kept that up and there were no nasty surprises along the way she probably wouldn't be going far wrong. Towards the end of her pregnancy she had been worried about if the two of them would get along and how she would provide for a child for the next 18 years. Would she blame her for keeping her from her father? Would they prove to be incompatible characters, frustrating each other by merely being in each other's company? But as they both lay there in the dawn of a new day Margot realised that to a certain extent all of that was out of her control. She couldn't alter what would happen ten years from now, she couldn't preempt their relationship or the path that their lives would take. She could only focus on the here and now, the feeding, the bathing, the cuddles and the snatches of sleep. The rest would come.

After the first few days of them being at the farmhouse Barbara had set to work sewing her a new sling which she assured Margot was the best way to carry Iris around in whilst also keeping her close. Margot liked the idea of being able to keep her near to her. Even walking into a different room within the house without her child felt like too far at the minute. Ever since she had been born Margot had felt an ache of anxiety at her only child being outside of her body as if every living thing in this world was a threat to them. Keeping her strapped to her chest felt like the closest thing she could get to having her back inside her womb and so she was keen to try.

Margot felt her strength gradually returning to her and despite the broken nights feeling long and draining she was still in a bubble of contentment over where her and her daughter had ended up. Things she realised just had a habit of working themselves out.

The new family of four settled into a comfortable routine with one another and the weeks began to merge seamlessly into one another. Before she knew it two months had passed and the house began to feel like a home. Truth be told John and Barbara were so relaxed in their way of life that it was hard not to settle in with their routine. She only hoped that she and Iris hadn't disrupted the status quo too much. She designated herself chef a minimum of three times a week and since Barbara was so willing to take care of Iris at every available opportunity it became a nice way to break the monotony of childcare and to feel like she was contributing to the household in some small way.

A keen gardener, Barbara grew a wide selection of vegetables in the garden so there was never a shortage of ingredients to pick from. Margot did however find herself struggling for inspiration having never had to cook for anyone other than herself for a number of years. Fortunately, Barbara had an abundance of well used recipe books, the pages crinkled over time on her favourite meals which Margot attempted to sift through to gather some ideas.

John more often than not was out of the house tending to the fields and the property. Never one to sit still there was always a job for him to finish or an errand for him to run. He and Barbara worked in perfect harmony, having settled into a pattern founded on 50 years of marriage together. He quietly took in everything that was happening around him, rarely commenting but always listening.

Whilst John clearly oversaw the running of the house there was no doubt that it was his much adored wife who called the shots. Barbara was one of those rare women who knew their path in life and bolstered all those around her on her way. She lifted the mood just by walking into a room with a gentle pat on the arm or the never ending offer of more tea.

Margot imagined that even as a younger woman she would have been quietly self assured and at her strongest when in her line of work delivering new babies into the world. Of all the people to have delivered Iris it was such a relief to have known that it was this woman. Initially Margot had been worried about stepping on her toes around the house, wanting to help but also not wanting to get in the way. However it seemed that her concerns were irrelevant as both women grew accustomed to the other very quickly. It was as if they had been waiting to become a part of one another's lives all this time and hadn't known it.

As Margot settled into life on the farm she familiarised herself with the routines and way of life of her adopted family. The two of them were early risers often up before dawn, John regularly headed straight out to tend to their small flock whilst Barbara preferred a more leisurely start to the day enjoying her breakfast around the large wooden table which dominated the kitchen.

It was at this table that Margot and Iris spent a lot of their time too. The kitchen was the hub of the whole house. The place they would all sit together and catch up with one another throughout the day. Considering there would usually just be the two of them Margot couldn't imagine they were ever at a loss for something to talk about and when silence did descend on the house it was such a comfortable relaxed silence that no words were necessary.

It was in the evening that Margot and Iris got some time to themselves. Having spent most of the day tending to Iris' needs and trying to catch the occasional nap Margot loved the evenings when she allowed herself the indulgence of sitting in front of the fire with only her thoughts for company. John and Barbara often headed to bed a lot earlier than she would normally retire and it was nice to wait up for Iris to have her late feed downstairs so that they could hopefully get a better stint of sleep when they did go to bed.

It was during these late night sessions in front of the fire that Margot's mind wandered sometimes to the past and all the events that had led her here, other times to what she could expect from the future. Whilst John and Barbara had offered her more than she could have hoped for by being able to stay here she couldn't take them up on their offer indefinitely. The last thing she wanted to do was to overstay her welcome but quite what her next move would be she didn't know and as things stood she desperately didn't want to have to move.

Just to have a quiet life would be bliss. Some security of knowing where the next few months and years of her life were headed. She missed her work and her colleagues and her home. She wondered how Nick was doing, whether they had made any advances recently and what they would all be making of her disappearance. Just to be able to sink her nose into a research paper again, dissolve into the arguments of scientists at the forefront of their field paving the way for the future. She was a shadow of her former self, in giving birth to a child she had given birth to a new form of herself. One with different strengths and flaws than before. She neither preferred one to the other, they were just different. She imagined she even looked different and yet on the rare occasions when she took some time out to look at herself in the mirror she was surprised to see the same brown eyes staring back at her. How could so much have changed internally and yet it not show outside?

The nights were the biggest struggle mentally for Margot. Having never previously been somebody who struggled to sleep she was now up regularly with her newborn infant. By the time that she had seen to Iris and she lay her head back down on her pillow, her body felt weighed down with exhaustion but her mind flicked a switch illuminating the memories of the past few months and trying to make sense of them. When sleep did eventually come it was broken by night horrors of aggressive shouting in her ears always in the pitch dark, her eyes straining to find the light.

She couldn't shake the dull ache of anxiety in the pit of her stomach that whatever she'd started wasn't over. Delivering her child safely had been her end goal and she had achieved that but where had it led her? She felt like she'd made a deal with the devil. She'd sold her soul in the hope of a healthy child but now that she was here she realised it wasn't enough. They had a lifetime together now and she would always have to fight to keep her safe.

Contentment felt like an unachievable goal in her life. Six months ago all she would have wanted was a healthy child. Now she had that she had all too quickly moved on to the next thing to worry about. Would she ever be able to relax? To enjoy the moment without worrying about the future? Perhaps if it was just herself she needed to be concerned for she could have found a way to adopt a more relaxed approach but the responsibility of her daughter's future lay all too heavy on her shoulders.

The events of the past few months had altered her

irrevocably. She was a fugitive now, a homeless, unemployed fugitive and a single parent to boot. Not quite what she had in mind when it came to setting a good example to her offspring, but if she wasn't all those things she would have no offspring to set an example for. Would she have made different decisions with the benefit of hindsight? Absolutely not, and that, she decided, was all the justification she needed.

No longer would she sit moping about where she found herself, she needed to embrace this unforeseen change of circumstances and shape it into something good and wholesome because that, she decided, was all that really mattered.

She attempted to smother the burning anxiety with a blanket of reassurance. They were safe, they were warm. She wanted to do more to show her appreciation to John and Barbara and decided that she would do something tomorrow however small to show that she wasn't taking them for granted.

Her gaze fell on the fire which she had neglected too long. The flames having long disappeared leaving only the glowing red remains of the last lonely log. She added another log from the basket in an attempt to keep her heat supply going a little longer but alas it looked like she hadn't yet acquired the skill set to bring it back to life. Frustrated with herself at not being able maintain the simplest of jobs she was muttering away to herself prodding and poking at the dying embers when she heard the heavy footsteps of John returning downstairs and entering the living room.

She hastily got to her feet, embarrassed unnecessarily at the thought of John seeing her so incapable.

'Barb is struggling with her chest again' her muttered his brow in a hint of a frown 'she might be coughing a lot in the night, might keep you up is all.'

'Oh don't worry about that, is there anything I can do?'

'No, she gets like this in the winter, seems to get a bit worse each year though, not that she'd admit it. I'm just going to warm up a bowl of water to get some steam into the room.'

He disappeared into the kitchen for a while pottering around putting the kettle on the aga.

Margot could hear Barbara upstairs now, her rattling cough echoing down the corridor. She hated hearing her unwell.

As John moved back into the living room he took the chair opposite her, a casual glance in at Iris' basket to check all was well. Margot loved that the whole household were so committed to her daughters wellbeing.

They sat in comfortable silence for a while, before John unable to stand it any longer moved over to the dying fire and began what to Margot seemed like the arduous process of getting it started again.

'Sorry, still haven't got to grips with keeping that thing going.' She added sheepishly

'It just takes a bit of time is all, I don't imagine there's much you don't pick up if given enough time.'

Margot smiled to herself. They both seemed to

have far more belief in her ability than she did.

'I don't know what I'm doing anymore John, I feel so lost.'

The words escaped from her before she'd even known she was feeling them.

John returned to standing and came and perched on the arm of the sofa, taking his time as usual to consider his response before he spoke.

'I remember after we'd lost our third baby and Barb realised having children wasn't on the cards for us, she lost herself a bit. Without knowing it we'd paved out a whole future for ourselves where we were parents raising a family of our own. It took a long time for us to realise that that had never been our story but over time it got easier. Truth is no one ever knows what's on the next page of their story, you've just got to keep on reading.'

'You're both so wise.'

John chuckled, his tanned face wrinkled at his eyes

'Another word for that would be old. It's amazing the wisdom that comes from years of mistakes during your youth. Don't ever worry about making mistakes Margot, just make sure you learn from them.'

She nodded absentmindedly, thinking of the many mistakes she had made in the past. She couldn't regret them, ultimately they had led her to Iris but what had she learnt from them? That would take a bit more consideration.

'We didn't see the two of you coming into our lives Margot but I can't tell you what joy you've both brought to us. It's given us both a renewed sense of purpose. I know it wasn't in your plan but it's the start of a great chapter in our story so thank you for that.'

Margot didn't know what to say, she hadn't considered that their presence would be anything other than a burden. It was a huge weight off her shoulders to know that they were not just tolerated there but valued and welcomed and her eyes filled with gratitude for the opportunity that had been granted to them. Maybe she didn't have to consider an imminent move after all. The thought that they might be able to stay for a while filled her with hope.

John wandered back over to the kitchen, re-emerging with a bowl of steaming hot water and a towel draped over his shoulder. The dutiful husband returned upstairs to care for his wife leaving Margot alone again with the now roaring fire.

Chapter 19

After giving Iris her late night feed Margot feeling the heavy weight of tiredness on her body headed upstairs to her welcome bed. Walking past John and Barbara's room she heard the repetitive rasping coughs interspersed by wheezing attempts to catch breath. For all John tried to play it down Barbara didn't sound healthy. Coughs often sounded a lot worse than they were though she reassured herself, relieved that Barbara had her loving husband by her side tonight. As she lay Iris in the moses basket she was aware of how awake Iris seemed. After her feed she normally fell asleep on the breast her mouth dropped open with a belly full of warm milk. Tonight, however it seemed she was resisting sleep for some reason. Margot had decided to take her upstairs anyway and at least try to get her down in the hope that she too might manage a couple of hours.

The hours that followed however were not restful ones. Margot only realised now how she might have taken Iris' sleeping habits for granted. She had grown accustomed to a sufficient amount of rest, broken usually by two feeds which in themselves were relatively short and uneventful. This evening though she was clearly not a happy infant. As the night dragged on she became more and more restless. Margot tried to stand with her and rock her, they sat in their chair together, she laid her down and rested her hand on her so she would know she was not alone. Nothing worked and Margot found herself still lying blurry eyed in bed rocking the moses basket next to her as the pinkish hues of dawn began to break through the sky.

She decided to give it up as a bad job and see if a change of scenery might help them both, along with a strong cup of tea. As they walked back along the hallway past John and Barbara's room she could hear that Barbara had not improved overnight. She was in fact sounding a lot worse, every few seconds interspersed with hacking coughs that seemed to rob her of her breath. There was movement within the room so she knew they too were up, no doubt having had no more sleep than she had.

She decided to go and make a pot of tea for them all along with some toast in case Barbara was feeling up to it.

Pottering around the kitchen she felt much better being able to do something. The demons of the night always settled in when all was dark and sleep was elusive however in the kitchen as the sunlight slowly seeped through the voile curtains Margot felt brighter and more hopeful. When John joined her in the kitchen a few minutes later however she could not say the same for him. His furrowed brow had settled into large indentations on his forehead, his shoulders stooped and his footsteps dragged slightly on the tiled floor. He looked every inch an exhausted man.

'Bad night?' she asked unnecessarily.

'I've called the doctor, I'm not happy with how her chest's sounding. She normally manages to clear it herself but this seems worse. Little Miss not happy either?'

'Sorry John I hope she didn't add to your bad night?'

'Not at all, there was no sleep happening for us last night regardless, it's not like her to be up though?'

'I know I'm not sure what's happening, I'm sure she'll settle during the day.'

Margot didn't want to be an added burden to John at this time. She knew that Barbara would have had some supportive words of wisdom had she been feeling better but for now she would just have to parent this one alone.

She offered John a steaming mug of tea.

'Thanks pet' he said taking a seat beside her groaning as he did so taking he weight off his feet 'the doc said they're sending someone out this morning to take a look at her.'

Margot struggled with the words that had been formulating in her head all night, no doubt worsened by the anxiety that came with the lack of sleep.

'John, you don't think that she could have caught

something from us? From Iris I mean?'

He didn't respond immediately, the thought obviously not being a new one for him.

'I can't see how, the little 'un's perfectly fine, we'd know if she was poorly and Barb get's like this sometimes. It'll be fine'

She wished she could feel reassured by his words but it sounded more like he was trying to convince himself of their truth. She couldn't live with herself if she had brought this on them. Every day since Iris' birth had been a reassurance that she had done the right thing, that all their effort and running around had been worth it, but what if she had been fooling herself. What if all along she should have heeded the advice of experts and professionals. What if she was single-handedly responsible for another nation wide epidemic? A new strain that didn't initially show in infants but gradually infected those around her? All of the studies showed that infants born with the gene would be fatally ill at birth. They would have known straight away if there were any risks. Wouldn't they?

Her anxiety was building in the pit of her stomach. She knew she was leaping to conclusions but it was hard not to once the seed of doubt was planted. A tired brain was always an anxious brain in her experience but there was little chance of any rest right now. She just needed the doctor to confirm it was nothing serious and then her and John could focus all of their efforts on building up Barbara's strength again.

John, unable to sit still for long, rose to a stand,

taking action to put an end to their worries 'the Doc'll be here soon and he'll sort her out. Will you keep an ear out and show him up when he's here?'

'Of course' she said sounding more confident than she felt.

John's abrupt way of closing down the conversation did little to alleviate her concerns but she understood his desire to not dwell on the possibilities.

She pottered around the kitchen that morning baking some fresh bread in the hope that it might in some way help. At the very least it was good to keep her hands busy whilst her mind was working so frantically. Intermittently Iris would cry out in need of additional comfort to soothe whatever it was she was struggling with. Thankfully she seemed a bit more settled now they were downstairs.

Eventually there came the knock at the door which Margot had been waiting for. With her hands still covered in flour and a tea towel draped over her shoulder she rushed over to the door to allow him entry.

Opening it with urgency she had her welcoming smile ready and waiting for the professional but her eyes opened wide with surprise when she found herself looking into the chestnut-coloured eyes of Sy.

He too had the courteous face of a tired doctor plastered on his face but after the briefest flicker of recognition his smile broadened as they found themselves back in each other's company.

'Sy! It's so nice to see you again!'

Inwardly chastising herself for being so enthusiastically welcoming, she realised that he would probably not remember the name of the random woman he had met once on a train over two months ago.

'Oh my God Margot, what a pleasure.'

She felt warmth radiate her chest as he seemed genuinely as pleased to see her as she was him.

'Come in please, thank you so much for coming out so quickly.'

'No problem at all, I take it you're not my patient today?'

'No it's Barbara, she's upstairs, she's been struggling for a few days now but she seems to be getting worse. I know John wouldn't have called you out if he wasn't really concerned for her so we're all really glad you're here.'

'No problem at all, do you want to show me the way?'

As he followed her through the living room to the bottom of the stairs Margot recalled their conversation all those weeks ago. Not hard when in truth it had been something she had replayed in her mind numerous times during the long lonely nights.

'I thought you were only visiting Newcastle?' She enquired, hoping it wasn't too obvious how much of their conversation she had committed to memory.

'I was but my mum's health declined whilst I was here so I decided to stick around for a little while. I've been doing Locum work for the time being to plug the gap. Did you come back after your holiday or have you been here the whole time?'

Margot felt a flourish of panic as she struggled to remember the exact details of what she'd told Sy that day.

'I decided to spend my maternity leave here in the end, like you said it's a place you end up falling in love with.'

'I'm pleased it worked out for you both, you look well'

Not knowing how to respond to the compliment she merely smiled just as they reached Barbara's bedroom door and she knocked on.

'John, the doctors here'

'Come in' he uttered. Margot could tell he was trying to maintain a calmness to his voice.

As they entered the room Margot could tell that even in the space of the morning Barbara had continued to decline. She looked so pale and weak it surprised Margot but she tried not to show it.

Deciding that introductions were probably not necessary in these circumstances she allowed Sy to enter and then retreated back downstairs to give them some privacy.

Returning to Iris she gave herself a quick cursory glance in the mirror, dismayed to see she'd spent the whole conversation with flour on her nose, she gave her hands and face a wash whilst waiting for his return and prognosis.

It took longer than she had anticipated for him to return which did little to alleviate her concerns, surely if it was a simple chest infection he would be able to diagnose medication fairly quickly.

She wiped down the surfaces and cleared away the

mess of her earlier baking whilst the bread baked in the oven, at the very least creating order out of chaos made her feel calmer.

Eventually she heard footsteps coming down the stairs and her heart quickened at the thought of hearing what he had to say.

From the look on their faces as they walked into the kitchen she knew instantly that something was wrong.

'What is it?' she asked unable to hold back the question.

'The doc isn't happy with her oxygen levels, he thinks we need to get her in to hospital for some more checks. I'm going to drive her over now.'

'It's far quicker than waiting for an ambulance these days' Sy added 'I certainly wouldn't want her to be waiting any longer than necessary as things stand and with her oxygen levels being as low as they are.'

'What can I do John?' Margot asked keen to try and be as helpful as she could, her heartbeat increasing with the unexpected urgency of the diagnosis.

'Can you show the Doc out for me Margot? I'm going to pack up some things and get her straight in the car.'

'Of course' she replied.

John took the doctors hand in both of his and held them for a second 'Thank you for your time'

'Not at all' Sy replied 'I'm hopeful that you'll see an improvement once she's at the hospital.'

Margot didn't quite know what to do or say, she

was nervous at the direction this was going and felt helpless.

John turned his back to take the stairs at a jog, clearly not wanting to waste any more vital time.

'Will she be ok?' Margot asked, aware that this was the million dollar question he must hear all too often.

'It was good that he called when he did.' Sy smiled at her unable to give anything more concrete.

Despite her worries about Barbara she felt her stomach do a little flip at the electricity of his eye contact. How long had it been since she'd felt butterflies at being in the company of a beautiful man.

Behind her Iris kicked her legs in the air and whimpered displeased with being left alone and out of the conversation.

'And who's this?' Sy enquired walking over to the basket.

'This' Margot smiled warmly 'Is my Iris'. She realised it was the first time she had introduced her daughter to anyone expect the two people that had helped deliver her. She hadn't expected to feel such pride in saying her name, claiming this wonderful human being as her own.'

'She's beautiful Margot, congratulations.'

'Thank you, we all certainly think so.'

'Well duty calls I'm afraid, but it was a pleasant surprise seeing you again Margot.'

'And you Sy. You're only the third person I know in this city so it's good to see a friendly face.' She didn't like the idea of him once again disappearing out of her life but couldn't think of a way to stop it.

'I'd like to know how Barbara gets on at the hospital, would you mind keeping me updated?' He produced a card from his jacket pocket and scribbled a number on the back. 'That's my personal mobile on the back feel free to use that.'

She smiled as she took it from him, conscious that he surely wouldn't provide his personal number to all his patients.

'Of course, thank you again for your time.'

As she showed him out of the door she felt hopeful that it might not be the last time she saw him, hopefully under better circumstances.

As she heard his tyre's move off down the gravel driveway she heard a thump upstairs as John attempted to pack up some items for the hospital. Sensing that he might need some help she scooped up Iris and headed for their bedroom.

Inside Barbara was still lying propped upright, her eyes closed, her mouth open, as she gasped for breath between coughing fits. John looked more fraught than she had ever seen him before. He had a bag open and was haphazardly throwing things in that he thought she might need.

Iris squirmed in Margot's arms and began to cry out again, more distressed than she had been all night now she was in their room.

It was clear that there was no logic to John's packing. She watched as he shoved a pair of shorts and a gardening glove into the bag and decided it was appropriate that she stepped in. With plenty of space in the king sized bed next to Barbara she placed Iris down on the other half, there was no consoling the infant at this stage and she rationalised that if she helped to get Barbara out of the house then she could devote her full attention to whatever it was that was causing her daughter so much discomfort.

'John, stop. Let me help you.' She figured a man like him would welcome an assertive tone in a crisis and it certainly seemed to do the trick.

'Why don't you let me pack the bag whilst you get her toiletries from the bathroom.'

John merely nodded in agreement. They had to practically shout now to get their voices heard over the infant's screams. If Margot thought lying her flat would help to alleviate her discomfort she was wrong.

Margot swiftly emptied the bag and then began quickly folding the necessary items and packing them in. What with Iris' screams, Barbara's hacking cough and John's anxiety there was a frenetic energy to the room. Margot wanted to focus on Iris but knew she needed to help here first.

As John came back in with his arms laden he tipped the wash bag up side down and the items he'd collected spilled onto the floor around him.

'Damn it.' He growled, growing increasingly frustrated with himself.

Margot moved to help pick them up but as she did Iris became inconsolable on the bed, writhing around in what Margot could only assume was pain. Suddenly panicked for her daughter having never heard her make a noise like that before she turned to try and pick her up. As she did so Barbara reached out a hand and rested it on the infant's chest.

Margot instantaneously felt her legs buckle underneath her, the room span and her vision blurred. She put out a hand to support her but there was no support to be had and she crumpled to the floor onto her hands and knees. She felt blood pound in her ears for a few seconds as a wave of heat swept through her body. She felt like she was in the centre of a tornado, the world was shifting all around her at a frenetic speed, the force of the earth's axis moving as she tried desperately to maintain her balance. She forced herself to breathe, unsure if she was going to vomit or pass out or both but as the breaths filled her lungs, she gradually felt the dizziness ease and her vision return. She was clammy and shaking and then suddenly as quickly as it had hit her it all came to an abrupt stop. She took a second to check in on herself, to reassure herself that she was OK and to focus on what had changed in the room.

There was stillness and silence. The complete polar opposite of what had been the case five seconds ago. Nobody moved, nobody cried or coughed. There was calm where there had once been panic. Warmth where there had once been a chill.

Looking up she could see both Barbara and John's eyes were focused on Iris. John had one arm out in the direction of Margot no doubt in an attempt to stop her from falling but something had distracted him before he had managed to get there.

With shaking legs Margot managed to get back to

her feet, keen to check that Iris was still OK and to establish why all was so alarmingly quiet.

'What just happened?' John asked the room.

'Iris just…' but then Barbara fell silent. It seemed there were no words to describe what Iris had just done.

'Are you okay?' Margot asked of the woman although it was clear that she was. She looked more alert and stronger than Margot had ever seen her. Although maybe it was the stark contrast from how she had looked a minute ago that highlighted the change so startlingly.

The absence of the rasping coughs and wheezes that had resonated so loudly in the room for the past few days left a sort of ringing in their ears.

Iris on the other hand lying on her back in the middle of the bed had stopped crying and was lying contentedly on the mattress. A serenity had washed over her as if she had finally been able to do the thing she had been yearning to do all night. She was gazing around at each of them blinking in the morning sunlight that streamed through the open curtains.

John looked over his shoulder at Margot who was now leaning onto the wall for support, more out of shock than because she needed to although her legs still felt weak.

'Are you OK?' he asked

'I don't know. I felt like all the strength went out of me for a few seconds. I don't understand' she turned her head once again to Barbara 'you look different.'

Barbara still couldn't take her eyes off the baby, confusion and awe wrapped up in her gaze all in one.

'I touched her and I felt her so viscerally. It was like she was a part of me, and then it just… went away.'

'What went away?' John was clearly torn between the action mode he had found himself in and the sudden change in tempo. Still holding a tube of toothpaste and a face cloth in his hands which he now wasn't sure what to do with.

'Everything… the pain, the cough. I've never felt better.'

She looked it too. Something about her looked more youthful and brighter.

Margot still feeling weak in the knees softly walked over to the bed to sit next to Iris. She picked her up and looked into her eyes, together mother and daughter stared into each other's souls. A silent conversation over something unknown they had just shared together. Iris had known what to do, she looked so sure of herself. The quiet self-assurance of a child who knew more about what had just happened than all the adults gathered together in that room but unable to communicate it.

Together they had just witnessed something that they were unable to put into words. John moved over to Barbara to wipe the sweat from her face that still remained from a fever she no longer felt.

As Margot held Iris close to her chest the infant closed her eyes and drifted off to a peaceful sleep, seemingly content with the work that she had done.

Leaving the three adults together to try and piece together the miraculous event they had all witnessed and the potential ramifications of what had happened here, this day, in this room.

Chapter 20

Despite them all being exhausted from the events of the night there was no chance of any of them attempting to get any rest that morning. Unable to put into words what they had all witnessed together the three of them decided to go downstairs and try to rationalise what had taken place.

'It could have just been a coincidence' Margot rationalised. 'Maybe you were over the worst of the fever and just recovered quicker than expected?'

'At exactly the same time that I touched Iris?' Barbara looked incredulous 'I know what I felt, it was like nothing I'd ever felt before. It was incredible, she's incredible'

Barbara still had a look of wide eyed awe on her face, suddenly filled with an energy she hadn't felt for years.

'And what about you?' she continued 'that was no coincidence, you were affected by what Iris did to me too and you were on the other side of the room.'

'I just felt dizzy that's all, it's no wonder after a sleepless night and then worrying about you.' Margot felt uneasy at the thought of Iris being incredible, she was perfectly happy with her being her beautifully 'normal' baby. Incredible implied different and different implied attention. They'd already had far too much of that.

John strode over to Barbara to check her temperature 'You don't feel hot anymore and your breathing sounds good. Maybe we should still take you in though just to be sure.'

'John I've honestly never felt better, I feel like I could climb Everest! It's a miracle.'

'Still love, I think it might be best to double check.'

'You cannot take a perfectly healthy person to hospital and say you want help because I used to feel poorly, you'd be laughed out of the place.'

'That's true, well if you're sure love. Maybe we'll just keep an eye on you and see how things go?'

Iris too seemed completely unperturbed by their discussions, sleeping soundly now in her moses basket peaceful and rested.

'If she did do it, and it's a massive if' said Margot 'how did she do it? Not only how did she do it, how did she know? She was so distressed when we were near you Barb it was like she knew you needed her and she knew she could help. She's a tiny little baby, I don't understand.'

'I'm not sure this is something we'll ever fully understand dear, maybe we're not meant to, but for the time being we can be thankful that you're in our lives and that we've had the joy of witnessing something truly remarkable.'

Margot tried to feel the peace and acceptance that Barbara was exhibiting, but she felt uneasy at the shift in balance. She was the parent, she was meant to be in control and have all the answers. Her daughter, already so new to the world seemed to be light years ahead of her and it left her reeling. She felt like she was fighting against a strong current to try and catch up.

She rubbed her legs trying to breathe life back into her muscles, the memory of her collapse still resonated within them and she still hadn't fully regained her strength.

'You look tired dear, are you sure you can't manage some shut eye?'

'No, my body feels tired but I think it'll take a while for my brain to calm down after this morning.'

'And a brush with a handsome young fellow to boot no doubt left you weak at the knees' John piped up from the corner of the room, he was clearly buoyant at Barbara's recovery and had the twinkle of mischief in his eyes.

'I don't know what you mean.' Margot replied unable to stop the corners of her mouth from rising and mortified to feel her cheeks burning. She was a grown woman for goodness sake!

'Oh John leave her alone, the poor thing has been through enough this morning, go and put the kettle on.' Margot reprimanded

John nodded in their direction and followed his orders leaving the two women alone.

There followed the merest hint of a pause

'He was a bit of a dish dear' Barbara piped up, unable to stop herself.

'Oh I know Barb, I know.'

The rest of the day passed with no further drama. No one could quite find the words to start the conversation that they all felt they needed to have. All of them lost in their own thoughts trying to piece together the events of that morning. Margot found herself going round and round in circles, the same questions plaguing her mind.

What happened in there? Surely it was all just a coincidence? If it wasn't what do I do with that? Who is my daughter?'

John and Barbara looked as if they too were trying to piece it all together but the overriding feeling coming off them both was relief. Relief that however it had happened Barbara was seemingly cured.

Iris unperturbed slept and fed her way throughout the day as if nothing had happened at all.

Barbara, thrilled to have been given a new lease of energy was apparently now also ravenous having not properly eaten for days and so had baked an enormous pie for them all to sit down to that evening. It was as they tucked in to their delicious dinner that John decided he was ready to broach the conversation.

'I don't think any of us can properly fathom out what happened today, but it's clear that something did and I for one am very grateful to the little miss for whatever she did.'

'I know I certainly am too.' The colour had stayed in Barbara's cheeks all day and she showed no sign of succumbing to another coughing fit anytime soon.

'I'm grateful of course Barbara that you're feeling better but I can't make any sense out of it. What if Iris gets poorly now because of it?'

'She's the picture of health Margot' John reassured her. 'She knew, don't ask me how and I know how it would sound to anyone else who wasn't in that room, but she knew what she needed to do and she did it!'

Margot understood, she'd seen it too. Iris' distress ever increasing whilst she was in Barbara's presence, clearly having wanted to be closer to her, to be able to touch her and make it all go away. But the logical part of her brain was screaming at her that this wasn't possible that they must be mistaken.

'It's all wrong, everything's so wrong' Margot uttered trying to find the words to express what her mind was processing. 'She was meant to have been a danger to society, a plague, a threat! She was never meant to have been born. Now, not only does she not have the virus but she's also some kind of prodigy too? If people find out about this are they going to want to execute her or examine her in a lab? I just want her to be left alone. I want us all to be left alone!'

She knew she was rambling, she knew her emotions of a sleepless night and a drama fuelled day were getting the better of her but she couldn't stop the fountain of words spewing from her mouth.

'Breathe deary' Barbara reached out a hand over the table and rested it on top of Margot's. 'We're the only ones who know about this and it will not leave this room. I'm forever indebted to that little girl and nothing is going to harm her whilst there is air in my lungs.'

'And mine' John chipped in clear to show his solidarity to them both 'Let's just take it one day at a time shall we? So long as we stick together no harm's going to come to you.'

Margot nodded trying to make herself believe the words. She opened her mouth to thank them when John held up a finger to silence her and turned his head towards the door.

Margot strained her ears, still unfamiliar with the sounds of the house to notice anything out of the ordinary but then she heard it, the sound of tyres on the gravel driveway making their way down the lane towards the farm.

Visitors were a rarity most days here with nothing but their house at the end of the long gravel road but at this time of night it was most unusual.

John stood and walked over to the window pulling the voile curtains slightly to one side.

'Two cars, formal looking' he said before turning back to them.

'Margot, we need to get you hidden, now'

Chapter 21

Margot didn't like John's tone. She trusted his judgement and he sounded unnerved. With her heart in her mouth Margot clung Iris close to her chest. She tried to convince her brain that it was all going to be okay but her heart was pounding. She chastised herself for potentially overreacting but she was nervous. She backed away from the door until it came to rest on the wall. There was nowhere to run, the only escape route from the farm was down the mile long driveway that the car was currently driving up and she was certain to get caught before she got to the end of it.

The engine noises got louder as they got closer to the house, it was probably nothing, she tried to reassure herself, an old friend or someone lost on their way into town maybe? But two cars? She questioned, who could possibly be visiting in two cars?

She felt like a rabbit in the headlights, unsure how to react or what level of panic was appropriate. She didn't want to hide, she hadn't done anything wrong.

The engines turned off and car doors slammed shut followed by a loud authoritative knock at the door. Her body began to shake with fear as adrenaline coursed through her body preparing herself for a fight she might be facing but could not win.

John walked towards her with a steely determination in his eyes. He looked twenty years younger and walked with a purposeful stride. He rested his hand on her shoulder

'Take Iris and hide in the dresser, you'll need to keep the little miss quiet, I'll deal with them, they'll be gone in no time you'll see'

She began to shake her head in protest but he was already ushering her towards the large wooden cabinet.

'There's no time to discuss it, hop in and I'll close the door'

She desperately wanted to find another solution but there was no time to consider anything now. She chided herself for all those long evenings where she'd been sat in the living room basking in the false security that she was safe, that they'd never find her. All that time when she could have been formulating an escape plan and now she'd put them all in danger all because of her lack of planning.

She opened up the two doors of the dresser which revealed a space just big enough for her to clamber into. There were piles of table cloths and towels bundled on the base which Barbara quickly gathered up and hid inside the washing machine.

It was going to be a tight fit. Margot sat inside and swung her legs in, bunching them up so they were tucked up by her chest. Iris lay sleeping on her chest tucked snugly with Margot's thighs resting on her back. Margot had to bend her head to one side and rest it on her shoulders so as to not push up the shelf above her.

She looked out at John and Barbara standing in the space and caught their gaze, taking a deep breath as they simultaneously closed the doors on her plunging her into darkness. She could hear her heart pounding and her panicked breaths seemed thunderously loud.

Through a small gap in the doors she could see John move across the kitchen and open the door for their visitors.

'Can I help you' he said in an unwavering tone. Margot couldn't believe how calm and relaxed he sounded.

'We're looking for a missing person, we've received intelligence she might be in the area. We wondered if you'd seen her?'

There was a pause Margot assumed whilst they held up a photograph of her.

'Fraid not, not seen nobody looking like that have we Barbara?'

'No don't recognise her sorry' Barbara replied tersely 'Don't get many visitors down these parts'

Margot clung onto Iris, the peaceful rising and falling of her chest a welcome sign that she was still asleep.

The man at the door took a small step forward

placing himself in the threshold of the kitchen. His voice was cold, monotone and he took his time, clearly in no rush to say what he wanted to say. Far from this having a calming effect on the situation Margot felt the palpable tension in the room.

'We've actually had intelligence that she's been staying here for quite some time'

Margot silently had an intake of breath. They weren't just scouting out the area they knew she was here. The only person that could have led them here was Sy. The realisation dawned on her like lead in her stomach, he had given her up.

'Must be some mistake lad, she's not been here'

Margot wasn't sure if John's use of the word lad was particularly helpful in this scenario, he didn't look particularly young and clearly thought of himself as somewhat of a big fish.

'Won't mind if we'll take a look around then will you' he said stepping once more into the kitchen. As he did so Margot could see two more men follow him in. Unlike the first these two did not look like government officials but more like thugs straight out of a boxing ring. Dressed all in black they towered over their companion.

'You will not step foot inside this house without a warrant' John thundered 'I know my rights and this will not be tolerated.'

John moved forwards in an attempt to stop them coming any further forwards but was intercepted by one of the gigantic men who shoved him backwards firmly.

'Get your hands off me!' John bellowed. Margot

had never heard him sound so fierce and authoritative and could suddenly envision him in his army days. He was not somebody she would have messed with but the three men seemed completely unfazed by his anger. In one swift move one of them bent his arm behind his back and kicked his legs out from underneath him so that he was kneeling on the floor.

There was a yelp of shock from Barbara as she attempted to rush to his aid but she was quickly grabbed by the second man and forced down next to her husband.

With them both now in Margot's line of sight through the gap in the cupboard door she couldn't bear to see them in such a vulnerable position. The two thugs stood motionless behind them, one hand resting threateningly on each of their shoulders. 'This is their home' she thought 'and they're being persecuted in it all because of me'. She moved her hand to rest on the inside of the cupboard door ready to push it open and reveal herself.

What would they do when they found her? Was there a chance they would re-test Iris for the gene or would they just kill her instantly? An image of Iris' lifeless body lying on a slab in the morgue filled her head and she retracted her hand from the door. There was no way she could move from her hiding place she had to hope they wouldn't find her and that they'd leave them all in peace.

If she survived this she would find somewhere else to go tomorrow, she wouldn't put John and Barbara in jeopardy like this again.

'The shorter of the three men moved forwards and bent his head closer to the elderly couple.

'We know she left yesterday, we just need to know where she's gone'

A stab of confusion broke through Margot's thoughts. Why were they so sure that she had already left? Whatever the reason though it gave her a glimmer of hope, surely now they'd question the couple and then leave them alone. She just hoped one of them could think up a cover story quickly enough to get them out of this situation.

'Please', Barbara implored 'All we did was give her some food and some clean clothes, we don't know anything about where she was going.'

'Now I know that's not true is it Barbara? She's been here for a good few weeks according to our sources, so why would you not be telling me the truth?'

'You won't get any more information from us sonny' John intercepted 'we know wrong'uns when we see them and from now on we'll be keeping schtum'

Margot couldn't believe their defiance. She felt tears welling up in her eyes at their solidarity and support for her. She only hoped that John's insistence on remaining quiet would encourage the men to leave sooner rather than later. She was now getting shooting pains down her shoulder where her head was bent at such an awkward angle.

She caught John casually reach out to take Barbara's hand. They both looked strong despite their years as they knelt there on the floor together, their love for one another binding them together. Margot suddenly felt very alone in the world. What it must be like to go through life with that constant companionship.

'Well, we're grateful for your time' the short pale man uttered. His expression unfaltering, almost with an air of boredom to it. He looked at his male counterparts and gave the merest hint of a nod before turning and walking slowly out of the door.

Margot dared herself to believe that they might have done it, that she might have escaped their clutches once more. She closed her eyes in the hope that when she opened them again they all would have left and she could breathe freely. But as she opened her eyes she witnessed the two men simultaneously reach into the waistband of their trousers and pull out identical pistols. Raising them at a 45 degree angle with both of their hands they pointed them squarely at the back of the John and Barbara's heads and pulled the trigger.

A cacophony of noise filled the small kitchen and Margot jumped so much her elbows hit the sides of the walls and her head hit the ceiling of her cramped cupboard space. She bit down on her lip so hard with terror that she tasted the metallic blood filling her mouth. Iris, also startled, had thrown her arms out to her sides, her reflexes responding immediately to the threat.

Margot instinctively closed her eyes and hugged Iris to her tightly. She could not bear the anticipation of Iris making a noise and them being discovered hiding in a cupboard like the coward she truly was.

This could not be happening, this was not real.

'Time to go' she heard the steely voice echo through the room.

There was a shuffling of feet and a click of the door closing to.

Margot could not move. Afraid that it was a trap, that they were still waiting for her. She remained where she was, frozen in fear and trepidation.

She sat there shaking as the silence enveloped the house like a thick blanket and still she did not move. If she stayed still, if she kept her eyes shut she could keep her life on pause, she didn't want to move, she didn't want to see what horror awaited her when she did.

Forcing herself to open her eyes she stared into the darkness of her cupboard the only light shining in from the crack in the doors. Her eyes settled on the small slither of kitchen floor she could see through the gap. Her gaze moved upwards following the lines of the tiled kitchen floor, past the wooden legs of the kitchen table and chairs over to the far side of the kitchen where two pairs of feet lay lifeless on the floor.

Chapter 22

Margot sat for a few minutes waiting. Waiting for something to happen, for something to stir her from the paralysed fear she now found herself in. Her mouth hung open in shock and fear as she tried to process the horrific reality of what she had just witnessed. She felt herself go weak and had to remind herself to take a breath. As she did so oxygen flooded her lungs and caught in the back of her throat making a gargled sound like a babies first breaths. Her eyes, wide open like a hunted animal, blurred as tears filled them.

She was terrified and confused and angry. What was happening? How had they found her here? Was she about to die? What had she done? How could she have brought this devastation to two of the most loving people she had ever had the good fortune to come across? People that she had grown to love.

Aware that at some point she had to move and with Iris becoming increasingly unsettled she slowly pushed open the doors and climbed out. Averting her gaze initially from the lifeless bodies she turned her back to them as she stretched out her neck, whimpering in pain as the shooting pains travelled across her shoulders. She placed her cheek down on Iris' head and held her close, their hearts beating together. She wanted her to know that she was safe, that her mother would never let anything happen to her.

The longer she stood there the harder it was to turn around. She felt sick at the thought of seeing them, like a horror film that you're unable to turn off. She didn't want to have the image of them in her mind but she owed them a debt greater than anything she could ever repay, the least she could do was look at the sacrifice they had made for her. Turning herself around she took a few deep breaths as she moved her eyes over to the far end of the kitchen. There they lay, the two of them side by side their hands touching, their bodies at awkward angles from the way they had fallen. John's eyes were open, Barbara's head was turned away from her and she was relieved. She didn't want to see her face, her beautiful soft gentle face, ravaged by her brutal killing.

Margot tried to breathe, tried to calm her pounding heart. It was too much to bear and her head was filled with questions, so many questions. She couldn't calm the noise, she couldn't slow her breath, she didn't know what to do or where to go. Her body responding to her panic, she wretched and just had time to turn to the sink before vomiting. Taking a breath, she placed Iris down on the worktop next to her, keeping one hand on her chest to stop her from being able to roll off she just had time to turn back to the sink before another wave of vomiting overtook her as she emptied her stomach.

Wiping her mouth she returned to standing. There were no answers to her questions right now but by God she was going to find them eventually. She would not let them both have died in vain and she would get answers for them. For now, however, she recognised that she had to leave. Would those men come back to the house? She figured not as there would seem no reason to but if they did she needed to be long gone. What would happen to John and Barbara? Who would find them? Surely there would be an investigation when two bodies were found with bullets to the back of their heads.

She had to get out now, she paced over to the stairs and went upstairs to her bedroom. Laying Iris on the bed she hastily grabbed a large holdall from the wardrobe and began to bundle their clothes inside. In the space of a few months she had acquired a number of thing for Iris, the majority of which she would have to leave behind. John and Barbara's beautiful Moses basket lay beside her bed, it had been a godsend in these last few months to lay Iris there and she had begun to settle for longer periods at night, contented to be on her own knowing her mother was always close by. But now she would have to leave it all behind. She wrapped her sling around her body and lifted Iris into place, now they were having to go back on the run it was imperative that she had her hands free. With Iris on her front and her rucksack on her back she was surprised by the weight she now carried but everything she had put in her rucksack was needed. The main difference from the last time she was on the run was that now she needed lots of items for Iris instead of just for herself.

She couldn't allow herself to cry, would not allow herself to cry. There was no time. There would be a time to grieve, a time to mourn, she promised herself that, but this was not that time. If she stopped now she may never get started again.

'Come on, you can do this' she muttered to herself through gritted teeth. The option to collapse into a helpless heap on the floor was so tempting, she was balanced on a knife edge of whether to move forward or just give in.

She had to move forward she knew, one foot in front of the other, step by step for Iris' sake. She may not know where she was going to end up in the next few hours but she had to keep going.

She moved downstairs and into the living room. The mugs of tea still on the side table placed down when they had been so abruptly interrupted by their intruders.

She didn't have the heart to walk back past them again so she turned right and went to the formal front door which she had never seen used in the whole time she had stayed there.

Coats hung up on the walls either side, umbrellas stood in the stand in the corner. Her own coat hung amongst the others, new looking and shiny compared to the weather beaten older versions behind it. She reached underneath her own and lifted out Johns, she could smell him on it and the material felt soft and worn in from the years of use. It felt heavier on one side and she reached into the pocket. A worn leather wallet and his mobile phone were nestled inside. A brick of a thing, John had never felt the need for a phone but Barbara had instilled in him that they had their uses and that he should carry one on him when he was out in case of emergencies. Now Margot decided she should follow the same advice. Putting the phone back in the pocket she draped his coat over one arm leaving her own hanging on the rack and let herself out into the crisp January air.

The cold wind hitting her face renewed in her an intense rage. How could they do this to them? As she began to try to piece together how this could have happened an icy clarity flooded her brain. There could be no coincidence, she rationalised, in bumping into the only other person she knew in the city one day and them being killed the next. She had trusted Sy and he had betrayed her in the worst possible way. She wanted to hurt him, to look him in the eye and see that he was not the man she thought he was. A tiny part of the back of her brain muted the idea that this might not be sensible but this was not the time for logical, methodical thoughts this was time for her to do something with the anger pounding through her veins. The injustice of the last twenty minutes, hell the last twenty years compounded within her and had now settled on the face of one man.

All too aware that the people who had just committed murder in the name of finding her would still be in the area she knew she needed to stay off the main road. Fortunately, her time on the farm had allowed her to familiarise herself with the local area and John had shown her a pathway through the woods at the back of the farm which would lead her eventually into the town centre. Anyone looking for her would never believe she would be stupid enough to head to such a built up area whilst on the run and she was relying on this train of thought to keep them both safe for the next few hours. She just needed enough time to see him, to look him in the eye. She didn't know what she wanted to say at the minute but to see him would be enough to start with.

After that she had no idea where she would end up. Despite the pain and anger, she recognised her behaviour enough to know that she was diverting her panic over her future onto something else but right now it seemed like as good a plan as any.

She wanted to scream. To shout out at the blustery wind that it would not take her down. That the world was going to have to try harder than that to stop her. She was incandescent with fury and was using it to power her through the walk, the bitter wind barely even registering on her skin.

Not knowing what they would have done to Iris had they found her was gnawing away at her thoughts. She had been allowed to believe over the last few months that the threat to her daughter might all be in her mind, but this had brought it literally to her doorstep. They wanted her, potentially wanted to kill her and Margot didn't know why. If Sy had been the one to betray them then he must have more information than she did and she was determined to get it.

Iris seemingly unaware of the cataclysmic events that had just altered the trajectory of their lives was attached once again to her mother, quiet, pensive, awake and taking in her surroundings allowing her mother the space to be consumed by her anger.

Margot's anger fuelled her entire walk, she did not waiver or slow, so determined was she to do something with her fear and anger, to avenge them in some way.

As she walked out of the countryside she found herself increasingly surrounded by more and more buildings. Taking herself into a more densely populated area she felt the creeping niggles of doubt start to work their way into her brain. She wasn't acting sensibly. She wasn't thinking of Iris.

But she pushed them further down into the pit of her stomach. She just needed to see him, just needed to hear what he had to say and then she would leave.

The hospital was on the outskirts of the city, fortunately on the same side that she was approaching it from so she didn't have to navigate the city centre.

As she got closer to the large white bricked building she realised that there was no way she could go inside without being detected by someone and so she sat herself down on an embankment by the edge of the car park with a clear view of the main entrance. He had told her that he would be at the hospital today and so she was pinning all of her hopes on catching a glimpse of him arriving or leaving at some point. She would wait here all day if she needed to.

Her breathing remained heavy, her mind still racing as she sat. Being here in such close proximity to so many people made her feel reckless and she relished it. She was ready for a fight, almost willing it to happen.

A group of younger people walked out of the doors one with his arm in a cast. They joked as they departed no doubt chiding themselves on their antics which had brought about a broken limb of a friend. Margot watched them with envy, their lightness of mood mocking her in the most antagonistic of ways. She wanted to hurt them for being so carefree.

Almost undetected to her a man walked out behind them and turned in the opposite direction. She could have so easily missed it but just before he turned a corner out of sight she caught his side profile and her heart rate increased, there he was.

She couldn't believe she'd found him so quickly. Was it really him?

She stood quickly and gave chase determined not to lose him. As she caught up to the end of the street where he had disappeared she was just in time to see him turn down another corner at the end of the road.

She had been worried that when the time came

she would be too nervous to take action but seeing his face, that smug, self assured face made the fury rise up in her once again. He was nothing compared to John and Barbara. She couldn't think about them now, she was emotional enough as it was and she did not want him to see her cry, she wanted to see him fearful, she wanted him to be scared just like they had been scared at the very end.

As she followed the road round the corner she could see that he had taken a short cut that would lead him onto the main road. Their current position was quiet and secluded. If she allowed him to reach the main road there would be no cover. She looked behind her, there was no one there, this was her opportunity to get him alone.

'Sy!' she shouted without giving herself time to consider the risk associated with her actions.

He turned his head to look behind him whilst still walking forwards, surprised to hear someone else down the quiet street.

A look of confusion briefly passed across his face

'Margot?' He stopped in his tracks turning to face her

She didn't reply, she wanted to watch his expression as she got closer to him she wanted to read his eyes before he had a chance to cloud her judgement with his words.

With every step she took closer to him his face remained passive and unreadable, no warmth, no fear. The poised face of someone who was trained to control their emotions.

She suddenly doubted herself, what if she'd called

this wrong, what if he knew nothing? The sudden onset of doubt made her furious with herself. 'Trust your instincts for once you pathetic weak little girl' a voice inside her muttered. The voice that had been gnawing away at her brain ever since she'd carved out this new life for herself. The voice that told her she was a hypocrite of the worst kind, who abused people's good faith to her own advantage, who offered nothing good to the world, only sucked the energy and life force from all that was wholesome and innocent. She despised herself and her choices and her past, but despite all this she kept making it worse.

Her teeth gritted together as she took the final steps towards him and he looked her straight in the eye

'Is everything OK?' He asked seemingly innocently 'you look not OK…'

The understatement of the century did not make her feel better and without allowing herself any other rational thought she let her emotions course through her muscles, drawing her fingers down into themselves, she pulled her arm back and with every ounce of fire she had in her blood she threw her fist forward into his face making direct contact with his cheek.

Pain exploded in her hand immediately, stabbing out through her fingers and down her arm and she liked it. She liked having a physical reaction to her pain, something real she could focus on. She wanted to hit him again but he had turned away from her and was bent low.

'What the fuck!' he shouted and she bared her teeth together again ready for a comeback.

He turned to face her still bent low his hands up in an immediate act of surrender. A trickle of blood seeped from one side of his nose which momentarily made her take stock. Her breathing came in rasping breaths unsure if she was going to lash out again, she wanted him to taunt her, to say something that would prove she was right, that would allow her to take her remaining anger out on him but he remained resolutely silent.

She watched as the trickle of blood slowly descended down to his top lip and despite herself she could feel her anger starting to ebb away already. She didn't feel better, she had hurt the man who had killed her friends and she didn't feel better which in turn made her feel worse. The realisation that no amount of retaliation would do the one thing that she needed to make her feel better, nothing would bring them back to her.

'How could you?' she screamed into the alley. 'How could you?' There was no other way for her to express her grief.

He looked her straight in the eye's, confusion now forming on his face.

'Margot' he said remarkably calmly for someone who had just been punched to the ground 'tell me what's happened.'

His hands were still raised, palms facing her which she found infuriating. If he at least shouted back it would give her reason to maintain her fury but his pathetic stance and her obvious advantage towering over him only made her anger start to dwindle.

'They're dead' she muttered, her vision blurred as her eyes filled with tears which she didn't have the energy to wipe away. 'You killed them.'

She didn't know what to expect in the form of an excuse or explanation, she was intrigued to know how he would try and talk his way out of it. What she hadn't expected was for him to say nothing. He lowered his hands, as he lowered his face and sat on his knees, his spine bent over looking utterly dejected, like all the life had been sucked out of him.

'I'm so sorry' he whispered

She continued to stare at him. Was this a confession? Was he admitting his involvement or just sorry that they had died? She waited allowing the silence to do the talking, allowing him to figure out what best to say next.

As he looked back up and their eyes met she saw that he too was crying.

'We can't talk here, you need to get somewhere safe' he muttered slowly rising to a stand.

She was momentarily surprised by his response, he was taking control of the situation which was exactly what she felt she needed but she still had no answers.

'You killed them!' she repeated shoving his shoulders and pushing him a few steps backward.

'Seriously Margot, the two of you aren't safe here. Think of Iris, you need to get her to safety.'

'Why would I listen to you? I can't trust a word that comes out of your mouth'

'You need to listen to me because I'm the only

person that can give you some answers, but not here and not now. You have no idea what you've got yourself mixed up in.'

'So tell me!'

'Margot, you're in the middle of the city centre, there are cameras everywhere and everyone is looking for her.' He pointed his finger directly at her chest.

She looked down almost surprised to see Iris there, her head turned sideways her arms up her hands resting on Margot's heart. It was the first time that she had put her own needs ahead of her daughters, bringing her here, putting her in danger to satisfy her own act of revenge.

'Why? Just tell me why they want her.' She pleaded now, desperate to finally get some answers to the questions that had been pounding around her head. 'She's just a little baby Sy.'

'You know as well as I do that she's so much more than that.' Their eyes met and a level of understanding passed between them. On some level he knew what she was capable of and she had to find out more.

'Do you have anywhere you can go?' He asked

Margot felt suddenly deflated. The anger she had felt had now dissipated and she was left confused, vulnerable and disorientated.

'No, there's nowhere. No one.'

Sy seemed to shake himself off. He wiped his nose on the back of his hand and then reached into his inner pocket and pulled out another of his business cards and a pen. He was scrawling something onto the back in rushed handwriting before handing it out to her.

'Take this, go to the end of the road, turn left and you'll see a taxi rank. Give them this address.' He reached into his jacket again, pulled out his wallet and produced two crisp twenty pound notes and placed them in her hand wrapping her fingers around them. 'I've written a name on the back of the card, ask for that person and tell them that I've sent you. Then talk to no one until I get there.'

She was being bombarded with information and she couldn't take it in. She'd come here to hold him to account for what he'd done not to become complicit in whatever it was he was involved in.

'I don't… I can't…' words escaped her as she struggled to string together an eloquent sentence.

'Margot you're in shock, you can't think straight right now and I need to get you to safety. We will talk I promise you but the longer you stay here the more danger Iris is in.'

He still held her fist with the money inside, her palms sweaty, her breathing still labored.

'I need you to go now.' He reiterated nodding and fixing her with a stare. She looked into his eyes, the eyes that she had thought about more times that she cared to admit and tried to find some truth in them, but the reality was she didn't know any more. She couldn't trust anyone, she couldn't rely on anyone other than herself.

'I'll see you there and we'll talk.' He repeated. Letting go of her hand he turned and walked away at pace down the alley, not looking back, not waiting to see what she chose to do and leaving her alone to ponder her next move.

Chapter 23

Alone and with no one else to turn to Margot attempted to quieten the noise in her head to enable her to come to some form of a rational decision.

Sy hadn't responded the way she had expected him to, he hadn't denied his involvement but similarly she had no more answers than she'd had beforehand.

She couldn't see a way of moving on with her life until she found out more about what was going on and she didn't see how she could do that without Sy's involvement.

It was a leap of faith, more truthfully it was a huge risk, but she knew that if she ran into hiding now she would forever be plagued with what truths were lurking out of her reach.

She owed it to John and Barbara, she owed it to herself. If Sy had wanted to hand her over to the person who had killed them then he had had his chance, she had offered herself up on a silver platter and he had walked away, she had to take some reassurance in that.

Feeling like she had no other option than to follow the breadcrumbs that had been laid out for her she took a deep steadying breath and followed his directions to the taxi rank.

There she found a long line of taxi's and headed to the car at the front of the queue. As she approached the passenger side the driver opened the window and she handed him the card with the address on it. He looked at it for a few seconds and typed the address into his navigation system. It clearly wasn't a place he was familiar with. When he viewed their destination he raised his eyebrows and nodded briefly to himself.

'Thirty six quid love' he leaned over to her with an outstretched hand.

One last opportunity to change her mind she thought and then before she had chance to consider it any more she handed over the cash, got into the back seat and settled in for the ride.

The driver took her out of the city, in the opposite direction to the farm and Margot once again felt the pull of grief and regret as she put a wider distance between herself and them. She would probably never see their beautiful farm again and she felt like another piece of her had died.

Her self-pity and despair once again took hold, clouding her mind and draining her body. What cruel twist of fate allowed her to still be here when all around her she was causing death and destruction.

She no longer recognised any of the landmarks

around her as the bustling city streets and high-rise tower blocks slowly transformed into leafy wide roads with numerous villages branching off either side.

Her sense of trepidation grew as she travelled further from the city. Despite hardly knowing anyone here she had become fond of the city even with everything she had been through.

Now she was very much headed into the unknown with only the word of a man whom merely an hour ago she had vowed to never trust again as her guide. Had she been a woman of faith she would have been praying to God right now that she was doing the right thing.

Eventually the driver turned off the main road they had been on and began to meander through a small town. This area looked a lot less appealing than some of the previous places she had seen. Tired shops, most with their shutters pulled firmly down displaying illegible graffiti and sprawls of colour, were dotted in between terraced houses.

The gardens were strewn with upturned children's toys and bags of rubbish, unable to be squashed down into the already overflowing wheelie bins.

Margot spotted random houses dotted in between that appeared to have been more conscientiously taken care of but they were a rarity and dishearteningly the further they drove the less frequently they appeared.

As they continued through the streets they turned down a road of terraced houses which looked like it dated back to the fifties. The houses all tightly packed in next to one another lined either side of a narrow road no longer big enough to withstand the modern day requirements of multiple cars per household.

Eventually even the houses faded into the distance until all that was left was barren waste land and a long winding pot holed road that meandered its way seemingly to their destination. The street appeared to be a dead end and Margot could see nothing from her vantage point other than an endless sky.

As they neared the end of the road however Margot found herself looking out onto the horizon and the vast expanse of the North Sea. Not having realised she was so close to the coast Margot was surprised to find herself faced with this mass expanse of blue.

Hundreds of wind turbines stretched out in the water, industrialising an otherwise natural scene. Some of them turning around methodically others sedentary as if exhausted from their daily grind.

As she turned her gaze to the right she saw a towering factory, dominant and opposing, casting the desolate grounds around it into shadow. There was an apocalyptic energy to the whole area. A place once no doubt vibrant and thriving now left to rot and decay lying quiet and stagnant in a state of disrepair. Windows were smashed, chimneys soared high into the grey clouds balancing precariously on their unstable foundations, weeds grew out of the walls in an act of defiance. Life will always find a way.

The driver stopped the car and turned around expectantly. Having not uttered a word to her the whole journey Margot didn't feel now was the time to question him on her whereabouts. If he had driven her to the address Sy had provided then she must be in the right spot, she was just struggling to see how that would be the case at this moment in time.

Nodding in thanks she gathered up her things and stepped out of the vehicle. Unsure what her next steps should be, she contemplated just getting back in the car and asking for it to take her back to civilisation before realising with a sinking feeling that the journey had cost her practically all of the money Sy had given her and she had no way of funding a return trip. She was well and truly stranded and suddenly, she realised with dread, very isolated.

As the taxi turned around and drove off she simply stood for a while taking in her surroundings. Vast ocean in front of her, barren land behind she felt a synchronicity with her surroundings having seemingly reached the end of the road. There must be something here she reasoned with herself. There would be no benefit in Sy sending her somewhere completely abandoned.

With no destination in mind she walked along the front towards the abandoned factory. At the very least it was of some comfort to be able to look out at the horizon for a short while. The still ocean calming her mind. A picturesque coastline view it was not but it was quiet and the salty air reminded her of happier care free times as a child with her parents by her side.

She stopped and closed her eyes. How long had it been since she had simply stopped. Allowing herself a minute to breathe deeply, to engage her senses, ground herself and try to take stock. The true repercussions of this day would reverberate with her forever more, and she was still living with too much fear and anxiety in her body to truly be able to think through the days events in detail but her emotions were bubbling just underneath the surface. She was scared to open the floodgates in case she was never able to close them again.

A solitary tear escaped her as she continued to take deep shuddering breaths in an attempt to keep herself under control.

Wiping it away she opened her eyes, making a decision to continue moving forwards on the road to nowhere. As she looked across at the factory she saw a solitary female emerge from the lower floor and begin to walk towards her. As the distance between them shortened she was able to make out more of her features. Tall with a determined stride she wore cargo trousers with a tank top tucked in highlighting her toned physique and muscular upper body. Margot felt too exhausted to be intimidated anymore but she was wary of this person, all too conscious that if she needed to protect herself physically against her she would definitely fail.

She wondered about turning back, heading back down the long empty road and trying to get herself somewhere less secluded but she hadn't seen anywhere inhabitable for at least a couple of miles and without knowing the area she could be getting herself into even more dangerous territory.

She continued to amble forwards towards the woman intent on appearing like she was innocently out for a walk.

'Can I help you?' the woman shouted in her direction, the sea breeze carrying her voice in the opposite direction so it only meekly reached her.

'No thank you I'm just having a look around.' She smiled attempting an air of nonchalant.

'Well this area's out of bounds to the public, you need to turn around.'

Margot wasn't sure at what point to drop Sy's name into the conversation to try and establish if that would make a difference. She didn't even know yet if she wanted to be here, and what being here even meant.

But she had come this far and she'd already established she had no funds for a taxi home so she may as well power through.

'Actually, a friend sent me to this address, I'm looking to speak to Dana.'

'Who sent you'

'Sy'

The woman stopped walking a meter away from where Margot stood, a wrinkle of a frown appeared on her forehead like she must have misheard. Before she opened her mouth again her gaze moved lower and focused on the baby cocooned onto Margot's chest, wrapped snugly inside John's coat which was large enough to wrap around them both. Only the top of her little hat was visible, safely protected from the cool air.

After a second she opened her mouth as if struggling to find the appropriate words.

'Oh my God, is that Iris?'

A cold chill spread through Margot's body as she realised suddenly just how vulnerable they both were. She put a protective hand around the infant, incapable of words she just nodded slowly.

'Quickly get inside' the woman ushered holding out an arm to guide them 'we've been waiting a long time to meet you.'

Chapter 24

Having jumped too far down the rabbit hole now Margot felt she had no choice but to carry on falling and follow the woman. How did she know Iris' name? Had Sy phoned ahead to warn them? What did she mean she'd been waiting a long time to meet her, she was a baby.

As they walked back in the direction of the factory she saw a metal perimeter fence all around the boundary which she hadn't been able make out previously due to the distance.

An open chain snaked around one of the adjoining pieces obviously where this woman had allowed herself out to challenge the apparent intruder. She slipped back through the gap and beckoned Margot and Iris to follow her. On the other side of the fence Margot took in her surroundings. The factory now loomed over her in a dominating fashion. Standing so close to something so large was oppressive and intimidating. Plus, she didn't have much faith in the structure of such an old derelict building and standing at the bottom of one of those towers when they collapsed wouldn't end well for anyone.

'Don't worry, she's an old bird but she's our protector, you're safe here.'

Margot would have felt more reassured by her words had her eyes not fallen on the chain which had now been securely wrapped around both fence panels and locked with a heavy duty padlock, the key for which had been put away somewhere that Margot hadn't seen. Was this to keep danger out or to keep her in?

'Follow me' the woman said still not giving anything away.

They walked around the perimeter of the outer wall before coming to a door which Margot assumed led to the inside of the factory. As they walked through the door however she saw that it led to a courtyard bigger than a football pitch. Margot couldn't get her bearings, she knew the factory was big but this was like stepping through a Tardis. The inside of the wall they had just walked around loomed over the courtyard but was less oppressive from this side allowing the late afternoon sun to shine in on them and radiate it's light and warmth over the area.

It appeared that this was used as some kind of base. There was a large marquee set up on one side fully enclosed with it's canvas doors zipped up. Tables were dotted around the centre and a number of tents and caravans were pitched up at the far end. It was it's own little village, completely hidden from the world outside.

'What is this place?' Margot wondered out loud.

'We'll tell you everything don't worry. First, I've got a number of people who are going to be very excited to meet you.'

She led her over to the marquee and as they got closer Margot could hear a number of people chatting inside. She felt intimidated at the thought of facing such a large number of people when she had been around so few for such a long time.

As her guide led the way she reached the side door of the marquee and unzipped it giving Margot a glimpse of the inside.

There were four long tables filled with people all eating what Margot assumed was their evening meal. Cutlery clattered on the plates, there was a hum of conversation from each table, some having larger debates involving all of them others splitting off into twos and threes having quieter discussions. No one had noticed them enter the marquee, all far too engrossed in what they were doing.

She held back not ready yet to immerse herself into such a large crowd.

The other woman sensed her hesitation.

'Wait here, I'll bring Dana out to meet you.'

She slipped inside leaving Margot alone for a minute. She caught a glimpse of her shuffling around the first few tables before squeezing in between two rows and moving sideways in between the women to reach someone further into the crowd.

After a short wait Margot could see her returning

with another woman in tow behind her. Margot would guess this woman to be in her sixties by the silver grey hair that she had cropped short around her ears but her physique and stature was that of someone much younger. She too wore cargo pants and a black vest, tucked in, showing off her toned physique.

They both stepped outside into the fresh air, the older of the two walking towards Margot held out her hand which Margot returned on auto pilot. The formality of shaking hands was not something Margot had experienced for a while and yet it was drilled into her to return the gesture, unsure yet on what this woman's intentions were for the two of them and if it was safe to take her hand.

As they touched, the woman took Margot's hands in both of hers and held it there, steadying her, looking her deep in the eye she spoke so that only the two of them could hear it.

'Are you ok?'

Margot couldn't find the words. No, she was not ok, not ok at all. The sound of the gun shots that had caused the death of her only friends hours earlier still echoed in her ears and she was on the point of collapse but how could she say that to a stranger? She merely shook her head slowly.

The woman nodded as if she in some way understood what Margot was feeling. She turned to the woman who had brought her out.

'No one must know that she is here yet, we need to figure out what to tell everyone.'

'We tell them the truth Dana, she's here, she's the

proof we've been waiting for.'

Margot was confused for a second what she would be able to prove, until she realised with a sinking feeling that they were talking about her daughter.

'We don't want to get everyone over excited, they'll have time to meet her, to hold her, all in good time but let's just wait for now.'

Margot bristled at the words. Who were these people? And who was this woman promising her daughter to them all as if they had some pre-determined right to her?

Iris would be held by no one and as far as she was concerned the two of them would be out of here as soon as she had some answers and had been able to speak to Sy.

Dana looked back towards the entrance of the dining hall, checking to see that no one had noticed their newcomers arrival.

Margot may not have agreed or understood a lot of what they were talking about but one thing she did agree with was that she wasn't ready to meet a large group of people. After months of it just being her, John and Barbara this sheer amount of people in that room was completely overwhelming. She was hot, she still carried her huge rucksack and her back was sweating underneath it. She was so thirsty and she just wanted to lie down with Iris somewhere and close her eyes. To take stock of all that had happened.

'Come with me, we'll find somewhere a bit quieter.' The woman said as she turned her back again on the tent and began to lead them away.

The lady who had brought Margot into the camp followed quickly behind them and placed a firm hand on the Dana's arm, stopping her in her tracks.

'Dana, you've got to tell them who she is, you know how long I've been waiting for this. Don't deny them now, you've got to stay, let them see her properly.'

'Sasha, we've got time. She's here now and we'll go through everything when the time is right but it looks to me like this young lady could do with a sit down and a cup of tea.'

Margot thought this was the understatement of the century but was relieved that Dana appeared to be on her side for her for the time being. She was getting pins and needles in her feet from all her standing, her hand still throbbed from her altercation with Sy and Iris was getting restless from being contained for too long, she must also, Margot realised, be long overdue a feed and a change too.

'They deserve this, we all do. It's been months of not knowing, months of waiting and now she's finally here! Celebrate with us.' Sasha protested, now raising her voice as she tried to walk along side them, keen it seemed to continue her emphatic speech.

'Sasha stop. I said no, that's the end of it.'

'OK fine, if you want to get her away from everyone take her to the comms room, we can talk there, I can show her what we've been doing.'

'You're staying here, I'm showing Margot and Iris to your caravan where they'll be staying tonight, I'll empty your things from it. I don't want to hear another word.'

Sasha looked like it was taking every ounce of her strength not to continue their disagreement however it was clear that Dana ruled here and ultimately had the last word. Dana put her hand on Margot's shoulder and gently chaperoned her away. Margot half expected Sasha to follow them and she wondered if she should be apologising to her for the inconvenience she appeared to unwittingly be causing her, but it was all she could do to be swept along by Dana and led away.

'You must excuse Sasha's enthusiasm.' She said as she led Margot back out of the marquee into the open air again. 'She's got a lot of energy and has been getting a bit carried away recently. I dare say she'll continue to be keen to talk to you as soon as possible.'

'I've got a lot of questions too' Margot replied 'But I don't think I've got much energy for it at the minute'

'I'll take you somewhere where you can have a sit down and put your things.'

'I'd appreciate that thank you.'

They began to walk towards the far end of the courtyard where groups of tents lay huddled around one another with a few caravans dotted in between.

'How long have you all been here?' Margot was exhausted but to find this group of women hiding out so close to where she had been these last few months had piqued her curiosity hugely

'The first of us moved in over two years ago. A lot

of us were working in hospitals or the civil service at the time. We were getting an insider view on what was going on and it was raising some alarm bells. We started to rally and protest and built up a bit of a community but then two of our main organisers went missing. The police weren't interested or couldn't help us. Maybe it was paranoia I don't know but we were starting to get the impression that our protestations weren't welcome in the city. We took the hint and decided to make less public noise for the time being but it just pushed us underground. We've based ourselves here ever since and as you can see the numbers have increased somewhat.'

'How do people know you're here to find you?'

'We still have a number of people working on the ground feeding information back to us. Some are working closely with the women who have lost their children. If they can see that they may be interested in joining us they subtly pass on our details.'

She thought back all those months to the sonographer at her scan. The uncomfortable manner she had when she was being delivered the news. Was she responsible for the note that had been slipped under her door?

''Why are you so interested in Iris?'

This was the question that was really haunting her. How did they know her name, why did they think she was special? Did they know she was different? Margot didn't want to divulge any information about her until she knew what information they were already privy to.

'We've got time for all that, and we'll go through it all I promise but honestly you look dead on your feet.'

They'd reached the caravans which were on the outskirts of what appeared to be the living quarters.

This one can be for the two of you, it's too big just for Sasha.'

'Oh please, I don't want to kick anyone out.'

'It'll be fine, she could do with being taken down a peg or two and anyway, we can't have a newborn sleeping in a tent now can we?'

Margot smiled in thanks and opened the door. It was modest in size, a small rectangular sofa at one end with a kitchen in the middle and doors at the other end, she assumed leading to the bedroom and bathroom. It was worlds apart from the farm house but hopefully it could provide them some respite for the night at least so that she could gather her thoughts.

'Thank you, we appreciate your hospitality.'

Margot was still unsure if she was staying at her request or at theirs and so decided not to mention at this point that she might only be here for the night. Would they even let her leave if she wanted to?

'Are you hungry? I'll ask someone to bring you some food shortly. In the meantime, help yourself to anything you need here, we don't condone individual possessions here, everyone shares everything so you're welcome to anything you'd like. I'll come and check on you before I go to bed.'

Margot nodded her head in agreement, no longer knowing what she was agreeing to, she was happy to be led along by someone else's momentum for the time being whilst she regained her sense of self.

She peeled the straps of the rucksack off her back which had almost become fused to her body after such a long time of wearing it.

She then removed John's oversized wax coat and felt the cool air swirl around her damp aching back.

Un-knotting the sling she lifted Iris free who immediately began to fuss for a feed. Margot moved over to the sofa and sank onto the soft cushions lifting her top and allowing Iris to latch on. She laid her head back on the cushions and closed her eyes, allowing the darkness and stillness to seep into her brain. To be still was all that she craved right now. It would take her years, possibly a lifetime to process what had happened today, but for now she needed to protect her mind and allow herself to just be in the moment, thankful that for tonight at least they seemed to have shelter and a relative amount of safety.

Chapter 25

After feeding and changing Iris, Margot took herself off to the bathroom for a long hot shower. She lay Iris on a folded towel on the bathroom floor where she dozed off to the white noise of the persistent flow of water. Margot was not willing to allow Iris to be out of her sight and so was able to allow herself to enjoy the shower with Iris being so close.

By the time she came out of the shower still feeling achy but at least devoid of sweat she noticed that a meal of sandwiches and an apple had been placed on her kitchen counter. She poured herself a glass of water from the tap and downed it, followed in quick succession by a second.

Her only visitor a few hours later was Dana as promised checking up on her before she went to bed.

Despite wanting to enquire more about her surroundings Margot found that having sat for a few hours with her thoughts she was sinking into a more melancholy mood, processing what had happened and what she had lost. So, it was a relief to her to find that Dana did not press her for information or details on what had led her to arrive with them that day.

She did notice however that Dana's eye's were drawn to Iris more than she would have liked. In the short time that she stayed to check they were settled and had everything they needed for the night her gaze repeatedly lingered on the babe, now settled on a makeshift cot on the sofa. Eyes that displayed a hunger that left Margot feeling unsettled.

Dana left them for the evening and Margot decided to get herself into bed, to close her eyes on the most traumatic day of her existence in the hope that sleep would allow her some respite from the traumatic images that played on a loop in her head. Her brain however would not allow her to let go of the trauma that easily and forced her to sit with her thought's way past the end of that day and well into the start of the next. She had thought that being attacked whilst she was pregnant was the worst that she could have felt but it turned out she could take a lot thrown at her but to witness those you loved being hurt was a torture like no other.

To that end she got up the next morning in her unfamiliar caravan, red eyed, with blotchy skin, a dull headache and an empty heart.

She wasn't sure if there was an expectation on her to leave her caravan and join the others in the marquee at some point but had no intention of leaving. She would wait here for Sy who she hoped would make an appearance in the next few hours and allow her to get some answers. As she tried to plan ahead however for what she would like to ask him she found that her brain was turning into a mush of confusion, no doubt from the lack of sleep and the rush of conflicting emotions she was dealing with. She was struggling to process her thoughts and gain any clarity.

With no thoughts to disrupt she didn't flinch when a knock came at the door. She had lost all track of time and couldn't tell what time of day it was. She had left all the blinds down in the caravan, keen to not be stared at like a zoo animal and not wanting anyone to engage her in conversation.

She acknowledged that she couldn't even muster the energy to stand and open the door. They'll just come in anyway if they want to she reasoned. Sure enough after another attempt at knocking, the door handle slowly turned down and Dana stepped through the open door.

The sight of Margot mustn't have put her at ease as she said nothing but walked over to them both. Margot once again got a prickly sense of unease as Dana chose to sit on the side of the bench where Iris lay, carefully peeling back her blanket to look on her whilst addressing Margot at the same time.

'Rough night?'

Margot simply nodded her head, aware that Dana wasn't looking at her but unable to form words all the same.

'I can take her for a few hours if you'd like to get some rest?'

'She doesn't leave my side.' Margot uttered as she

clenched her jaw, hoping that she was making it clear that they came as part of a deal and that they would never be separated. She felt anger trying to fight through the exhaustion she felt deep down in the pit of her stomach. She knew she had nothing yet to base this anger on but she wanted to aim it in Dana's direction all the same.

'I understand' Dana said, though still did not remove her gaze from the sleeping child. She was not alleviating Margot's concerns with her actions, nor did Margot feel comforted by her apparent concern for her child. How different it felt to when Barbara had first held Iris. Something intangible, in the miniscule, imperceptible movements of a person, in the very air they shared told Margot that this was not the safe space she had once known, that she needed to be cautious, that these people may not have Iris' best interests at heart.

'Breakfast is in the main tent where you were yesterday, it'll only be out for another half an hour or so though so you'd better get moving if you're hungry.'

'I'm not, I just want to be alone.'

'Well, I'm afraid that's not how it works here. Everyone pulls their weight, everyone contributes. I can give you another day to wallow but then we will need you to muck in.'

Margot was surprised at the change in tone from yesterday when Dana had appeared to be on her side. She hadn't asked to come here. Did she want to be inducted into this group of women and contribute to their lifestyle? She needed answers before she could even begin to think about those questions.

'Is Sy here yet?' She was hoping that he would be waiting for her ready to put her at ease.

'Sy? No, we don't see him here very often. We try to avoid regular visitors so that we don't draw unnecessary attention to ourselves.'

'He said he'd come so that we could talk.'

'Well, I wouldn't hold your breath on that being any time soon, he's a busy man.'

Margot rubbed her forehead trying to ease out the knots of tension that were forming. She was relying on him being there today. After he had seen her distress yesterday he would know how important it was to her. She could feel her anger rising once again, churned up with the anxiety and grief she was attempting to process. She would just have to be patient, not her forte at the best of times but a skill she would have to practice.

Dana, recognising that she was not going to get much conversation out of Margot today, stood up to leave. Both women appeared to be holding back, neither apparently keen to be the first to engage in conversation.

'I'll ask one of the women to bring you some lunch later on.' And with that she left them to be alone once again.

The day dragged ahead of her. Iris continued to be the only thing she cared about, drumming up enough energy to feed, change and soothe her and then returning to her almost catatonic state. Another knock at the door came later in the day but this time they had the consideration to not barge in when she didn't answer. Instead, a voice she didn't recognise spoke softly through the door to tell her there was a plate of food outside for her should she want it. She didn't want any food, couldn't muster the energy to even consider if she was hungry, but again she acknowledged that she needed fuel to sustain another person, so after a while she timidly opened the door to find a covered meal ready for her.

This wasn't like her, she was not ungrateful for the support and shelter that she had been given but she felt disassociated with herself as if trying to create a distance from her own life in order to protect herself.

As day faded to night her anger at Sy began to grow again. Why had he not come to her knowing how much she needed him? Knowing how much her grief had consumed her and how much he owed her an explanation for all that had happened. He was clearly in no rush to answer her questions, despite him knowing how distraught she must be.

She had a momentary rush of adrenaline as she remembered him giving her his card with his number on, before she realised that she had chosen John's coat over her own and had left the all important number in her coat pocket.

She couldn't even leave without asking for the permission of the women around her to open up the gates. Were they her rescuers or her captors? She still couldn't tell. Despair and anxiety wracked her body, she moved through cyclical patterns of having no energy to do anything to being overcome with anger and wanting to take immediate action of some sort.

Eventually Margot settled down to yet another restless night. This time interspersed with dreams that tormented her mind and once again leaving her drenched with sweat.

Chapter 26

Two more days passed with no word from Sy. Margot felt she was completely at his mercy. Unable to move forward without answers but unwilling to stay somewhere so unfamiliar to her. The caravan the two of them now found themselves in had become both their refuge and their prison cell. Having still not built up the courage or the energy to leave and interact with the group of people around her. The blinds had remained firmly down and with the cold wind buffeting the thin walls each evening her imagination was getting the better of her, each howl of wind or branch snapping sounded like someone coming to get her, the outside world felt more threatening than ever before.

It was becoming too much she realised. She was not coping with her situation well and she was sinking into the depths of her grief. If Sy wasn't coming to her she needed to figure out what she was going to do. If it weren't for Iris she would have succumbed to the weight of despair. She would have returned to bed and pulled the duvet over her head for as long as it took to want to be in the light again. Although, she realised to herself, if it wasn't for Iris she wouldn't be here at all. She would probably still be in her lab, drinking coffee. Would she be aware that this was ever a possibility for her own existence? She felt guilty at even acknowledging the unequivocal truth that Iris had been her greatest gift whilst simultaneously setting her life on a trajectory of heartache and conflict.

She was fearful of what was outside her door. What she would face if she opened it, what would happen to her and Iris if she didn't. Despite Dana's words of warning about her needing to involve herself with the army of women she had not had another visit trying to encourage her out. Twice a day however there was a plate of food left for her on her step. A gentle knock accompanied each time by that quiet timid voice she did not recognise, informing her that she had food should she want it.

Eventually towards the end of her third day, having established that no one was going to pull her out of this pit of self-wallowing other than herself she decided to take the first steps towards moving her life forwards. Bone achingly tired despite having done nothing for the past three days she stood up, got the two of them dressed and attached Iris once again into the sling. Iris felt hotter than usual as she picked her up. She hoped she wasn't coming down with something. Now she thought about it she had been sleeping more than usual the past few days. Margot hadn't considered it before now having been so locked inside her own head.

Opening the door of the caravan she felt the breeze hit her face and she closed her eyes to bask in the weak sunshine that fell across her skin. She hadn't realised how musty the air had become until she breathed the outside again.

Retracing her steps from three days ago back across the compound she was struck again by how developed it was. This wasn't a temporary base or a rushed set up, it had taken time to become so established. There were what appeared to be sleeping quarters around the outside, mostly made up of tents forming a circle, enclosing the various different living areas in the middle. Rudimentary signage had been put up marking some of the larger tents and their purpose such as medical and washing facilities and at the far end Margot could see vast rows of vegetable beds with an abundance of crops.

She wondered again what had brought so many of them here and why they had decided to stay living such a simple lifestyle.

There were women wandering around, heading in and out of the various areas. Some clearly with a purpose, a hamper of laundry in their arms or wearing work gloves and carrying tools. Others appeared to be having recreational time walking the perimeter or sitting at the far end around a fire, reading or talking. The mood was calm but not light. There were no peals of laughter erupting from the low hum of conversation. It occurred to Margot that these women might once have led very ordinary lives, perhaps they simply had nothing left to laugh about anymore.

Closing in on the larger Marquee where Margot had first stood when she had arrived, it appeared that she had missed the evening rush of dinner. As she walked through the makeshift door she saw the last few stragglers finishing up their meals, mostly the more elderly of the group, clearly happy to take their time and enjoy their meal. At the far end near the serving hatch Margot could make out Dana talking to a petite woman serving up some food.

She wandered up to them, embarrassed to be appearing before them after days of being locked away, like a petulant teenager returning home after an argument. As she drew closer to the two women who had their backs to her she began to pick up their conversation.

'This is the last time, don't ask me again. She eats here or she doesn't eat at all, understand?'

The slight woman nodded whilst loading up a tray with a plate of food and two pieces of fruit.

Margot didn't need to be told that she was the source of Dana's displeasure and was grateful that the timid stranger had been continuing to bring her food over the past few days despite it clearly not being a popular decision.

'There's no need, I'm here' Margot announced, ready for whatever jibe Dana was going to throw her way for having remained locked away for so long.

Dana however merely glanced over in her direction, locked eyes with Margot for a second or two before nodding approvingly and continued with her task of scrubbing the large serving pans.

'I assume that's for me?' she gestured to the tray

The woman nodded, looking embarrassed at having been caught in the middle of their exchange.

'Thank you. I'm guessing it's you that' been bringing me food for the past few days too?'

Another embarrassed nod

'Well, it has been appreciated. I'm sorry I've not been able to say it until now.'

Margot took the tray and holding it out in front of her to keep it away from Iris snug in her sling she took herself over to the nearest table and sat down on the bench to eat her meal.

She anticipated Dana joining her, attempting to engage her in conversation again but fortunately she was left in peace to eat her meal. She kept her back to the serving hatch and faced out over the multiple rows of tables that ordinarily seated the large group of women.

By the time she had finished there was no one left in the hall. All having decided to move onto their final tasks of the evening or make the most of an early night.

Picking up her empty plate she returned it to the hatch. She no longer wanted to be pandered to, she needed them to know that she was more than capable of looking after herself.

'Where can I wash this up?

'Leave it there we'll sort it' Dana shouted, with her back turned to her. 'We'll assign you your own rota of tasks from tomorrow and I'll show you the ropes'

'I'm not planning on staying actually, I just need

to talk to Sy and then I'll be leaving. Has anyone got his number? Could someone just phone him for me please it's really important that I speak to him.'

'Even if we had his number we couldn't call him, there's no phones here.'

Margot was getting irritable talking to her back as she continued washing up the large pots from dinner.

'Well then I'll need to leave and find a phone to call him, it can't wait any longer.'

This appeared to get Dana's attention enough to make her stop scrubbing. She exhaled louder than she needed to and turned her head, her hands still submerged in the soapy water she finally looked at Margot.

'If he said he'll be here, he'll be here. He's a man of his word, but like I said to you the other day he's incredibly busy. This is the safest place for you both right now so I suggest you settle in a bit.'

Margot relented, not sure it was worth arguing her case further right now.

Dana spoke out to the shy woman 'Ailsa, Why don't you show Margot to the pit where she can meet some of the others.'

Ailsa nodded meekly, reddening again at the mention of her name and being given the extra responsibility of looking after their new guest.

She carefully untied her apron and came to meet Margot on her side of the serving hatch.

'Hi Ailsa, it's nice to properly meet you.'

Ailsa just smiled in response, clearly unsure if conversation was also an expectation of the tour

As they walked back out through the marquee Margot realised that this might be her best opportunity to get more information on exactly where she was now living.

'So how long have you been here Ailsa?'

'Two years now.'

'Wow, that's a long time. Do you mind me asking what brought you here in the first place?'

Ailsa paused, clearly pondering her answer. She didn't seem to rush anything she said, seemingly running it through in her mind before she let it out into the open.

'I used to work in a bank and a friend of mine there used to tell me what she'd read about what was going on in the hospitals with the virus. She was approached one day by Dana and asked to join the sisterhood and she brought me along with her.'

'You just left? What about the people you left behind?'

'I don't have anyone on the outside, she was my only friend. Now I've got a whole family.'

'How often do you go back home?'

'We don't. Once you choose to join, you've joined for life. We can't risk people coming and going too much.'

'And has the group grown much in those two years?'

'Marginally. We're very selective about who we bring in. I was fortunate to know my friend who fought for my place here but most now are specifically recruited for their skills or knowledge. Dana says that being self-sufficient is a balance between having enough bodies to do the work whilst not having too many mouths to feed.'

It was making sense to Margot now why Dana had been quick to request for Margot to pull her weight. She had her own civilisation here that needed to be maintained, no newcomer could be allowed to upset the status quo.

As they made their way over to what Dana had referred to as The Pit, Margot could see people dotted about in small groups. Some warming themselves close to the fire in the centre others sitting further away cross legged like they were back in primary school sharing a story with the teacher.

Margot wasn't sure if it was her imagination but as she walked past each little group she sensed their conversation dip as they acknowledged her. Just before she was out of their earshot she picked up on whispered murmurings no doubt discussing who she was and where she'd come from. From what Margot had seen so far there were no other children on the camp aside from Iris. This in itself made her uncomfortably aware of how much the two of them stood out.

Ailsa led them to a group of women and led the polite introductions. There was no way that Margot would remember their names but she nodded and smiled at each one in turn

As Margot sat amongst the group in front of the fire she began to settle in a bit and focus in on their energy which was quietly passive and restrained, but in the air there also hung a heaviness of sorts too. Margot wasn't sure if it was sadness or resentment but she felt like these women weren't completely fulfilled in their lives here. Was the camp a retreat for them or were they running away from their lives on the outside just like she was? Did they too feel the oppression of the world outside the factory walls closing in on them.

Over the course of the next hour what felt like the majority of the women joined the group. Margot assumed this was part of their daily routine to end the day together and reflect on their time.

As the stars began to appear above them and the wind picked up, Dana stood and led the group in an evening prayer. Collectively the group bowed their heads, some clasped their hands together whilst Margot somewhat caught off guard tried to listen to the words that bore no sense of familiarity or comfort to her. As she took in the group she noticed one other head raised, looking straight ahead of her. Sasha met her gaze, she raised one eyebrow in mock exasperation and the two shared a conspiratorial smile.

Returning to her caravan shortly afterwards Margot tried to make sense of the group and the new home she had found herself in. They seemed pleasant enough, if a little deluded. But Margot could understand the desire to not be owned by the state anymore, to be in control of their own destiny, even if it was purely within the confines of these vast factory walls.

Dana on the other hand she couldn't quite put her finger on. There was no doubt that she had built a successful community but to what end? She had a sense that her intentions were ultimately good however and felt like her and Iris were safe in their company for the time being. Nevertheless, she knew better than to take people at face value and remembered back to the hungry look Dana had on her face when she had observed Iris.

Unfolding Iris from her sleeping cocoon she laid her down on the sofa whilst she methodically checked each and every window was closed and locked. She pulled all of the blinds back down encasing them once again in their little bubble away from the world.

Picking up Iris and holding her close to her chest she breathed in her beautiful scent. She hadn't properly looked at her for the past few days, so consumed had she been in her grief and getting through each hour. She felt frustrated with herself for not showering Iris with the love and affection she deserved but consoled herself with the fact that she was still here, that she was doing the best she could under the circumstances.

Making her way back across the living area she double and triple checked the lock on the door before finally accepting that they were safe and headed off to bed.

Chapter 27

The following morning Margot woke feeling a bit brighter. She had slept properly for the first time since they'd arrived having only being awoken at the now familiar intervals for Iris' feed.

She took her time getting dressed, in no hurry to engage once again with the group but pleased with herself for making it to the food tent in time for a quick round of toast before the days jobs commenced.

Dana came to meet her as she was taking her empty plate to the washing station.

'If you're ready I'll give you the full tour and we can plan you out a schedule of duties.'

Margot just nodded in agreement. She was interested to see more of the camp and not opposed to having some tasks to complete in order to distract herself whilst she waited for the elusive Sy to show up.

As the two of them walked around the yard though she realised that in the small amount of time she had been here she had already seen most of what the camp had to offer.

Dana smiled as she walked past the groups of women, clearly proud to show Margot the fruits of her labour.

'I established this community as a place of healing for those who had suffered trauma. The world is not supportive or understanding of what women are going through and I wanted to create an environment where those women could come to heal.'

Looking around Margot could see that she had provided that. From the outside looking in everyone seemed content in their little bubble.

Behind the main marquee was a set of wrought iron steps that led their way up to a walkway that wrapped itself around the interior perimeter of the camp. Margot had seen a handful of people up there in the time she had been wandering around but it didn't appear to be accessed by the majority of the group.

'What's upstairs?' Margot enquired.

'We have people on watch day and night in case of unexpected visitors.'

'Do you get many?'

'It's rare for people to come down this far, it's why we based ourselves here, we've had the odd group of youths stumble across us by accident but Sasha's been quick to scare them away.' She added with a wry smile 'but it's been months since we've seen anyone new, until you came that is.'

At the mention of Sasha's name Margot wanted to

attempt to glean more information.

'Why was Sasha so interested in Iris when we first arrived?'

Dana paused

'There have long been rumours that the testing programme is not all that is seems. Understandable, I suppose when people have lost so much that they'd be looking for someone to blame. But your scan changed everything.

On the day you received your final scan there was an anonymous post on a whistle blowing forum showing the anomaly on the timestamp of your scan results. Rumours continued to swirl when it was announced that you'd subsequently died under mysterious circumstances. The story gained traction online and you became somewhat of a martyr for the cause.

Sasha in particular has been an avid follower of the conspiracy threads and believed that your scan was a catalyst for change. When she then heard from Sy that you were in fact alive and had delivered a healthy child it solidified in her mind everything that they'd been theorising about you.

Sy has convinced her, for your safety, not to publicise the fact that you're alive as of yet, but I think it's taking all of her will power to keep it to herself.'

Margot struggled to take in everything that had been happening behind the scenes whilst she had been struggling to survive. She hadn't anticipated that anyone might know about her, let alone be interested in her story but now that she could see it through others eyes she could appreciate why people might feel like she held answers for them.

'Sasha mentioned that you had a comms room. Is that where she has been reading these threads?'

'We have one computer here to allow us to keep an eye on outside events but we limit its use. Most of the women are perfectly happy not knowing what's going on out there. Sasha oversees our security though and spends quite a bit of her time in there.'

Margot was reluctant to get drawn into conspiracies and part of her relished the idea of burying her head in the sand and embracing the healing journey that Dana was offering here but there was also no denying that hearing the rumours was piquing her interest.

'I'd like to speak to her if I can, I'd be interested to get her insight.' Margot wasn't quite sure why she was asking permission but it was clear that she needed to get Dana on side if she was going to be spending any time here.

'You'll get a chance to speak to one another of course, but Margot I need to speak frankly and I hope you can appreciate why. I won't allow anything to disrupt what we've built here, it's taken too long and it means too much to too many.

Sasha's perception of the outside world is not an accurate representation of what is truly out there. Our individual perception of the world is perpetually biased based on our past experiences or what we're looking for the world to be and Sasha wants there to be more to her story.

She, like most people here, lost a child and she is looking for answers as to why that might have happened. I indulge her to a certain extent, after all we all cope with trauma in different ways but, it's important to establish that I don't believe there to be any truth in what she is researching and I won't have these women dragged into her warped version of reality. They need contentment now and peace, they've earnt that.'

Margot merely nodded. She wasn't even sure herself what she wanted to achieve from her time here other than to speak to Sy but she could appreciate that Dana needed some reassurances from her.

'I understand Dana, and I appreciate you allowing me to stay. Honestly, I just want to talk to Sy and then I can decide what we're going to do.'

Dana nodded although she continued to fix Margot with a steely glare.

'Well considering you've got Iris to care for I wonder if it's best to ask you to contribute to some light chores initially. The garden always needs an extra pair of hands if you're in any way green fingered?'

Margot grimaced, without wishing to appear ungrateful she wasn't sure she would be able to bring much skill to their crop growing.

'Or just simple pot washing might be more up your street?'

Margot smiled at her, 'Pot washing sounds great'.

Dana left Margot shortly afterwards having

concluded their tour and seemingly content having delivered her speech. Margot didn't hold it against her for wanting to maintain a peaceful lifestyle but she couldn't commit to doing the same until she knew more about what was going on.

If she could be guaranteed a quiet life here for the rest of her days she might be tempted to take Dana up on the offer but something told her that her past was going to catch up with her at some point one way or another.

What she wanted to do now was talk with Sasha.

Dana had casually forgotten to show Margot into the comms room after their conversation about it but she hadn't mentioned that it was out of bounds either so Margot decided to go and have a closer look.

She surreptitiously waited until it was quiet around the entrance to the steps leading up to the walkway before making her way up. She wasn't sure why she was adding an air of mystery to it, no one had said she couldn't go in there but she still felt she shouldn't be drawing too much attention to herself.

Heading to the top of the stairs all of the doors looked resolutely closed but as she wandered along the walkway she heard the rustling of movement behind one and so she gave it a timid knock.

There followed a few seconds pause before it opened up and Sasha's disgruntled face appeared. It was clear she was in the middle of something and not happy to be interrupted, but upon seeing who her visitor was her eyes lit up and she pushed the door open wider for the two of them to enter.

The room was purposeful with not a lot of tech. Dana hadn't been lying when she said there was only the one computer for them all and it looked like that was at least a decade old.

'So this is your comms room?' Margot enquired

'Yep, this is where I spend most of my time' Sasha added with a wry grin. She looked like it was taking every ounce of her strength not to burst into a tirade about research and strategy. She'd clearly been warned not to scare Margot away and Margot sensed she was practising her restraint. She had an intimidating physique but a youthful face.

'I'd like to learn a bit more about what you've been working on if that's ok?'

'That depends, do you want the Dana approved version or do you want warts and all?'

'Warts and all please'

Sasha nodded her head appreciatively

'OK, well that'll take some time but if you start to come up here regularly I can take you through it all methodically. It's only when you start to put all the pieces together that it makes any kind of sense.'

'Just give me the bare bones for now, tell me what it is you think is going on'

'Well, a lot more than we've been led to think that's for sure. We've got hundreds of examples of falsified documents, research papers that have been buried under mounds of false papers. Clinical professionals that have lost their jobs when they've started asking too many questions.'

'Well, they'll have some answers for us surely why can't we just track them down?'

'We've tried. They're gagged by NDA's, given a healthy payout if they promise to stay quiet or the threat of never working again if they don't. These people have money and power and that's proving hard to fight against.'

'So what does that leave you to go off?'

'Well, you, for a start. You're the only person who's worked in the labs who isn't still employed by them or denied your freedom of speech. You're the only person who's successfully evaded them when a termination has been ordered and you're the only person who has then gone on to have a healthy child despite them saying she was a carrier. We need to tell the world that you're alive Margot, more to the point that Iris is alive. She is the catalyst for change. If we put it out there they can't hurt you anymore you'll be protected by the truth.'

'No I won't' Margot struggled with the words as it brought up the fresh memories from the days before 'They won't leave us alone even if we go public. You said it yourself, they've got money and power and if they've made a mistake with Iris, if they were going to terminate a healthy baby in error and if others begin to think their child may have died unnecessarily there will be an uprising. They will never allow that to happen.'

'I think it's bigger than that Margot. I don't think Iris was a mistake.'

Margot looked at her trying to establish what else she knew

'The time stamp on your bloods. That can't be passed off as an error. Those blood works were generated hours before you arrived for your appointment. They were falsified, they must have been. I just wish you'd been able to come to us straight away when you went on the run. We'd have been able to find you shelter and could have organised our own blood tests, then we could have truly known what your results showed.'

Margot hesitated unsure how much she could trust Sasha, but her enthusiasm for finding out the truth was palpable and Margot was feeling more reckless than usual following the events of the last few days and irritable by Sy's continued absence.

'I know what the results were'

'You can't trust what they showed you Margot, they could have been anyone's results, they could have been made up entirely.'

'No, Sasha I'm not talking about the results they showed me. I'm talking about the ones I did on myself the day before my scan. The ones that showed Iris was a perfectly healthy baby.'

Sasha stared wide eyed at Margot, at the news she had been waiting years to hear. Confirmation at last that she hadn't been going crazy.

'Holy shit'

Margot simply nodded allowing Sasha the time to let it sink in.

'This changes everything. This is why you went on the run?'

Once again Margot merely nodded

'Please tell me you've still got the copy of your results.'

This time Margot despondently shook her head

'I couldn't risk it. I was only testing myself so that I had some reassurance. I'd had a tough time at work and I just needed to know everything was going to be ok. I had no idea that life would take the turn that it did.'

'Damn' Sasha muttered under her breath. She was back in her own head, her thoughts whirring inside her brain as she began to put the pieces of the puzzle together.

'We need to go back and look through everything again, with a fresh pair of eyes, knowing what we know now to see if it sheds a new light on any of it.'

She began to clear the table in front of them enthusiastically. Margot felt swept along by her enthusiasm, not sure what they were looking for or what all of the paperwork referred to but she was thankful to have a distraction, for something to throw herself into.

They were so engrossed in what they were doing that a sudden knock at the door made them both jump as Dana entered the room already beginning to speak.

'Sasha, have you seen Margot anywhere…'

She stopped abruptly, gazing at the two of them bent over the table strewn with schematics and newspaper articles. Her face and the room turned instantly icy.

'What is this?' she questioned accusatory.

'Margot was interested to know about some of my theories. We're just talking Dana, that's all'

Margot could see Dana was in turmoil. Part of her wanting to stamp her authority on the two of them and another part of her attempting to channel her calm compassionate side. Like a mother chiding her children Margot felt a sense of guilt seep in. She could see that it upset Dana for her to be showing an interest in Sasha's work and she didn't take Dana's hospitality for granted but she couldn't let that stop her from learning more about what might be going on.

They stayed where they were, waiting for Dana to make her move. Was she going to demand that Margot and Iris leave? Was she going to grab all the papers and rip them up? In the end she took a despondent breath accepting that they were going to do this with or without her consent.

'Margot, I think you'll want to come downstairs. Sy's here'

Chapter 28

Margot was temporarily thrown, unable to gather her thoughts. She'd spent days waiting for him but her conversation with Sasha had temporarily wiped him from her mind for the first time.

She trained to regain her composure. She wanted to make sure she was in the right head space to face him, she wanted to ask him all of the questions that she'd been holding in for him. This might be the last time she saw him for a while so she needed to make the most of it. She wished she'd written all of her thoughts down during those long nights when she'd been lying awake so that she wouldn't forget to ask him something important.

Having been so fired up over the past few days her anger had started to ebb since she'd met the other women but she didn't want him to be able to get away too lightly, he still had a lot he needed to be held accountable for.

'I've shown him to the food tent, he's waiting for you there.'

Margot nodded in response before turning to Sasha 'we'll pick this up later if that's ok?'

Sasha nodded enthusiastically clearly keen to continue what they'd started.

Margot found Sy sitting at one of the furthest tables from the marquee entrance. She bristled to see that he'd been served a fresh hot meal and was hungrily tucking into it. He was clearly considered as somewhat of a VIP around here, no one else would have something cooked to order outside of meal times.

He stood to greet her as she walked over to him, his face acknowledging that they had a lot of ground to cover.

She took pleasure in the fact that he was still showing the signs of where her fist had made contact with his cheekbone four days earlier. She wanted him to be in pain, to have a reminder of the pain that he had caused others.

'It's good to see you Margot, I'm pleased you made it here ok'

'I made it here fine, I still don't know why I'm here Sy. I've been here for four days, just waiting for you to grace me with your presence, to put me out of my misery'

'I know, I'm sorry. After the farm there was a hive of activity, they knew you were close, they were interviewing anyone that might have been in contact with you, I couldn't risk leaving and drawing their attention to this place. They still don't know you've given birth Margot. You're due date is this week and they're hoping they can still catch you in time.'

His eyes rested on the top of Iris head nestled against Margot's chest

'She really is a miracle Margot, you don't know what this means that she's here, and that she's ok.'

Margot was irritated once again by his calm and compassionate nature. She wanted a fight and she was going to do her best to have one with him.

'Enough Sy. Talk, tell me everything right now.'

'Okay....Okay' Holding his hands up in submission as he took his seat again. He looked weary with dark circles under his eyes.

'You need to know that you were never meant to be involved in this. The day you went on the run changed everything. It kick started a series of events that no one could have predicted.'

Margot already had questions but kept her mouth resolutely shut, if she was finally going to get to know what had been going on over the past few months she wasn't going to interrupt. She sat herself down opposite him, ready to listen.

'There's a lot you don't know about me Margot, a lifetime of things you don't know about me in truth, in the same way that I know very little about you. But what I should probably start by telling you is that whilst I am a surgeon I also work as a civil servant, I provide information back to the Government about cases I have come across or people that I have met.

The day we met was no coincidence. There was an unusual amount of interest in your pregnancy from the beginning and you were on round the clock surveillance. I happened to be on the team the night that you ran and it was up to me to build a rapport with you and try to establish what you were doing.'

Margot's face must have displayed her confusion without her even needing to say anything.

'There are ways and means of controlling someone's decisions without them knowing it Margot. The only effective way of introducing yourself to someone without raising suspicion is by making them think they've done it all of their own choosing. You were always going to sit opposite me that day on the train and you were always going to strike up a conversation with me, you just didn't know it at the time.'

Margot simply shook her head at his self-assurance. More annoying to her was that it had actually worked.

'I was meant to build a rapport with you, try to establish what your plans were and where you were going. That in itself was strange. Anyone else that had gone on the run would be tracked down immediately and the termination carried out, but with you there was a very clear directive to let you continue on your way.'

I put a tracker on your bag that day and from that point we monitored you remotely. Until suddenly we lost you, you just disappeared. We assumed you'd been tipped off or got wind of something untoward and decided to bail?'

Margot still bore the scar of that day where she had been knocked unconscious and had all her wordly goods stolen, the day she had thought she was going to die, the day that led her to John and Barbara.

There was a pause in the air as Sy waited for her to elaborate on the details of how she had eluded them but she stood her ground and let the silence engulf them. This was not her time to talk this was her time to listen, to get answers.

Eventually Sy took the hint and continued.

'I'm not trying to make excuses Margot believe me but at that time I truly believed I was doing the right thing. I'd seen the despair of those who had lost children, I'd seen what the disease had done to those who weren't immune. They told me that I had a duty to protect others from being harmed and I agreed with them, it's why I went into medicine in the first place, to help people.'

Margot so desperately wanted to believe his innocence in all this. He appeared so genuine in his turmoil but ignorance and naivety were not an excuse and if he had in any way contributed to John and Barbara's death she could never forgive him.

'A few of my staff had spoken to me about the rumours they'd heard, the conspiracy theories that were being passed around at the dinner tables. I didn't think to pay them any attention, there were always those that longed to see deception behind every act of altruism. Then one day, a few weeks after we first met on that train, a young research scientist came into the hospital, she'd suffered a small fracture and needed an x-ray. When we were alone she confided that she'd been sent to see me to share with me information that she thought I'd be interested in. She showed me your file Margot.

Your file on the most part looked to be what I would have expected, your medical history, your log of the boosters you'd received and your early scans. But she pointed out to me an anomaly in the last set of blood works. One that quite honestly I'd have missed if I wasn't told about it or hadn't been specifically looking for something out of the ordinary. The time of your test.

Margot thought back to the day of the scan, 'they changed my appointment at the last minute, it was meant to be first thing.'

'Well, your blood tests were carried out first thing, or at least they have been made to look like they were.'

Margot looked into his eyes to try to establish if she was being played, what was his agenda? But something in the pit of her stomach told her that he was on her side. She had spent countless hours going over this in her head trying to figure it out. If her own test results had been accurate and theirs hadn't then this would at least go some way to explaining why. They must have forged them and forgotten to change the time. Okay if she was being really considerate there may be a slight chance that they'd accidentally picked up the wrong results but they were in her name and made to look as if they were carried out during her original appointment time. However it had happened it raised serious question marks around their agenda.

Sy was observing her too, no doubt wary if she was contemplating another right hook.

'Margot, the woman that came to see me said that your appointment had been purposefully changed so that they could evidence that this was happening. She told me that blood works were being falsified for hundreds of women but they didn't know why. She asked me what was important to me, did I want to spy on women who were trying to keep their children alive or did I want to help them uncover whatever it was that was actually going on behind the scenes. And so, from that day onwards I've been trying to do both.'

'A double agent?' Margot scoffed, balking at the absurdity of their conversation.

'Well if you like, yea. It's not quite as cool as they make it out in the movies but I've been working for both sides trying to figure out what is really going on.'

'And where has that led you?' Margot asked still keeping up her tough exterior not wanting to let him see that he was chipping away at her resolve.

'It led me to you Margot. Yes, that train journey was staged but that was the real me you met that day. I could see that something didn't fit, that they had been following you even before the test results showed that Iris was a carrier. I knew there was more to the story. So, from that moment on things got more complicated for me. I tried to play both sides whilst not letting on to either what I was up to.

Meeting you at that farm was pure chance but you don't know how lucky you were that it was me that made that house call. By this point your picture was up in every hospital, police station, hell every street lamp had your face plastered all over it. They were happy to let you run initially but by this point you were very much a wanted woman. I tried to buy you more time Margot, I went back and told them that the old couple had mentioned they'd had a young woman staying with them but that you'd left. I expected them to be questioned and released, they weren't important to anyone. I couldn't believe it when you said they'd been killed.'

Margot was looking down at the floor now struggling to hear them being spoken of in such an impersonal manner.

'They were important to me.' She uttered, feeling the sense of longing and despair rise up in her again.

'I know that, I'm sorry, I just meant… I just meant they should never have died.'

At that Margot felt the grief begin to leave her body as the reality of their loss finally began to sink in. She had been pinning all her hope on feeling better once she had spoken to Sy, once she had a better idea of what was going on, but in reality there was nothing. Only answers that led to more questions and no way to bring them back to her.

She let silent tears leak down her cheeks as she felt the anger disperse from her body only to be replaced with an aching sadness. Sy remained steadfast in front of her, clearly unsure if her anger had dissipated enough to allow him to offer her comfort. Unable to stand the weight of her sorrow any longer she bowed her head and wept for all that she had lost. Sy reached out across the table and held her hand allowing her the space to grieve, allowing her to let them go.

Chapter 29

Despite how she had been feeling towards Sy over the past few days she couldn't deny that it only took a short amount of time being in his presence for her to feel like she trusted him once again. He had a way of putting her at ease, of speaking so compassionately and sympathetically that she couldn't help but feel like he was on her side.

The truth was she would never truly know who he was but she couldn't deny that he'd brought her here to relative safety and that her and Iris now had a base to plan out their next steps.

Once they'd sat for a while and Margot had composed herself, talk turned once again to discovering more about what was going on outside the factory walls.

'Who was the man who came to the farm? Who was responsible for killing John and Barbara?'

'Honestly, I don't know' Sy responded 'but in truth whoever they were, they were just following orders. They may have pulled the trigger but someone much higher up gave the execution order'

'I won't stop until I know who did it Sy, it's my fault they died, it's the least I owe them.'

'It's not your fault Margot, you're caught up in something that we don't know the full scale of yet. The priority now is keeping the two of you safe.'

Iris awoke with a muffled cry no doubt wanting a feed. She was spending more time awake these days in between feeds which Margot was enjoying. She removed her from the sling and allowed her to wake up a bit turning her to sit on her knee so she was facing Sy.

He looked down at her, reaching out his finger for her to hold in her grasp.

'How is she doing? She certainly looks healthy'

'She's amazing. I've got nothing to compare her to but as babies go I think she's pretty much perfect.'

'Has she been checked over at all since you gave birth? Do you want me to do any checks on her?'

Margot hesitated. Part of her was keen to hear that everything was okay with Iris that she hadn't missed anything glaringly obvious but she was also reluctant to hand her over. She may have softened towards Sy this afternoon but trusting him with Iris was altogether different.

'I don't think she needs it, she's got a bit of a cold or something at the minute but on the whole she seems fine, thanks though.'

He hesitated as if wanting to give her reason to reconsider but then seemed to think better of it and relented.

'What about her newborn vaccinations and things,

do you want me to see if I can arrange for her to have those?'

Margot had always been an advocate of immunisations, knowing what a difference they had made to the population over the years. Right now though she felt that everything she had previously known was in question. Plus, Iris was different, there was no doubt about that, there was something fundamentally different about her and Margot didn't know what the repercussions of that would be for her in the future.

'I'm not really in the right head space to think about it right now Sy, but I'll bear it in mind. If this cold doesn't clear up soon I'll see if Sasha can pick us up some medicine.'

He nodded again, acknowledging that right now he was better giving her some space.

'So, you've met the ever-enthusiastic Sasha' Sy said with a smile

'I have. Have you known each other long?' Margot was keen to establish the extent of their friendship

'About a year or so now. Once I was introduced to this place I started to help out a bit as and when I could. I try to bring some medical supplies over when I can and provide a bit of an ad hoc GP service for everyone. Sasha has always been keen to discuss what's going on out in the world with me whenever she can. Her hearts in the right place.'

'Dana doesn't seem to agree with what she's doing'

'No, Dana started this place as a way for people to

avoid conflict and Sasha's interests and research put that in jeopardy, so she's understandably wary. The irony though is that Sasha is probably closer to finding out what's going on than anyone else is. She starting to pull together the threads from lots of different sources. I just hope she's doing it sensibly.'

'What do you mean?' Margot was disappointed in herself to find she was a bit jealous of his concern for Sasha. She wondered if there was more than a friendship lingering there.

'We've both seen what happens when people get too close to the truth. If she's in any way on the right track with what she's looking into then she needs to make sure she's doing it very quietly.'

They sat in silence for a while, both pondering the lifestyle they had unwittingly fallen into.

Sy mopped up the last few mouthfuls of his dinner and took his plate over to the kitchen.

'Feel free to leave it on the side' Margot called after him 'It can be my first task as the new resident pot washer.'

Sy chuckled 'Don't be daft, I'm not above clearing up after myself' as he rolled up the sleeves of his crisp light blue shirt and began to fill the sink with soapy warm water. Humming away to himself as he did so, a tune that Margot didn't recognise.

Margot took the opportunity to feed Iris, anticipating that her cries for a feed were not far away.

Having cleaned up his dishes Sy returned with two glasses of icy water and put one down in front of her 'Important to drink lots whilst your breastfeeding' he told her before promptly downing his own glassful.

'Always the doctor' she smiled, warmed by his concern for her.

'Right, I'd better head off' he announced.

'Do you have to leave so quickly?' Margot responded. She had taken more comfort from his visit than she had been expecting and she didn't want him to leave.

'Afraid so, I'm only meant to be out on a house call so I need to be heading back. I am sorry it took me so long to get out to see you Margot, you've been constantly on my mind, you both have.'

She wanted to believe him, so strong was her desire to have him in her life right now, looking out for her.

'Will you be able to visit again soon?' she asked, somewhat embarrassed by her apparent need to see him again.

'I'll do my best, hopefully within the next week or so I'll be able to get away.' He walked over to her side of the table where she sat still nursing Iris and gave her a soft kiss on the top of her head before turning and walking away from her.

'Look after yourselves, I'll see you soon' he called behind him as he disappeared out of the tent, rolling his sleeves back down as he went, returning to his other life.

Which one was the real Sy though? Where did the real Sy start and the fake one begin? Margot found it hard to distinguish the many different versions of him.

She remained there long after Iris had finished her feed, drinking her water and contemplating what she would fill her time with over the next few days.

She needed to distract herself she decided and resolved to return to see Sasha as soon as she could to continue the conversation they'd started.

In the meantime though she was happy to sit there in the quiet, while the heat of his perfunctory kiss slowly faded away.

Chapter 30

It was the following day before she managed to catch up with Sasha once more. Her new job kept her busy after everyone had eaten their dinner and Sasha seemed particularly difficult to pin down. Margot wondered how often she left the site on her security walks.

Just before lunchtime however she noticed that the door to the communication room was slightly ajar and so ascended the stairs to the upper level.

There she discovered Sasha once again in the little office, more papers strewn all over the table some of them spilling over onto the floor.

How does she work like this? Margot wondered before remembering with a pang of nostalgia her own desk at work compared to Nicks. She wondered now how Nick was doing and what he would make of her new line of work.

Sasha barely acknowledged Margot before picking up the conversation as if they had never had a break, so keen was she to move forward with their discoveries.

'I've got a bit of a network of women now that I speak to regularly online. The trouble is the sites that we use are constantly being tracked and shut down so we have to keep re-establishing new ones and tracking each other down again.'

'How do you know that everyone on there can be trusted?' Margot enquired her senses tingling always conscious that danger could be lurking behind every conversation.

'We don't' Sasha muttered matter of factly. But that's why we don't put anything personal on there. I don't know any of their names or where they're from and vice versa. Even if someone was on there to spy on us all they'd be able to read about is our own conspiracies. They can't put us in jail for that.'

Margot wasn't sure she knew what they could do anymore.

'There are some who go public but it normally doesn't take long before they go quiet. They've probably been forced to stay silent, paid off or worse, but I like to think that some of these anonymous women are them under cover. Still fighting the good fight'

Margot was surprised to hear how Sasha spoke so lightly about the situation. Was it possible that more people were being murdered or was her imagination getting the better of her?

'There was a research paper published a year ago that was only online for a day before they took it down from the web, but not before someone had made a copy of it and it's been doing the rounds online ever since. They can't clamp down on it quick enough but they keep trying which tells me that there's definitely something to it.'

'Can I take a look?' Margot was itching to have something that she could sink her teeth into. Something that would allow her to utilise her brain, to remember who she once was.

'Of course, I've got a printed copy of it somewhere you can take back to read. It's quite in depth and a lot of it went over my head so it would be good to get your insight on it.'

Sasha started an excavation of the paperwork in front of her. Haphazardly shoving documents to the side and scattering them into an even bigger mess on the floor in her attempt to find what she was looking for.

'Have you ever considered a filing system? Margot asked in jest

'Oh sod off' came the retort 'Organisation dampens my natural spark'

'If you say so.'

A few minutes later there was the cry of success as Sasha emerged from the rubble of paper with a document in her hand.

'Told you I'd find it!' she cheered enthusiastically.

She handed over the paper with a flourish and Margot took it shaking her head with a smile.

Sasha wasn't lying when she said it wasn't a small document, flicking through the pages Margot could see that this would take her a while to work through but she was desperate to get started. Would this confirm anything for her? Would this give her any answers about Iris? Something she hadn't yet discussed with anyone since arriving at the camp. Something which no one else appeared to know anything about.

As she closed the document and scanned over the front page the name of the author jumped out to her as being familiar.

'Dr Fenwick, I recognise that name'

'Really? Did you work with her at some point?'

'No not professionally' It took Margot a second to think back to why she had a connection to her.

'I sent her a message on a forum months ago, before I'd had Iris. I was trying to do some research of my own and her name kept cropping up so I reached out. A stupid idea now looking back and knowing what you've said now about the forums being monitored the way they are.'

'Did she respond?'

'I've got no idea, I was beaten unconscious and went into early labour later that day so it kind of slipped my mind.'

'You were what?' Sasha stared at her wide eyed and open mouthed in disbelief

Margot forgot how little everyone knew of her story, how difficult it would be for everyone to process all that had happened to her.

'It was quite the day'.

'You're telling me!'

'Well, why don't we take a look. Can you remember what the forum was?'

'No, I can't to be honest, I'd looked at so many by that point and I was clutching at straws just for some way of getting some answers that I made a bit of a rash decision. But this is great' she said holding up the paper 'now I can see for myself what she was all about and if there was anything in it all, I can't wait to get started.'

'Do you want me to watch Iris for a bit so you can read in peace?' Sasha offered

Once again Margot felt her walls go up. She was only going to be reading, why would she need someone to watch Iris for her so that she could do that?

'No don't worry we'll be fine thanks. She's still got a bit of a temperature and she's a bit restless. I'll start it tonight once I've put her down.'

Sasha contemplated the two of them

'You've got to let some of us in at some point Margot. I probably don't know half of what it is that you've been through over the past year or so but you have to start trusting people again at some point.'

'Why?' Margot muttered feeling her frustrations starting to rise 'every time I've put my trust in someone it's either ended up in them getting hurt or me getting screwed over. I can't keep doing that.'

'Nor can you keep up this hyper independence that you're so insistent on. I may not have bought into Dana's vision completely for this place but what I have seen is people coming together and supporting one another. Not because they're doing anything particularly special but because slowly, over time, that trust is built and a bond is formed. It's mutual Margot and it's done gradually so that you can start to heal some of that trauma you're carrying around with you. Christ, I sound like a right hippy, don't tell Dana she'll have me leading evening prayer before we know it.'

Margot smiled in spite of herself. She could see what Sasha was getting at but she wasn't going to change her mind anytime soon. The one thing she could never let happen was for Iris to be put in jeopardy. She also knew however that Sasha was not one to let something rest easily and she was sure she hadn't heard the last of it from her.

'Thank you Sasha, I appreciate it honestly I do. I will give it some thought'

This seemed to pacify Sasha for the time being and she let it go, returning to her table of paper trying to return it to some kind of distorted order.

Chapter 31

That evening Margot stayed up into the early hours reading the paper. It appeared to cover years worth of research. Margot tried to follow the logic behind the route that had taken Dr Fenwick from one test to another. Tried to establish what her area of interest had been.

She was so desperate to get answers that she flicked to the back at one point in a vain attempt to view her last published paper. But like skipping to the last chapter of a book it didn't seem to give her any answers without the context of the pages in the middle.

She would have to do this methodically.

She returned to Sasha bleary eyed the next morning with a head full of thoughts.

'I need to talk to Dr Fenwick, I need to know if she has anything to back these claims up with.'

Sasha didn't seem surprised by Margot's train of thought or her lack of formality and greeting.

'Can you remember yet what chat room you used

when you reached out to her?'

'No, but it can't be that hard to retrace my steps. I'll just need to go through them all one at a time and see if any of them look familiar.'

'If we had another computer it would be a lot quicker' Sasha added, her frustration seeping through at the conditions they were forced to work in.

'Let's just be grateful we've at least got one form of communication. We'd have no way of reaching out otherwise.'

'Dana's threatened to take this one away from me before now. Anytime she thinks I'm getting too carried away she brings it out like a veiled threat. Make sure you keep up with your chores so she doesn't feel you're getting too distracted.'

Margot realised with a pang that she hadn't held up her end of the bargain, failing to attend any of her washing up duties the day before. She wondered if her name was already mud amongst some of them and vowed to pull her weight more that day.

'So how far did you get with the paper last night? Did it tell you anything new?'

'Not really. It's clearly not the finished article, she must have felt like she needed to publish it before she'd been able to draw any conclusions about what she'd found. She seems to be focusing on the prenatal boosters. I think she might have developed a vaccine that works. But then why would anyone not want that publishing? It doesn't make any sense.'

'OK well let's see if we can find that forum, it can't be that hard surely.'

And so they methodically started the process of working through any and every available forum that Margot may have reached out to.

It felt like another life when Margot had first written her comment online. She remembered how vulnerable she had been at the time, no idea if her child would even survive the birth. How much had changed since then.

There were a few pages that looked familiar to Margot but she remembered looking through a lot of them before deciding to reach out to Dr Fenwick.

'Search for Dr Marsha Fenwick forum' I remember I used her full name in the post.

Sasha did so, her fingers swiftly gliding over the keyboard with ease.

The top result brought up Margot's message.

'There, that one!' Margot shouted unnecessarily

'Annnd perforated ear drum' Sasha added sarcastically rubbing her ear lobe in mock indignation

She clicked on the top link which led to them to the page that Margot now recognised. Her heart leapt as she realised there was a response waiting for them.

Happy to discuss further, will be live on here most evenings.

Margot realised that this had been posted months ago though, it was unlikely she was still using the website that frequently.

'Let's ask her if she'll meet online so that we can talk to her.' Margot turned to Sasha 'We need to know it's actually her.'

'We can't risk you being on camera Margot, the whole country is looking for you'

'So, you meet her then. I'll stay behind the camera. I'll prep you with the questions '

'In what world do I look like a research scientist?' Sasha asked incredulously

Margot took in her shaved half head of hair and nose ring

'Some of us are cool!' she replied in retaliation.

Sasha grinned 'If you say so! Just give me the script and let me go over it a bit this afternoon. I'll make it work.'

'She might not even respond, it's been ages since she put that post up.'

They needn't have worried though. Within twenty minutes of them putting up the request on the page they had a response to say she could be online at 11pm that evening.

'Is that worrying that she replied so quickly?' Margot asked Sasha apprehensively looking for deception at every turn.

'She must have it set up to alert her to any updates. Perhaps she wants to speak to us as much as we want to speak to her.'

Sasha was adamant that Margot return to the camp that afternoon and be actively present amongst the other women. Everything that they were trying to do was dependent on them staying in Dana's good books and nothing would make Dana happier than Margot integrating herself into the group.

Margot however was frustrated at not being able

to prep for the meeting. This was the first time they had started to make any kind of progress and if Sasha made any mistakes it might shut the door on the one and only lead they had.

The day crawled along whilst Margot washed and dried the remnants of lunch and helped to set up for dinner, interspersed with feeding and changing Iris. Some of the other women attempted to make polite conversation with her but she found herself shutting them down quickly, preferring to work in silence, alone with her thoughts and making a mental note of everything she wanted to remind Sasha to ask that evening. She was aware that she wasn't making a good impression with most of the women here but it really wasn't her priority right now. She didn't need friends she needed to make progress.

Eventually dinner was served, although Margot didn't feel like she was able to eat any of it. Sasha, she noticed was nowhere to be found. So much for being an active presence around camp she grumbled.

She excused herself from the table and returned to the comms room where she found Sasha sitting in an unusually tidy space. A black drape had been hung behind her, covering the wall which ordinarily plastered with newspaper clippings and schematic drawings. The table had been pushed against the end wall so that it was out of sight. Sasha had managed to remove anything that might give someone an indication as to where they were or what they were doing. It occurred to Margot that maybe Sasha was as nervous about doing this as she was.

It was a long wait until 11.00pm. The two of them

passed the time by discussing what they wanted to get from the conversation and Margot attempted to give Sasha some tips on how to present herself more like a research scientist would.

Fortunately, their preparations helped the time move more swiftly and before they knew it they were online waiting for her to appear on the website live chat.

Margot had positioned herself out of the shot but still within eyesight of the screen so that she could witness what was going on.

As the clock struck eleven they got a notification to say that Dr Fenwick was in the chat room. Margot had to hand it to her, she was efficient.

'OK' Margot turned to Sasha 'Ready?'

Sasha just nodded, words failing her for a second

'Remember you're just a normal woman wanting to ask her a few questions'

'I am normal' Sasha replied with mock indignation

'If you say so' Margot smiled before leaning back and ensuring the camera wasn't picking her up.

Sasha clicked the mouse and after a brief pause a woman appeared on the screen.

She looked almost exactly like Margot had pictured her in her head. Short greying hair, cropped into a tussled pixie cut around her ears. She wore a pale blue blouse with the collar pulled up at the back and held a pair of tortoiseshell glasses in her hand which she hastily slid onto her face when the call connected.

Sasha slipped immediately into role

'Dr Fenwick, thank you so much for meeting me.

I really appreciate it.'

'You're welcome. I'd like to get straight to the point if that's ok though, I'm not sure if this is a particularly good idea.'

'Of course I understand. I wondered if you could give me a bit of insight into the paper that you published. I've been doing a bit of research myself and I think your findings could help'

'That paper was published too prematurely. I thought I was onto something and that I was going to be shut down. I shouldn't have acted so rashly, it turned out I was wrong.'

Margot frowned. This wasn't what she was expecting. Sasha too seemed momentarily thrown. This wasn't a script that they had rehearsed.

'I'm sorry, are you saying the paper isn't accurate?'

'Yes, that's right, after completing further research I discovered that there was nothing in it after all. I wish people would stop sharing it.'

Margot couldn't fathom it. There was no denying her research had been valid and it looked like she was onto something. Why now the sudden change of direction?

Sasha too seemed to be of the same mindset.

'Dr Fenwick are you safe right now?'

The lady paused and stared directly into the screen

'Yes of course, I'm fine.'

Her eyes however said differently. There was fear there.

'I really need to go. I'm sorry I couldn't be more useful.'

Margot panicked. There was more to this and she

needed to know what it was. She couldn't let her slip through her fingertips now.

As Dr Fenwick reached forward to end the call Margot took a step to the side and moved herself into the frame so that she could be seen. Dr Fenwick paused at the movement and locked eyes with Margot. Recognition and surprise dawning on her face.

'Oh my god'

Margot didn't say anything. Hoping that just making herself visible would be sufficient to gain her trust.

'The baby?' She looked worried. Nervous even to ask the question, fearful of what the answer would be.

Margot reached over to the bassinet where Iris lay sleeping and lifted her out.

Sasha clearly concerned about the speed with which this meeting was progressing held out an arm keeping Margot at bay

'You sure about this?'

Margot nodded, knowing in her bones that this was the right thing to do. She stepped back into the shot, Iris in her arms allowing Dr Fenwick to see her.

The scientist brought a hand up to her mouth.

'Do you know what this means?'

Margot nodded but the truth was that she didn't feel like she did truly appreciate the enormity of it yet. The truth lay just out of reach for her, enticing her forward.

'I don't want to know where you are but do you

feel like you're safe? Can you stay there for the time being?'

Margot looked at Sasha questioningly. She was certainly starting to feel more settled here but the truth was she wasn't ever truly safe.

Sasha clearly took this as a personal affront at her security measures.

'They're both perfectly safe here.'

Dr Fenwick nodded. Now apparently deep in thought. Without warning she stood up and walked out of shot for a second before returning with a notepad and pen.

'Do you have a secure email?'

'Use mine' Sasha announced 'It's encrypted'

She read out the details whilst Dr Fenwick hastily scribbled them down.

'I'm sending something across Margot. What you choose to do with the information is up to you.'

'OK' Margot was unsure what was happening or why there was a sudden sense of urgency 'can we meet again once I've seen it? Can we discuss it at some point?'

'I won't be contactable again, If I'm going to do this I'll need to leave tonight. Once you have this document Margot you'll have some answers but there's no going back. You can't un-see this. Are you sure you want to go down this route?'

'I'm sure' Margot forced the words out of her mouth before her brain would have time to consider it. She needed to know.

Dr Fenwick nodded as if their fates were sealed.

'Ok, I'll send it across shortly, good luck Margot

and take care of that little one'

Margot bristled as she always did at the insinuation that strangers may care about her child's welfare as much as she did. So many people seemed to feel as if they owned a part of her.

The screen went black before they had time to say their goodbyes or issue any pleasantries leaving Margot and Sasha in a stunned silence for a second.

'Well, I think I handled that exceptionally well' Sasha added sitting back in her chair.

Margot still felt dazed by their fleeting encounter but rolled her eyes at Sasha all the same.

They didn't have long to wait to receive the mysterious email. Following a tense moment of Sasha thinking she'd given her the wrong details and after multiple attempts to remember her password Sasha finally accessed her account to find an email awaiting them.

'You ready for this?'

Margot wished everyone would stop asking her. They were words on a paper what was the worst that could happen?

'Just open it' she replied tersely

Sasha double clicked on the document and brought up a folder containing hundreds of documents.

Margot knew there were too many to go through all at once but she was desperate to get started and see what this was all about. She asked Sasha to move over so that she could have control and clicked on the first folder.

'It looks like they're patient files. It's all of their

blood works from the 24 week scan. Look can you see, it shows their markers are all below the threshold, none of these babies were carriers.'

'What happened to them? Did they survive?'

Margot scanned to the back page of the first document looking for signs of what had happened. Two words signed off the document, underlined and in bold

SUBJECT TERMINATED

She felt her spine stiffen as the words sunk in. She closed that document and opened the next, similar results all below threshold, not a carrier, she turned to the back page

SUBJECT TERMINATED

Page after page after page, different patient, same result. Healthy babies, terminated.

This was is it, this was the proof that she'd been looking for. Her insight into what would have happened to Iris had she attended that appointment.

She looked over at Sasha who was still trying to follow Margot's line of thought.

'Margot what does this all mean?'

'It means that Iris wasn't the only one. All of these babies tested negative. None of them had to die.'

'So why did they? What does anyone gain from killing a healthy child?'

Margot shook her head unsure herself of what possible reason there could be to do what had apparently been done.

She looked down at the numbers allocated to each file. Seemingly indicating that this had been the case for thousands of children. She wondered if every one told the same story. How many had been killed?

She returned to the first case file and looked at it more in depth. The first page of the file appeared to list the vaccines that had been administered before the blood works were taken.

'What are all these codes Margot? Are these the boosters we all had to have?'

'No, they're something else.'

'What do you mean something else?'

'I think they've been injecting women with something, it doesn't appear to be anything to do with the virus though. It's something different.'

Margot flicked to the next patient file and saw they too had a similar note. Vaccinations administered in early pregnancy but this one was slightly different.

As she continued to flick through the different cases, she could see that no two files were the same. Each woman had been administered something different. They all followed the same timeline, each one documenting one woman's 24-week pregnancy journey. The personalised cocktail the mother has been administered, the subsequent blood works completed at the 24-week scan, and the termination date the following day.

'They were using healthy babies as lab rats, injecting them with something, I don't know what, but whatever it was they needed to cover their tracks. These babies were killed so they wouldn't be caught.'

If these files were correct, it affected more people

than she could have ever first contemplated. She thought of the women below in the camp, all of whom had lost a child. If these files were correct then they could have all gone on to have healthy children. Children that would have gone on to lead healthy lives.

Every day that Iris lived was a day that would have been taken away from her had Margot followed the professional advice she was given. She held her closer to her, more grateful than ever that she had taken the path that she had.

'We need to tell Dana about this.' Margot added, feeling like she was a child wanting to confide in a parent.

'Margot she'll shut this down. She doesn't want anything to do with the fight, she's not interested.'

'She will be when she hears this.'

Sasha looked unsure, nervous almost at confessing to Dana what she had been doing in her spare time.

'If we're going to tell her then we should tell everyone else at the same time. We have strength in numbers Margot, this is too big for the two of us now.'

Margot felt a deep sense of unease at the thought of dropping this bomb shell on everyone here. If Dana knew the upheaval that she was going to cause when she allowed her and Iris to join the camp she felt sure that she would have turned them away and closed the door. She sympathised with Dana's desire to bury her head in the sand but this was no longer about Dana. This was about every single one of those women and what had been taken away from them.

'We'll wait until everyone's together tomorrow evening and do it then. We need as many of them as possible to hear it at the same time, then Dana won't be able to stop us.'

Margot nodded in silence. Dr Fenwick had been right, there was no way of taking back what they had seen now.

Chapter 32

The following day Margot's sense of unease was deepening. It had been one thing to come into the camp and not tell everyone her story but that was personal and she felt, her choice to make. Now however, her and Sasha were sitting on information that no longer just affected her and Iris. What was the kinder thing to do, leave them in their bubble as Dana would have it or tell them everything they knew, most likely breaking their hearts in the process.

She felt like a traitor every time someone attempted to make conversation with her, knowing that she was going to drop such a huge bombshell on them in just a few hours. She also dreaded Dana trying to engage her in conversation. She didn't think she would be able to keep her face from betraying that she was hiding something from them.

Fortunately, she managed to avoid Dana for the first part of the day and after lunch Margot decided to escape to the caravan for the afternoon, citing

Iris' fever as a reason for them to have some downtime. This however meant that she also didn't get a chance to speak again with Sasha. She wondered if she too was questioning if this was the right thing to do. Having lived here far longer than Margot had and knowing the women here a lot better than she did she suspected that the weight of the moral conundrum would sit heavier for her.

It was only that evening when Margot walked across to the communal area that she spotted Sasha and could see that she was also indecisive about their decision. Her brow was furrowed and she sat quietly amongst the group. A noticeable change from the life and soul of the party that she usually was. For years Sasha had towed the line with Dana, conceding to her leadership even when she hadn't agreed with it. Would this now be the time she stood up against her? Would she lose her home and her community as a result of it?

It appeared however that Sasha had made up her mind despite the angst it was causing her. As soon as she saw Margot had joined them she rose from the crowd and whistled with her fingers to get everyone's attention.

Conversations halted mid-sentence as all those sitting around the fires turned to look at her.

Sasha cleared her throat.

'I wanted to speak to you all tonight whilst we've got everyone together' she spoke clearly and loudly so her voice travelled to all those sat around her.

'We welcome newcomers to the group every now and again but we've recently welcomed Margot who has brought with her our youngest recruit, Iris'

Those sitting around Margot turned and smiled at her warmly

'The truth is you don't know the real reason about why Margot and Iris have joined us and I don't think that's fair on you.'

Dana rose to a stand quickly and glared at Sasha.

'Sasha I'd like a word please.'

'No, Dana I'm sorry. I value you and your opinion but you can't keep everyone in the dark anymore. They don't get to see what's happening out there and they need to know.'

Dana took a few steps towards Sasha in an attempt to continue the conversation more quietly 'They've come here for peace Sasha, not to get dragged into your dramatic conspiracy theories.'

Sasha had clearly decided that she wasn't going to be swayed as she kept her voice loud and clear 'They're not conspiracy theories, they're the truth and they deserve to know!'

'I have never understood you Sasha, you've got the perfect opportunity here to move on, to form friendships and community, to live in peace and you won't allow yourself to have that, why?'

'This is not peace. This is hiding in the corner of the playground hoping the bullies won't come to find us.'

The crowd were following the argument enraptured, moving their heads from one side to the other like an argumentative game of tennis.

'You have filled your head with these ideas in an attempt to alleviate your pain and I understand that

Sasha but this has got to stop' She was raising her voice now, losing her calm demeanour

'It's not just me. Margot knows about it too and she's got proof'

Sasha looked over at Margot in anticipation. Margot however froze in response.

'Margot, tell them!' Sasha yelled at her.

The crowd of heads turned in her direction in unison as an anticipatory hush descended on the group.

Margot looked around at their faces. She could speak up or she could continue to hide.

'It's okay Margot' a voice near her spoke quietly 'we'd like to hear your story.'

And in that moment, she knew she had to speak. Whether they believed her or not it was her duty to share with them all that had happened to her and all that she now knew in light of it.

And so, as the night enveloped them and the fires crackled higher, she told them all her story. All the facets of her story just like she had with John and Barbara, however this time she was putting it out there to a much larger group, publishing her life, her achievements and her regrets in the most public counselling session she could have imagined.

She shared how she had tested herself before her scan and found out she was negative and the subsequent positive result, followed by her escape North which eventually led her to John and Barbara. The only area she omitted was Iris' seeming ability to heal Barbara. She no longer knew whether she believed that herself and with no one else alive who had witnessed it she decided to keep her doubts to herself for now.

Dana in spite of herself remained silent, being drawn into Margot's story herself and eager to hear how she had wound up arriving with them. Whilst she continued to stand as Margot spoke, her shoulders lost their tension as the adrenaline of the argument with Sasha dispersed.

Margot spoke of John and Barbara's death in a matter-of-fact way, not wanting to allow herself to get swept away with the emotion of it all. She owed it to the two of them to tell people clearly and concisely how brave they were and how barbaric and unnecessary their deaths were.

Some of the women raised their hands to their mouths in shock as she spoke, others became emotional on her behalf wiping away an escaping tear.

The more Margot spoke the more she realised how important it was that she was doing so. Her story needed to be told, as did John and Barbara's. To keep it to herself would make it appear like it hadn't happened at all and would make it all too easy to be swept away and die with her.

She also began to appreciate that it wasn't just her story. The events of her life were so closely interwoven with all of theirs that it belonged to them too. She held the key to unlocking all that had been kept secret from them, they just didn't know it yet.

As she reached the part of how she had found the group and settled in here she could see a few starting to mutter amongst themselves assuming that she was nearly done. Sharing their shock at what one woman had had to endure in order to find her way to them.

She glanced across at Sasha who gave her an encouraging nod to continue, to say the words that would affect them all profoundly.

'Since I've been here, I've been spending time with Sasha who has been doing her own research. We've shared stories and tried to piece together some of the rumours that have been getting passed around. Yesterday we spoke to a research scientist who has managed to get hold of some paperwork from the labs. She's since gone into hiding as it's too dangerous for her to remain out in the open now.'

Dana looked in between Sasha and Margot. Her surprise at what they had been getting up to behind her back evident.

'These papers, which I believe to be genuine show that babies, possibly some of your babies, were being injected with something without your knowledge.'

The silence was so heavily weighted that Margot could feel its pressure weighing down on her. She could see that they did not understand what she was saying and so continued.

'We were all offered prenatal boosters, yes? These were meant to support the baby's immune system and help protect them from the virus. The truth however appears to be that these were not boosters at all. They were trialling something, I don't know what but whatever it was they were so keen to test it that they've bypassed all the usual testing methods.

It would appear that they've moved directly onto human trials'

Reality began to set in on some of the faces near her. Even Dana looked taken aback by the bombshell she was dropping.

A voice a few rows away from her spoke up, slightly shaky

'Was it these injections that made my baby poorly? Is that why she was a carrier?'

Margot took a shuddering breath, aware that she was on the precipice of breaking their hearts.

'If these files are correct then your babies weren't carriers at all. They all tested negative for the virus. But they were evidence of the unlawful testing that had been going on. That's why they were killed.'

Margot wasn't sure what kind of reaction she had expected but she soon realised that there would be no immediate reaction. So huge was the bombshell that she was dropping on everyone it settled onto the group like a fine mist.

She stared out over a sea of faces looking back at her. Unsure what to do with the information they had been delivered.

Margot was worried she hadn't been clear enough, that they might not believe her, that she might be told to leave immediately for causing such upset but the silence just continued.

She looked across at Sasha in the hope that she might be able to offer some words of support.

'None of them needed to die' Sasha spoke up and all heads revolved in her direction once again 'They took them from us to cover up something that they'd done.'

'What though? What is it they're meant to have done?'

'We don't know yet' Margot answered 'We literally found this out ourselves late last night but we couldn't keep it to ourselves. This is news that affects you all profoundly and it's only right that you're all aware and are able to process this at the same that we are.

What I can promise you though is that I will find out, I won't stop until we know exactly why they were killed and to get you all some kind of justice'

'Justice?' Someone shouted up from the back 'what justice is there? There's no bringing them back.'

'You're right' Margot continued 'Justice is the wrong word. I can't ever bring them back but I can at least get you the truth. I can give you that at least.'

'I will too' Sasha agreed. The two of them stood facing one another across the sea of women sitting amongst them. 'If you'll have me, I want to help you in any way I can. Let's get the bastards'

Margot nodded, she was grateful of the friendship she had formed with Sasha in such a short time and would welcome her support.

'And me' A woman rose to Margot's left. It was an elderly woman Margot had seen gardening most days but had not yet spoken to 'I'd like to support in any way I can Margot. I may be an old fart but I'm not giving up just yet.'

Margot smiled and rested her hand on her shoulder in appreciation

'Me too'

'And me'

Women stood one after the other all in support of what they were doing, all ready to come out of hiding and take back control of the life they had been living.

As each of the women in front of her followed suit she felt such relief and pride swell up inside her. They believed her, they didn't consider her to be a nuisance or upsetting the status quo, they wanted to join her, they wanted to know what had really happened.

As the talk grew in volume and as people began to break off to discuss emphatically the news that had been delivered to them Margot was able to take a deep breath.

There was one face however that was no longer in the crowd, Dana appeared to have taken herself away to be alone.

Chapter 33

The weeks that followed brought about a noticeable shift in camp. Life no longer revolved around the day-to-day chores or idle gossip. There was a wider purpose and drive for them all. They had cried over their lost children, they had wept and mourned and found a way to move forwards without their children. What was left, was a desire to hold to account those that had taken that version of their life away from them.

Margot could see that they were still shocked. There were in depth discussions taking place morning, noon and night about what this meant for them all and where Margot's investigation might take them next.

Margot spent the time fully engrossing herself in the documents that she now had at her disposal. There was so much of it she found it quite overwhelming and the weeks blended into one another as she methodically progressed through all of the information.

She also wasn't immune to the weight of responsibility that now lay on her to continue what she'd started. It wasn't enough to have told them of the injustice that had taken place, she now needed to be able to explain why it had happened.

Despite that however she felt a lightness over being accepted for the first time as her authentic self. She had confessed her deepest darkest secrets and they had continued to welcome her with open arms. She wondered if her and Iris had finally found their people.

The evenings were when Margot could most notice the change in the group. During the days people still had to keep camp running, they still had food to prepare and crops to tend but as the now warmer spring evenings descended, everyone was united as they spent time together. There were no longer little cliques of individuals. Everyone intermingled, they shared stories, they included one another ensuring that everyone was involved in the discussion, they were already aware that their strength lay in their number, in them all being united. It was heartwarming to see them pulled together in this way. They spoke with passion and determination, finally with an outlet for their grief and anger which had been suppressed for all these years.

It was as evening fell one night, whilst Margot moved between the groups of women, dipping in and out of their conversations, she became conscious of the sound of tyres slowly rumbling closer outside and she wondered with a flutter of anticipation who they might belong to. With visitors to the camp being scarce at best, Margot had become fine-tuned to the sound of someone's arrival. At this time of night and arriving by car too she held out a faint hope that she might know who it would be. She didn't however look around, keen to appear as though she was still engaged in the conversation in front of her.

After a few minutes he picked up the sounds of a distant conversation behind her, with a voice that she felt she recognised.

After a few seconds she felt a hand lightly rest on her shoulder and her heart fluttered as she turned to look into Sy's eyes. He looked relaxed and at ease and held her gaze without saying a word, the now all too familiar boyish grin appearing on his face as they acknowledged one another. There was a comfort between them now which had not existed earlier and she chastised herself inwardly as she acknowledged with a thrill that he appeared to have sought her out as soon as he had arrived in camp.

The rest of the group were keen to see him too and quickly engaged him in conversation wanting his opinion on the information they were now privy to.

He looked confused clearly not in the loop about what had been happening over the past few days but slipped naturally into their conversation whilst remaining at her side but removing his hand from her shoulder as he did so. Margot realised she liked it a lot more when he left it there.

She acknowledged that the mood in the camp was in quite stark contrast from when he was last here, when talk primarily revolved around the vegetable patches and who wasn't pulling their weight on the duty rota. Now however there was an energy to their discussions. The previously disconnected group of women had one united front, one topic of discussion, one purpose drawing them together.

It seemed to please Sy as he stood amongst them watching their interactions.

'You seem to have had quite the effect' he leaned in and murmured into her ear.

She smiled warmly 'I don't know what you mean.'

'Where's this paper that you've found? I've not heard of it before' he questioned.

'I've got a copy inside if you want to take a look?' she asked

He seemed genuinely interested to see what information they had pulled together and nodded eagerly.

Margot on the other hand was more excited at the prospect of getting him alone. He seemed to be in so much demand all the time, people always keen to get his attention or his opinion. He was certainly a man held in high regard here and Margot felt the thrill of having him all to herself.

They stood up to leave and Margot went to pick up the basket with Iris sleeping snugly inside.

Sasha reached out a hand and rested it on Margot's

'Don't disturb her she's just gone off; I'll watch over her. You two go an enjoy some grown up conversation' she said with a smile as she gave an extremely unsubtle wink.

Margot mortified turned to see if Sy had noticed but was relieved to see he had his back to her, engaged in another conversation.

'Oh, control yourself, you're meant to be a grown woman' Margot smiled in spite of herself feeling like she was thirteen again.

'Go on, scratch that itch.'

'You're insufferable do you know that?'

'That's why you love me' she replied with an impish grin. It was impossible to be grumpy with Sasha when she was in one of these moods.

'Are you sure?' Margot, for the first time, found that she felt comfortable with the thought of it, knowing that Sasha was more than capable of watching her for a short while.

'Yes! Be off with you!'

Margot took a deep breath.

'OK, thanks'

She turned to Sy to see if he was ready.

'Shall we?

As they arrived at the caravan Margot led the way over to the table where she still had the paper open at the last page she'd been reading. It was also accompanied by a number of other documents that she was reading in collaboration, trying to piece it all together. She realised her working space was now in a similarly dishevelled state to Sasha's and she smiled at how similar they were becoming.

'These are the documents that Dr Fenwick sent over to us, they clearly show some form of testing being done on the children and you can see the correlation of the testing, followed by their negative blood works and their subsequent terminations.'

They both reached for the article together and their fingers rested on one another. Margot again felt the thrill of electricity at their touch and left her hand there in the hope that he wouldn't retreat, that he would feel the same, that he would offer her the comfort of being close to another human being that she hadn't realised until now she so desperately craved. His hand remained in place too and as the seconds ticked by it became obvious that neither wanted to break the connection. She turned her head to meet his gaze and gave a half smile of invitation. This apparently was all the confirmation he needed as he moved his hand to the back of her neck and pulled her face close. He kissed her deeply and passionately as if he had been waiting to do so since the first time they had met. Margot caught off guard by the sudden intensity felt herself stumble into his body, but he held her close against him taking her weight along with her worries and insecurities and for the first time Margot allowed herself to forget. She allowed herself to become fully present in the moment, in their kiss, in the heat of their bodies pressed closely together.

Having never relied on a man she had underestimated the importance of physical contact and the sheer joy it could bring in the moment. She moved her hands round to his back and held on to his muscular physique, her slender body cocooned in his broader frame. The insecurities of not knowing if he wanted her as much as she wanted him melted away as she realised she wanted him more than she had ever wanted a man before.

Her hands edged underneath his top as she felt his smooth skin and the ripples of his faint muscles underneath his torso whilst, simultaneously, he reached up to the straps of her dress and deftly slipped them off her shoulders allowing it to fall from her body and drop to the floor. She had worried if this moment ever presented itself that she would feel vulnerable in his presence but he continued to kiss her with such passion that she felt her insecurities disappear, she was more of a woman since becoming a mother than she had ever been and whilst her body showed some of the war wounds of that process she embraced her new physique with the confidence of someone who was proud of what her body had achieved.

The external noises became distant, her thoughts quietened as she pulled her lips from his and looked into his eyes. Unable to break the bond of connection their bodies had formed she delicately traced her fingers down his forearms and intertwined her hand in with his. With the moonlight dancing across her semi naked body, she led him by the hand into the bedroom.

Chapter 34

Later as their bodies lay wrapped in one another, their limbs intertwined, Margot felt a peace she had not experienced before. The heavy weight of his thighs resting on hers the only blanket she needed on that warm night, she felt protected and safe. No words could express her feelings for what they had shared, and as he gently kissed her shoulder she took comfort that he felt the same.

Reluctantly she shuffled out from underneath him.

'I'm going to get Iris, I'll be right back.'

He nodded and lay back on the bed.

Margot dressed hastily, keen to get Iris and return to him as quickly as she could. She had been on a roller coaster of emotions with Sy but the attraction she had felt with him had been instant and it thrilled her that they appeared to feel the same way about one another.

As Margot walked back into the camp there were

still a few people milling around. The warmer evenings elongating the time they could spend in each other's company. The clear night sky looked breathtaking and Margot felt a deep sense of serenity at where her life had brought her to.

Sasha sat next to Iris in her bassinet, keeping conversation with others nearby but standing resolutely by the small child. Margot was certain she wouldn't have left her side and made a mental note to start to trust her more moving forwards. She had been right, she could do this alone but it would be so much harder and she had good people around her who she could trust. She needed to embrace that.

Margot anticipated having to field multiple questions from Sasha about her time alone with Sy but she was uncharacteristically discreet, giving Margot the merest hint of a knowing smile when she arrived. Margot was relieved, she had a bed that she was very much looking forward to getting back into as soon as she could.

'Hasn't stirred once' Sasha stated proudly as she handed the bassinet over 'I thought babies were meant to be hard work?'

'You've obviously got a gift! Thank you, Sasha, I appreciate it'

'Anytime' she added

Before anyone else could catch her attention she picked Iris up and headed back over to the caravan. Iris still felt warm and whilst she'd been feeding throughout the day Margot couldn't help thinking that she had been sleeping more and more recently. She rarely woke in the night these days and whilst

Margot knew this was something most mothers craved she felt it was unusual. She decided to ask Sy what he thought when she got back and ask him if he could bring some medicine for her to try and bring her temperature down the next time he came to the camp.

She arrived back and headed into the bedroom to lay Iris down for the evening. She was surprised however to find Sy out of bed, fully dressed and hunting around for his keys and wallet.

She wasn't sure what to say, she had assumed he would be staying the night, that they would sleep together and wake up together the next morning.

'Margot, I've got to get back' he was now lifting up the fallen bed covers from the floor searching for his one remaining shoe that had been discarded in their rush to get undressed.

'Why?' She muttered, frustrated with herself for not sounding as relaxed and carefree about his departure as she would have liked.

'I've got a long drive, I need to get ahead of the traffic' He wasn't even looking at her but was putting his shoes on with a pace that implied he couldn't get out of there quick enough.

Margot couldn't think what to say, this seemed to be in such stark contrast to what she had experienced only a few hours ago she was momentarily thrown and incapable of speech.

She moved across and lay Iris down in the crib next to the bed, in which time Sy had made his way to the door and was preparing to walk out.

'I'll see you around.' He said and with a passing

wave of the hand turned to leave the room.

'Wait' she called after him, unsure what she was going to ask him to wait for.

He turned almost reluctantly barely meeting her gaze as his eyes were drawn down to the worn carpet below. His expression one of unease.

'Kiss me' she begged, desperation seeping out of her as she craved any affection from him. He smiled uncomfortably took two strides over to her and gave her a perfunctory kiss, before turning his back to her and leaving without another word.

Margot sat on the edge of the bed with an emptiness in her stomach as she heard him move through the caravan and out into the camp. The gravel under his feet crunched with the pace of a man who was in a rush followed by the sound of a car door slamming, an engine starting and then disappearing into the night.

Margot sat for a while unsure what had just happened. Had she imagined the intimacy they had shared? Had she been naive to expect him to want to spend the night? She felt tears begin to pool in her eyes as she was caught off guard by the hurt she felt. She did not give herself over to anyone lightly and she felt the sting of rejection at his abrupt departure.

She shook herself off, she was old enough and thick skinned enough to not let this bother her. She should have known better than to give herself over to someone so easily, of course that's all he wanted from her. Why would he want anything else? Why would anyone?

Her bed felt contaminated by him, his scent still on her pillow, her bed sheets in disarray. She didn't want to lie here, she didn't want to think about him if he wasn't going to be thinking of her.

The concept of sleep now was inconceivable and in desperate need to distract herself she decided to sit up for a while longer and do some work. There was a document that she wanted to re-read that she had left that afternoon in the comms room so she decided to go and get that.

As she walked back across camp once again the stars appeared to mock her. Laughing down at her and her vulnerabilities for even thinking that she had a chance at happiness.

The last few remnants of the group had dispersed now, all retiring to their beds for the night. She was relieved she didn't have to speak to anyone.

Dejected she climbed the stairs to the gangway above and entered into the Comms room. This would at least give her something to distract herself with for a few hours. Then hopefully she would be able to sleep and forget this whole evening ever happened.

Walking over to the table where the papers lay she noticed the screen that they kept on for updates was flashing at her with a new message on the forum website. Ever since they had spoken with Dr Fenwick they had agreed to keep the website open so they could keep an eye on it. They were hopeful that despite her saying she needed to go into hiding that she might at least find some way of getting a message to them to let them know that she was okay, but it had remained resolutely quiet for the last week which Margot could only hope was a good sign.

The flashing icon on the screen told her that they had missed three video calls that evening from a number she didn't recognise. Someone was clearly trying to get in touch with her quite urgently. The last call had been over an hour ago, was it worth trying to call them back? Margot couldn't think of anyone else who would be calling them through this page other than Dr Fenwick, might she be in trouble or have more information for her? Margot knew it was risky but felt she couldn't not respond. She was feeling impulsive and rash following Sy's departure and was faced with an opportunity to act on those feelings.

Without giving it too much thought she hit the redial button and waited with baited breath as it connected.

After three rings the video opened up on the screen and Dr Fenwick appeared in front of her.

From one look at her Margot could see that something was wrong. This was a different woman to the person she had spoken to the previous week. She was pale, she looked like she hadn't slept in a week but there was a nervous energy about her which was unsettling. Her eyes kept darting around whatever room she was in never settling.

'Dr Fenwick? Is everything ok?'

'No Margot everything's changed. I've found something, I can't sit on it, I don't know how long

I've got before they catch up with me. I need to see you.'

Margot was temporarily stumped by the change in her demeanour.

'Okay, just take a breath, it's okay we'll figure this out.'

'Margot can you get out? I need you to meet me. I can't stay long it's not safe but you have to come.'

Margot knew it wasn't that simple. She didn't feel imprisoned in the camp any longer but choosing to leave was not something that someone did lightly here.

'I don't think I can, can you send me anything across?'

'No there's too much, there's not enough time. Iris doesn't have time'

The hairs on Margot's arms stood to attention at the mention of Iris' name

'What do you mean she hasn't got time?'

'Is she unwell Margot? Is she showing any signs of being unwell?'

A deep sense of foreboding was beginning to seep into Margot's body

'She's a bit poorly at the minute, she's been sleeping a lot'

'It's happening' Dr Fenwick appeared to be lost in her own head mumbling words and muttering half sentences.

'Dr Fenwick, what is it? What do you think Iris has got?'

'It's not what she's got, it's what she's not got'

'I don't understand, you're not making any sense'

Margot could feel her frustrations rising now as she struggled to grasp what was causing Dr Fenwick so much anxiety.

'Margot, I know that Iris is different'

She tried to keep her expression neutral not wanting to give anything away

'I don't know what you mean.'

'Yes, you do. Who else knows?'

Margot paused she felt like a rabbit in the headlights not knowing which way to turn for safety.

'Margot this is important' she raised her voice 'Who else knows about Iris?'

'No one.' Margot paused 'No one alive anyway.'

'Okay, good. Keep it that way. This is bigger than either of us could have imagined.'

'What is? What's going on?'

'You need to come and see it for yourself, there's so much to go through. I don't know how secure this line is. You need to come and meet me tonight'

Margot didn't know whether she could or not. She didn't even know if she should. It was all happening so fast.

'Margot it's imperative that you meet me, for Iris' sake'

These words left Margot with no choice as to her next actions. She felt she could trust Dr Fenwick and if she held the answers as to what was wrong with Iris then she had to find out more.

'OK, I'll find a way. Where are you?'

Having hastily scribbled down the address that Dr Fenwick had given her Margot sat for a second pondering her next moves. She wanted to go and tell Sasha straight away, she would be insistent on coming with her she was sure and they would have to leave soon if they were to get there in time. Dr Fenwick had told Margot that she would be there until midnight but after that she would have to leave. It didn't leave Margot with much time and she needed to figure out how she was going to get there. Her only option was one of the rusty community cars. The only trouble would be getting hold of the keys.

Margot decided to go and speak to Dana straight away. If she could get the key for the car she could then go and get Sasha and they could head straight off. She just hoped that Dana wouldn't make this too difficult for her. She knew she wasn't going to be keen on the idea of Margot leaving.

Dana slept in one of the only other caravan's on site. Margot hadn't visited it personally before but she knew which one it was. There were no lights on as she approached it which gave Margot a deeper sense that this was not going to be easy. Asking a favour of someone was a lot harder when you'd also just woken them up.

Margot took a deep breath before approaching deciding that honesty was going to be the best way forward here especially as she was working on a tight timescale. She knocked hard on the door keen to exhibit the urgency of the situation. On the second round of knocking a small light came on at the far end followed by footsteps and the door opening onto the bleary eyed face of Dana.

Margot didn't wait for her questions.

'Dana, something's happened and I need to leave urgently. I wondered if I could borrow the keys for the car please, it's really important.'

Dana's brow furrowed deeper as she processed the request whilst still appearing somewhat disorientated.

'No, that's not possible.'

Margot wondered if she had expected that this request would come from Margot at some point and had an answer already prepared.

'Dana I don't ask this lightly, this is important, please.'

'Why do you need it?'

'I need to meet Dr Fenwick, she's got something important for me, something to do with Iris'

'No, it's too dangerous Margot'

'I'm sorry Dana but that's not your decision. I just need to meet her and get whatever else it is that she's found and then I'll be back.'

'No you will not' She rubbed her face, wiping her eyes and looked directly at Margot. 'I welcomed you here, allowed you to integrate into this community that I built and all I asked from you was compliance. You have brought nothing but anger and discourse into this camp and I will allow it no longer.'

'That's not what I've done Dana, I've just told people the truth and yes they're angry but they're also empowered now too. Isn't that what you wanted, empowerment and ownership of their lives.'

'Don't tell me what I want, you haven't seen the struggle it's taken to get here. You haven't witnessed the countless women I've had crying on my shoulder because of everything they've lost and the journey they've been on, all the while trying to find a way to heal themselves. And they've managed that because of their faith and their acceptance of their circumstances and making an active decision not to allow grief and anger to control them.'

'Why aren't you angry?' Margot was shouting now in frustration 'why don't you want justice for everything they've taken from you, for everything they've taken from every single one of those women out there. Why won't you fight?'

'What is there left to fight for?' Dana now fully awake glared at Margot. 'They've taken everything from us, there is nothing left to fight for Margot and if I don't find a way to move on from that then I may as well just give up now because it will kill me. Do you understand? I cannot live with that pain every day.' Dana's eyes pooled with water but she wiped them ferociously before they could drop.

Margot took a breath, aware that neither of them were in the wrong but were both on very different paths to one another.

'I do have something left to fight for Dana, and I will fight for her with every breath that I have. All I ask is that you lend me the car. I will return it when I'm done and if you really don't want me to return to the camp I'll respect that, I'll leave'

Dana looked conflicted. She clearly thought life would be smoother without Margot in it but she also did not condone what Margot was about to do.

Margot could see the conflict in her face and

knew she held the card that would convince Dana to let her go now.

'If you give me the keys now, I won't tell Sasha. I'll go without her. You can tell her I decided I didn't want to be here anymore, you can paint me out to be the bad guy, what ever you want. If you let me go now you can keep her safe.'

They locked eyes for a few seconds. Dana clearly toying with which was the lesser of two evils in this case. Sasha would be livid that she had been left behind but to know that she was not being put in harms way would make Margot feel a lot better too. Too many people had been hurt along the way and she needed now to make sure there were no more casualties because of her actions.

After a few seconds Dana reached behind the door she was holding open, pulled off a single key and handed it over to Margot.

With no words left to say and having lost so much time already Margot took it from her grasp and shoved it in her own pocket. She dashed over to her own caravan to grab an extra layer for Iris, along with the bassinet that she now couldn't live without. She hoped she could collect the rest of her items when she returned the car. Knowing Dana, she wouldn't be surprised if she returned to find they'd already been bundled up into bin bags and placed outside the front door.

After grabbing a few essentials she darted back out of the caravan and headed for the rear entrance where she knew the car was parked.

With Iris in the bassinet she wedged it into the

footwell of the passenger seat and vowed to drive as steadily as she could to keep her safe. At this time in the evening she hoped she wouldn't come across too much traffic.

She now only had twenty minutes until she was due to meet Dr Fenwick and she was pretty sure that the destination was a good half an hour away. Would Dr Fenwick be willing to wait, would she trust that Margot would follow through with her promise and turn up when she said she would?

Margot turned the car around and drove as calmly as she could over the dirt track that led her back towards the main road. Not wanting to look back and see what she was leaving behind, only looking ahead, returning once again to civilisation, to the bright lights of the city and to Dr Fenwick who she hoped would give Iris what she needed.

Chapter 35

As she drove away from the safety of the camp the niggling feelings of doubt were starting to creep in. Was this a good idea? Especially with Iris in tow. She didn't however feel like she had been given any choice. Iris wasn't well that much was clear and if there was more to it than a simple bug then Margot needed to find out what was going on.

She worried though that she was once again uprooting them from relative safety into the unknown. Where would she go now that she had vowed to Dana that she would leave.

Perhaps this was the catalyst she needed for a complete change. After she had met Dr Fenwick she could travel further North perhaps, somewhere even more remote. She hoped that she might be able to get a message to Sasha once she had settled somewhere. It would be nice to think that she might want to join her. The two of them might even be able to find some peace.

She took a wrong turn in her haste and swore

under her breath turning the car around and righting her mistake. It was hard navigating in the dark when everything looked different and it had been so long since she'd done this journey in reverse.

She glanced down at Iris who was still snugly wrapped in her blanket in the basket on the floor. How much of this would she tell her when she was older Margot wondered. It was nice to think she might grow up in a world where she didn't need to know any of it.

Slowly the landscape around the car began to become more built up again. Even at this late hour there were a few people walking down the streets, some carrying bags of food, others clearly out for an evening with friends or lovers. What she would give to be oblivious like they were. To be able to live a life without fear and suspicion lurking around every corner.

As she got closer to her destination she started to be on the look out for Dr Fenwick. If she had decided that Margot wasn't coming she may already have left. If that was the case there was a small chance they might pass one another as she was leaving.

As Margot drove however she didn't see anyone that she recognised. She hoped this meant she was still waiting for her.

Arriving at her destination she drove around to the back of the building where there was space for her to park the car. She decided the safest thing to do was to leave Iris where she was. If anything happened she wanted to know that she could jump straight back in the car and drive them both away to safety. Iris remained in a deep sleep but her breathing Margot noticed slightly alarmingly was speeding up and becoming more shallow. Margot hated seeing her unwell and was desperate to know what Dr Fenwick had been alluding to so that she could try to help her.

Nothing about this situation gave Margot good vibes. She was out of her depth, she had no control and she was completely at the mercy of another who seemed to know so much more than she did.

Parking the car as close to the shrubbery as she could to make it as inconspicuous as possible she turned the engine off and leaned over to Iris resting a hand on her chest to feel her breaths she whispered over to her 'I'll be right back sweetheart'.

Stepping out of the vehicle Margot looked around her for any sign of movement, for any rustle of bushes or footstep to indicate someone nearby.

The area looked deserted. There were streetlights in the distance that provided a weak orange glow to the air around her but Margot was unsettled by the many dark spaces around her where the light couldn't reach.

She didn't know exactly where she wanted them to meet, or even if she was still here but Margot was reluctant to move away from the car. She decided to take a brief look around the corner of the building to see if there was another entrance or to see if Dr Fenwick was waiting for her closer to the road.

As she walked along the red bricked wall that stretched out ahead of her there was a fire exit door that she could see was slightly ajar. Looking back at the car she couldn't hear any noise from Iris but she already hated the fact that she had put a distance between them. I he courage failed now she could return to camp but Iris might get worse. What if there was something she desperately needed inside that building?

She decided to go and take a look, but rationalised that if she couldn't see her inside then she would return to the car. The silence was unsettling and something about this felt off.

As she reached the door she managed to slip her fingers between the small gap and pull it towards her. It looked to be a warehouse of sorts, with shelving units and tables dotted around. The weak light from outside seeped onto the table nearest to her, revealing files and documents scattered haphazardly but it was impossible to see further into the room as it dissolved into complete darkness.

She felt around the walls beside her for a light switch but found nothing. She hadn't thought ahead to bring anything useful like a torch. She wondered if there was one in the car.

Margot thought she heard a noise from outside and turned to exit the room but as she did so one of the files on the table caught her eye. It was the same as the files that Dr Fenwick had shown her but there were far more of them here, enough she calculated to add up into the hundreds.

Was this what Dr Fenwick had wanted to show her? More evidence of yet more murders, more deception and cover ups?

She reached out to pick up the file closest to her when a voice from the very depths of the room spoke out and she leapt in fright dropping the file on the floor and scattering the contents.

'Well well well, the wanderer returns.'

Margot squinted into the dark not initially recognising the voice that spoke out to her, her heart pounding in her chest as she tried to establish it's origin.

'I'm so pleased you finally decided to return Margot.'

Margot followed the sound of the voice as it got closer to her, the faint outline of a person walking slowly and calmly towards her emerged.

'And here I was thinking that we might never be reunited.'

The figure of a man slowly appeared, as her eyes continued to adjust to the darkness and slowly a dawning realisation came crashing down on her as she recognised who she was facing.

'I think it's about time the three of us had a little chat don't you?'

Margot found herself looking into the eyes of Ben, the man she had once adored, the man who had fathered her child.

A satisfied grimace settled onto his face as he looked down into his arms where he held the sleeping bundle of their daughter.

Chapter 36

Margot couldn't process what she was seeing. Why was he here? Why did he have Iris?

'Ben? I don't understand, what's going on?'

'Oh, I could write a book about what you don't understand Margot. You've caused me quite the headache recently.'

Iris wriggled in his arms and gargled out a cry.

'Ben can I have her please, she's not well'

Ben ignored her and moving Iris out of the crook of his arms held her out in front of him to look at her. Her blue and white crocheted blanket that she had been wrapped in fell to the ground and Ben continuing to walk forwards stepped full footed on top of it leaving it in his wake covered in muddy footprints.

Iris now looked red and feverish and she cried out in pain at whatever it was her body was currently fighting off but Ben seemingly unperturbed continued to hold her out in front of him like a prized trophy.

'I've waited a long time to meet you' he spoke to the crying child. There was no empathy or softness to his voice though. It felt cold and calculated.

Margot looked at him, he was so vastly different to the man that she had once known. Something about him was changed.

'Ben what is going on? Please just give her to me she needs me'

Iris began to cry out louder now, a cry that Margot had never heard before. It was clear that she was hurting and it broke Margot to have to listen to it unable to help.

A door banged shut behind her plunging them into the pitch dark. Iris' cries continued but as Margot listened to them willing her eyes to adjust to grant her some limited vision she felt the cries begin to move away from her.

'Ben where are you taking her? Ben bring her back here right now.'

The cries were getting further and further away from her and she fumbled around in the dark trying to follow. She banged into a table and bent double trying to regain her balance.

A door much further away from her on the other side of the space banged closed again and completely muffled out the sobs. She could now no longer hear Iris at all. They weren't in the same room as one another anymore.

'Ben!' Margot shouted

With a blinding flash all of the lights suddenly came on basking what she now saw was a vast warehouse space with stark white light. She held a hand over her eyes and squinted around to see where Iris could have gone only to notice Ben still standing where he had been a few moments ago. His arms empty, Iris no where to be seen.

'Where is she? Bring her back right now, she needs me' Margot's voice grew hoarse with the effort and strain of the emphasis she was putting on the words.

'She no longer needs anything from you Margot, you gave her the last of what she needed from you a long time ago'.

Margot tried to piece together what he was saying. Her panicked breaths and racing mind preventing her from thinking straight. There was more to this than she had first thought. Why was Ben here, what did he know?

'What have you done?' she asked pointing an accusatory finger towards him.

'More than you could ever know.' He added with a smile

Suddenly she saw that it was all linked to him. He was the central cog in this whole machine. He held all the answers.

'It was you' she said in shock 'you faked the results, you've been testing something on women and killing the babies to cover your tracks. It was all you?'

He remained passive, maintaining eye contact with her. Neither confirming or denying anything which in itself was all the confirmation she needed.

'All those women. All those babies that should be alive. I've seen the codes you've given them, you've reduced them to letters and numbers. Is that to desensitise yourself so you don't have to feel the ramifications of what you've done?'

He maintained her eye contact the entire time, the ghost of a smirk emerging on his mouth. She sensed he wanted to gloat, that far from being worn down by his misgivings he was bolstered with a sense of entitlement from them.

'Why don't they have names?' she repeated. This in particular jarred with Margot. To have done what he'd done was one thing but to erase their very existence was a crime like no other.

'Because they don't exist on paper, they are a figment of your imagination, a prototype, an experiment no different to the ones you used to carry out in your lab.'

'You're comparing these children to rats and blood work… How can you not see the obscenity of what you've done?'

'I have worked all my life to establish the boundaries of what the human body is capable of, I refuse to be bound by the archaic mindset of the narrow minded fools who refuse to do what is necessary to secure the future of the human race.'

'Nice speech, you've been practising that one in your bedroom I can see?'

'I have done what…'

'You have done what countless other people could have done but the difference is they had a conscience. They knew where the line was and they stuck to a moral code. You are nothing more than an abusive child killer.'

Margot was long past caring about a game plan of trying to keep her cool. She was disgusted to be in his presence and the longer she spent with him the longer she despised the shared air they breathed and the further away Iris was from her. The diatribe coming out his mouth was sickening and yet he said it with such conviction she realised that he believed every word.

'I have made strides forward in the field that others only imagine is the source of fiction.'

'You have achieved nothing! They're dead, for nothing! There is no cure, no development, no progress, only death. Death where there should have been life.'

This time he didn't even try to hide his smirk, a sickening smile spread across his face. He walked forward towards her, intimidating and self assured until he stood within a few centimetres of her, looking down at her with disdain.

'You're a fucking idiot' he said 'those files weren't the end of their story, they were the beginning'

Margot rolled her eyes at his inability to see the errors of his ways before she played over his words and struggled to make sense of them.

'What do you mean?'

'I didn't kill them Margot, I gave them life. A life beyond something you could ever imagine.'

Margot found she was holding her breath, on the brink she felt of discovering something monumental.

'I can't take all the credit, I accept that initially it was a discovery made by accident, although I like to think that a higher power was at work. We lied about the vaccines initially just to try and ease the public's growing trepidation. There was no cure, no booster that would prevent fetuses from carrying the virus, we were helpless, merely trying to prevent a nationwide panic from setting in. People blindly believed us too, they were so desperate for hope, for the comfort of believing someone was in control of the pandemonium that was happening all over the world. Do you realise that over 90% of pregnant women took us up on the offer of a booster. Blind trust from a nation of complete imbeciles.'

Eventually I came to realise that the only benefit of the boosters was that it gave us access to the fetus from a very early stage in it's development and so I began to consider what I could do with that.

As the population developed their herd immunity we found less and less fetuses were testing positive but I became less and less interested in the virus. It did however provide me with the perfect cover to continue my research. To adapt the vaccines to include a little extra something.

By 24 weeks gestation the mother had become obsolete, the child had been adapted to my specification and would be able to survive outside of the womb. Enforced terminations gave me the permission to take what had now become rightfully mine. They just didn't know that they were delivering a sedated child as opposed to a dead one.'

He still stood overwhelmingly close to Margot, their chests basically touching. He spoke quietly but enthusiastically as if it were a privilege that she should be let in on the secret.

'But they were negative' she croaked, her brain unable yet to process the myriad of information he was feeding to her.

'Test results are easily adapted.' He added dismissively, 'As you well know.'

She glared at him as she finally processed the confession she had waited over a year to hear.

'It changed everything Margot. I have grown the most incredible family, all gloriously unique and overwhelmingly impressive. Their skills, their power, their cognitive ability, it's mind blowing, it's unprecedented and I've only scratched the surface of the modifications that can be made.'

'They're alive?' Her voice was barely more than a whisper now. She was scared to even say the words out loud, to make this warped reality real. All those children? All those grieving parents and those children are alive, out there, somewhere?

'My children are alive and well' he announced it like he had been waiting years to finally be able to tell somebody what he had achieved. He puffed his chest as he stood up straighter, he was proud and exuberant in his announcement.

'You ripped children from their parents? You let parents grieve for their babies whilst all along they were alive and being raised by you? In what, some form of obscene concentration camp?'

'I gave them a life their parents would have been proud of, away from the judgemental ideologies of a broken world. I have given my creations new life, one where they can achieve their potential, in an environment where they will be accepted and nurtured. They are grateful I've removed them from the cretins who gave them life. They don't even share the same DNA anymore so there is nothing to link them to those who were once their parents. It may not fit with your idea of a normal childhood but it is not the abhorrent crime you believe it to be.'

Her head was starting to hurt, so overwhelming was the tirade of lunacy that was being hurled at her. She couldn't correlate that this was once the man she had fawned over, she still expected some one to jump out of the sidelines shouting that this was some elaborate hoax. It couldn't be real.

'My only growing regret was that I didn't have a child of my own.'

At this Margot felt the walls begin to close in on her. The dawning reality of her life finally slotting into place. Her eyes wide with fear staring into the eyes of the father of her child, the monster.

'The one thing I craved was a biological child of my own. To see my image, my creation intertwined with my vision was a dream I thought would never come to fruition. My own wife, having been told that she could not carry a child, wanted us to adopt but I had many children already that she was not aware of. It was easy to become the man that she grew to despise, gradually distancing myself from her, she was after all the reason that I could not achieve my life's ambition. And then you came into my life, gullible, naive Margot. It was like you came to me knowing what I wanted and laid it all out on a platter. I thought I'd at least have to play the conflicted husband card for a longer period of time to make it seem all the more believable but then you got pregnant after one night? Some might call that divine intervention.'

Margot grimaced as she looked at the man who once made her weak at the knees and now made bile rise in her throat.

'I see you looking at me like I'm a piece of shit on your shoe.' He said to her with mock indignation 'You had no right to get involved and fuck everything up. You were only ever meant to be a vessel to hold her in until she was ready to be with me.'

Grabbing her cheeks between his fingers and thumb he pushed his fingers deep into her skin forcing her lips forward in an obscene pout. She began to shake with the realisation that she no longer knew what he was capable of.

'She was never yours, do you understand?' droplets of spit escaped from his mouth as he enunciated every word with fierce aggression. 'You ran off with my child, with no idea of who she was or what she was capable of and she was never yours to take!'

He kicked her feet out from underneath her with no warning so that she fell to her knees in front of him, her kneecaps hitting the concrete floor with brutal force. She realised now that he would make sure that she would not live to tell this tale but before that happened he would satisfy his narcissistic desire to have her at least recoil at his life's work. Her disgust at what he had achieved satisfied his desire to shock and surprise.

'Where is she?' Margot croaked. Unable to voice the words that she so desperately needed to be heard. She knew she couldn't fight him, she knew that he had won. She alone was not enough to take this on, she had been protecting her daughter from all of the many evils in this world without realising that the one person she needed protecting from was the only other person in this world who had given her life.

'My daughter is safe, my daughter will grow to know her place and she will take that rightful place at my side. My daughter will not know you, she will not know the weak, pathetic woman who tried to keep her from me. The woman who hides in the shadows, and who belongs on the floor, on her knees, at my feet, in the dirt. She will be told that she had no mother just like the rest of them, that they were abandoned by women who were not strong enough to do what must be done.'

The lie stung Margot's conscience more than any of the other diatribe he had come out with since she had first arrived. The concept of Iris growing up believing that she had not been loved by her own mother was more than she could bear. Margot's life had changed the moment Iris had made her dramatic entrance into the world but the reality was that regardless of the bond they had built, Iris would never remember this stage of her life. Should he so wish there was nothing stopping him from completely erasing her from Iris' life.

A guttural roar developed in her throat as she

attempted to get onto her feet, refusing to go down without a fight, but he was waiting for her to give him a reason to finish her off. With one swing he brought the back of his hand down onto the side of her face and she fell to the floor. Before she had chance to move again she felt hands close around her throat and squeeze.

She scratched as his hands desperate to claw them as much as possible to make him relinquish his hold but he didn't seem to be able to feel her, so strong was his desire to remove her from this world.

And yet the small fire of resistance inside her chest had not yet been extinguished. Until her last breath she would put every fibre of her being into fighting her way back to Iris. In a desperate attempt to find anything that might help her she brought her hands down to the floor and frantically felt around for something, anything that would come to her aid. Her nails scraping in the dust and the dirt of the concrete flooring, nothing but empty space surrounding her. As her vision blurred the edges of her fingertips touched something cold and hard. With no idea what it was and with little care she pulled it millimetre by millimetre towards her, knowing that this was her last chance. If she lost her grip on it now it would all be over. As her brain began to burn with the lack of oxygen she rested her middle finger inside what she could now tell was a pole of sorts and dragged it towards her. As the rest of her fingers were able to wrap themselves around it her vision disappeared altogether. She tightened her grip and used her last remaining strength to grasp it tightly lifting it up and swinging it round in front of her until she felt it make direct contact with the side of his face with a sickening crack.

With a rush of oxygen and light flooding her senses she took rasping gasps of breath, each one regenerating her body, flooding her muscles with the energy to fight back. She raised her head to see him holding the side of his face, blood seeping down his cheek.

Seeing him in pain gave her renewed energy, he was cut, he was bleeding, he was not indestructible, she just needed to find the inner strength to do what she needed to do. She still lay on the floor, she was still gasping for air waiting for it to fuel her body with life. With every breath she took her throat burned unbearably.

Dazed but not willing to give up he lunged towards her again. She was not going to let him get his hands on her throat again so she deftly moved herself to one side so that his body weight fell slightly to one side of her. His head came down on the right side of her own and by instinct she turned her face towards his, opened her mouth wide and bit down hard on his ear lobe. She clenched her jaw down like a vice, determined not to let go, as she felt the warm thick blood fill her mouth. His emanating scream filled the room and only goaded her more, how weak and pathetic do you think I am now? With determination and a fire in her belly she had not felt before she snapped her head away from his with speed and she felt the lobe detach itself completely from the side of his head.

He rolled off her screaming, both hands cupped around his ear, the blood now seeping through the gaps in his fingers. Margot managed to scrabble to her feet and take a few steps away from him. Taking in her surroundings, trying to establish an escape route if there was one. There were hanger doors at the far end that had been closed and padlocked behind them and the windows were too high for her to able to climb out of. It was going to end in the death of one of them, or both of them. Piece by piece she would take him apart if she needed to.

She rubbed her throat as she tried to ease the fire that continued to rage inside her whilst she attempted to breathe. Talking was out of the question.

Ben stood with his back to her still clutching his ear taking deep breaths that made his back rise and fall. Then he lowered his arms and walked away from her. She watched him cautiously, unsure what his next move was going to be as he allowed the blood to now flow freely from his ear. He moved across to a table on the far side of the warehouse and picked something up before turning to face her again and walked with purpose back in her direction. His face set, his eyes full of rage, her stomach flipped over as she saw the steely glint of the knife in his hand.

She still had the metal pole in her hand but she didn't fancy her chances against his strength and that knife. She tightened her grip as he got closer. Her heart beating faster as the distance between them grew shorter. She planted her feet readying herself for the fight, the blood rushing in her ears full of adrenaline.

His stride didn't falter, he didn't slow at all as he drew level with her and raised the knife to strike. She struck the first blow with her bar but it was as if he'd lost the ability to feel anything, so strong was his determination to kill her.

He raised to strike again and she attempted to deflect but at the last minute he changed his trajectory, swung underneath her arm and plunged the blade deep into her side.

A gargled gasp erupted from her mouth as she stumbled away from him. He was panting for breath, the effort of their struggle having taken its toll, Sweat pooling on his forehead

She grasped at her side, fear and desperation flooding her body now as she began to accept her fate. When he was ten paces away from her he faltered and turned his head to the side having heard something she had not. In response she followed his gaze only to see the hanger doors implode inwards as a car exploded into the warehouse with an cacophony of noise. It collided with everything in its path, knocking over tables and cabinets and headed directly for Ben causing him to dive out of it's way.

Margot in a state of shock watched as it came to a stop in front of her.

'Get in!' someone shouted as the rear door was opened for her from the inside.

Not needing to be asked twice she leapt into the rear of the car, scrambling at the door trying to close it as they reversed at speed back out the way they had come. The car bounced up and down as they drove over the hanger doors they had just knocked off their hinges and she was thrown to the side as they violently spun around in a cloud of burning rubber. Margot now in a heap in the foot well clung on to anything she could rest her hands on as the car sped off into the night.

Chapter 37

Margot kept her head down in the car, her hands held over her head in the brace position anticipating a further impact. Her adrenaline pounding, her senses on high alert. The car was still screeching away from the warehouse, swerving around corners and cutting through lights from the sound of it based on the horn of indignation that followed them. Margot was relieved that they seemed to be putting distance between her and Ben but she felt panic rising in her chest as she realised she was being drive away from Iris. She let out a strangled cry unsure what to do or how to act.

'Margot, it's okay we've got you' she heard a familiar voice say.

She looked up to see Dana on the back seat next to her, offering out her hand to help her out of the foot well.

Margot felt a rush of emotion. After everything she'd been through with Dana, the fact that it was her face she was now looking into was overwhelming. Everything was overwhelming. The pain, the loss, the deception, the unexpected friendship.

The pain in her side was unbearable as she clutched at her side and felt it hot with blood.

Dana, bending over to help her up saw her dark crimson hand pull away.

'Sasha, put your foot down she's bleeding'

'What the hell happened in there?' came Sasha's voice from the drivers seat.

Margot attempted to speak to try to find the words but just gasping for breath was more than she could manage. Her hand dropped away from her side onto the floor as the noise and the lights and the world around her as she knew it melted away and she collapsed unconscious on the floor.

When Margot next opened her eyes she was lying on a bed. There was a hive of activity around her as women tended to her and ran around getting supplies.

She attempted to raise her head and found the pain in her neck made that impossible.

She felt a hand rest on her arm and looked into Dana's eyes. She attempted to speak but Dana shook her head.

'There's time Margot, rest up and catch your breath. You're safe now, we've got you.'

'No' she croaked, fighting against the fog in her brain that made her want to sleep for eternity and the fire in her throat that roared with every rasping attempt at speech. She had to make sure they knew.

If she took her last breath in this bed she had to make sure that someone had heard her message.

'He took them'

'Who Margot? Who was that man? Did he take Iris?' Dana looked worried, obviously concerned for the child's welfare.

'He took all of them, your children'

She could see a few of the women around her looking from one to another. Some with mild looks of confusion, others with looks of pity. They obviously thought she was losing her mind, that the head injury had been worse than they'd first anticipated.

'I think she's saying that that man whoever he was is responsible for the terminations. Was it him Margot? Did he lead the testing programme?

'No.' She was getting frustrated now, did they not realise how much effort it was taking her to talk, that all the extra noise in the room was making her feel nauseous. That if they would just listen to her she could make them see, then they could start to feel how she felt.

'Ben didn't kill the babies. He was injecting them with a serum but it was nothing to do with the virus. He's developed them, changed them. He didn't kill them, they were sedated when you delivered them… they're alive.'

Like a fog descending on the room a silence spread through the women. Some were still busying themselves around her as she had been speaking but as her words sunk in, their backs, still bent over medicines and bandages, stiffened as they processed her words. Most continued to stare at her, unable to comprehend the reality of what she had voiced. Some further back had caught only parts of what she had said and were now checking in for clarification. Those nearest her were in silence, barely a breath was taken.

Margot knew the impact of what she had said but she needed them to understand. A part of her still felt like she was in grave danger, she could not yet compute that she had been saved from the grips of death and that she was in any way safe. Whilst she believed she was still at risk of harm it was imperative to her that she made them understand. She couldn't be the only one that knew the truth.

'You're lying' Sasha announced breaking the silence. 'He was lying to you. I saw my son, I delivered my son and he was dead.'

'Did you hold him? Did you feel him not breathing? Did anybody?' Margot's vision had started to come into sharper focus as she put all of her energy into this conversation.

'They didn't let us, they said the risk was too high.' Someone muttered from further away. The dawning realisation setting in that nobody had proof otherwise.

'They're alive' Margot repeated, knowing how hard it was for them to hear what she was saying. 'He's raised them, he said they've all been developed differently, all been given a slightly different cocktail but they're alive.'

The noise steadily grew, most started crying. Some tears of joy at the resurrection of their children, others tears of confusion, anger and disbelief at the years they had lost. Everyone had a burst of energy as they frenetically discussed what this meant, and what they would do and how could they find them and could they get them back. Their lives from this moment would never be the same again, after all these years they finally knew the truth and Margot forgotten and alone in the corner of the room slumped back onto the bed and let the black wave of unconsciousness once more crash down upon her.

Margot slept solidly for the next two days. Depleted of all emotion, energy and fight, her body had subconsciously decided to go into hibernation. People kept coming in to check on her, give her fluids and medication to block the pain in her head which still throbbed relentlessly in the background and check the stitches that had been put in whilst she was unconscious. When she finally did open her eyes she was overwhelmed by the light and the noise that attacked her senses and so she closed them again and drifted off once more.

Eventually her body began to awaken itself and she caught snatches of conversation from the women around her as she flitted in and out of sleep. There was a buzz of energy around her, she could feel the desperation from those around her for her to wake up and tell them more about what she knew.

Margot knew the second she was visibly back in the land of the living she would be expected to lead, to have hatched some marvellous plan that would bring all their children back. In her dreams Iris was lost in a sea of children and when she finally caught hold of her hand and tried to pull her back her daughter looked at her like she was a stranger and pulled herself free to return to the sea of floating limbs.

She heard the door open and more mumbling of whispered conversations reached her ears. She kept her eyes closed once more but she was more awake than she had been in a while and her breathing became less shallow as her body began to feel more energised. She heard a stool being dragged to her bedside and sensed someone sitting down close to her side before a hand came to rest on her shoulder.

'Margot, it's time to wake up now.'

Even these words set Margot's mind racing. She didn't want to wake up. Like a child being awoken before a Monday morning at school she told herself if she just kept her eyes closed she wouldn't have to face the responsibilities that loomed over her, threatened to engulf her.

'Margot, I know you're tired, but it's time to come back to us, we've got a lot to do.'

Margot kept her eyes closed but a traitor tear gave her away, escaping smoothly from the corner of her eye, slipping down her cheek and coming to rest on her pillow. Unable to keep up the pretence any longer she wiped her face slowly and turned her head to the other side to look into the eyes of Sasha.

'They're alive?' Sasha whispered, her eyes searching for confirmation of the words Margot had stumbled over when she'd first returned, 'you're sure?'

Margot nodded her head, even this slow movement brought back piercing hot pains in the back of her head.

'That's what he said.'

'You believe him?' Sasha wasn't going to allow herself to hope until she had seen from Margot herself that it something worth believing in.

'He was killing me whilst he told me, it was something he wanted me to take to my grave. It was his proudest secret.'

Sasha's grip tightened on her shoulder, the ramifications of the confirmation she had just received seeping in.

'Sasha, I can't do this. I was going back to fight for Iris but it's too big now. There are too many people involved and I can't be the saviour that you all need me to be. I know you're going to be angry with me, I know you're going to try and tell me to sort myself out, but I can't fight anymore.'

In spite of herself she looked into Sasha eye's, anticipating the frustration that she was bound to find there from her inability to carry on. Instead she saw compassion and grief and empathy.

'I don't mind admitting that I was jealous of you and everything you had when you arrived here. You had everything I ever wanted and I envied you. But then I began to see that you have been through so much more than we could ever understand. You have been so brave Margot and you protected Iris so well and I'm so sorry for what's happened.'

Margot just listened. A few more tears escaped

her but she had no control over them and her face remained passive. She couldn't muster the energy to be angry, sad, forgiving or anything else. She wondered if a part of her had died, if she had lost, perhaps forever, the ability to feel anything.

'I'm done Sasha, just leave me alone please.'

'No, I'm not going to do that, you were there for us and now we're here for you. We're not asking anything of you this time Margot but I need you to know that we've got your back. You're one of us and you've done more than should have ever been asked of you. I want you to try and stand up if you can, I want to show you that you don't need to bear the weight of this on your own anymore.'

Margot wanted to do whatever it was going to take to get Sasha to leave her alone. To let her return to the void that was the world she now found herself in without Iris. Despair was easy, effortless, and she wanted to let it wash over her, allow herself to sink below the surface until eventually she wouldn't need to actively think about sinking, she would be pulled effortlessly down to the very depth of the blackness where she would gladly disappear forever. That's what she wanted now to just simply slip away. To go somewhere she hoped there would be peace for her aching soul. Yet Sasha was pulling her reluctantly back up to the surface using her own strength to drag both of them out of the depths back to the oxygen and back to the pain.

She tentatively sat up and swung her legs around to the side of the bed. This small movement made the room spin and she closed her eyes whilst the sensation took over her. Sasha physically took her by the hand, put another around her back and took her weight. Her bruises were already starting to heal but the emotional effort of just moving her body, of engaging her brain to elicit movement was too much for her to handle and she was grateful for the support.

Taking slow steadying steps the two of them walked out of the hospital room together out onto the gangway and looked down onto the central area of the camp. Whereas this had once been a sedentary relaxed space for people to meet or hold light discussions it was now a hive of activity. Multiple tables had been set up, each with a team of women working around it talking enthusiastically, engrossed in building layouts or research papers. No one noticed her above them looking down on them and for that she was grateful. It was the first time she had sensed hope radiating out of the group. They were no longer just angry, they were determined, focused, methodical and from the looks on their faces, driven to succeed.

Margot watched them work for a minute. They were changed now she could see that. No longer looking for a leader to show them the way, they were taking control of their own destiny. Now there was the possibility of their own children being returned to them they had a renewed purpose. At the far end of the room she saw Dana move from one table to another moving between teams, co-ordinating their work, nodding in approval.

'Why did Dana come for me?'

'I think she realised as soon as you'd left that she'd made a mistake. She came to find me to tell me what had happened and I went upstairs to see if I could find out where you'd gone. There were messages from Dr Fenwick I recognised the code name. She was telling you not to go, something had spooked her, she thought it was a trap. So we decided to go get you back.'

'The car? How did you get me out of there?'

'Well, that's why it took us a bit longer to get to you. We had to walk into town and flag down a taxi. Dana brought the spare car key though so when we saw it abandoned by the hedge we were able to get it started and bust you out.'

'You must have been there just as they were taking Iris away. Did you see anything when you were coming in?' The talking was now making her throat dry and burn with the effort but she had to know if there was any way of finding where Iris had been taken to.

'No, we didn't see anything, I'm sorry. By the time we got there it was just you and that man.'

Margot lowered her head again to look at the women. Desperation for all that she had now lost seeping into her bones.

Dana, walking around the room below her however had never looked so energised. She, like many of the women around her, finally had something to live for. Their lives here were no longer about hiding and healing. There was an uprising amongst them, they were an army in the making.

As Dana raised her head to speak to someone her eyes were caught by the movement of people above and she noticed Margot and Sasha.

She smiled warmly at Margot, a smile that conveyed her thanks and gratitude in the same way that Sasha's had done. Margot was no longer their conflicted leader which in turn now allowed her to be her friend.

Dana brought her hands up and began to clap, keeping her eyes on Margot. Bewildered, the women closest to her followed her gaze and upon seeing Margot they too began to join in. All smiling, all in awe of the gift that she had given them. The clapping spread throughout the room, interspersed with cheers and whistles. The noise, whilst somewhat overwhelming to Margot's still aching head, was warm and comforting. Never before had she been in a room with this group of women without there being conflict and tension. But today it seemed that all of that had been forgotten, today they were as one.

'This isn't just your fight now Margot' Sasha turned to her speaking over the noise of the crowd below 'you've been alone all this time but now you've got us and we're as invested in this as you are. You're in pain and we've all been where you are now, we know it's debilitating strength and we also know that you will rise from it. But whilst your shackled in grief we will carry the load. We've processed our pain, our waiting is over, now it's our time to rise. You're not alone anymore Margot. It's time to go and get our babies. We've lost them once, we've got nothing else to lose and everything to gain. That makes us a pretty fierce force to be reckoned with.'

Margot looked back at the group below her and could see that Sasha was right, but for now it took all of her strength to remain standing. She gripped onto the rail in front of her for support whilst the clapping died down and the women returned to their task at hand.

Sasha acknowledging that Margot was now struggling to support her own weight once again put her arm around her and supported her back into bed. Margot collapsed onto it, breathing deeply as if she had run a marathon.

An elderly woman came over to support her, lifting her legs to the centre of the bed and plumping her pillows to support her shoulders. This woman was bent over and frail looking and yet was capable of far more than Margot was right now. She despaired at her pain and lack of energy wondering if she would ever get back to her former strength.

As Margot closed her eyes and prepared to drift off to sleep once more she felt the old woman take her hand. Her fingers despite their age were strong, her grip firm. Her silky soft papery skin wrinkled under Margot's course cold fingers.

Margot looked up into her watery blue eyes enveloped by laughter lines from years gone by. The lady's frail frame straightened itself up in front of her, her determination and energy palpable as she tightened her grip on Margot's hands, a wry smile escaping from the corners of her mouth.

'Sweetie, he's got no idea of the wrath that is about to rain down on him.'

Chapter 38

In the days that passed Margot slowly began to heal physically. Her bruises developed a rainbow of colours all over her body and her stitches began to tighten as her skin began to fuse itself together. Being able to visually see the effects of her interaction with Ben validated in her mind that it had really happened. But once the bruises faded away and the stitches had been removed she would be left with no less hurt. She would still have the pain of separation from Iris and the gnawing anxiety of what was happening to her.

The only small glimmer of hope that she had to hold onto was that in his own twisted way Ben didn't want any harm to come to Iris. He would, she hoped, have given her the medicine she needed for whatever fever it was she was fighting and no doubt have her hooked up to all kinds of machinery to research whatever modifications he had given to her.

All Margot could do was remind herself of this,

convince herself that Iris would be okay for the time being and allow herself the time she needed to build up her strength again to go and get her back.

She had not heard from Sy once since she had returned to the camp. She assumed he must know that something had gone down, with all of his connections and involvements on both sides. Perhaps he had been playing her all along, perhaps he had come into some difficulty and had to go into hiding himself. Margot found that she couldn't muster up the energy to wonder too much about him. He was an anomaly to her. Someone who compounded her insecurities and gave her more questions than answers.

From her hospital bed Margot looked across at the clock on the wall, it was five am but she knew that any hope of sleep was long gone. Having done nothing else but sleep over the past week her body clock was completely out of sync. She felt like her blood was itching, her feet were twitchy, she needed to get up. What she needed she realised was fresh air and head space.

She had started leaving her room occasionally over the past few days, attempting to do so at a quieter time of the day so that she didn't have to see or speak to people but it appeared that the sedentary way of life around camp was truly over. There was a constant buzz of energy day and night from the women. It seemed like there was nothing that could dampen their spirits now they knew their children were out there. Even now at this ungodly hour she could hear people milling around and talking.

Tentatively swinging her legs out of bed, she slipped out of the room and walked along the elevated walkway. She had always known that there was a route somewhere to gain access to the roof but had not been up there before herself.

Walking around the gangway she noticed a ladder at the far end that must, she assumed, provide her access. She wasn't in the best condition to be climbing but something in her craved solitude and exploration.

Climbing the ladder made her wound sting with every step but she didn't care. She gritted her teeth against the pain and ascended through a caged tunnel leading to a hatched door above. As she pushed the hatch open she felt the light early morning breeze float down to greet her and she felt instantly better.

Emerging onto the roof of the factory she looked out onto the expanse of the North sea stretching ahead of her and the most incredible sun rise breaking over the horizon. For a second it took her breath away. She had forgotten that the world could be beautiful.

The colours radiating from the rising sun brought warmth to her soul and gave her more hope than any of the words that had been spoken to her over the past few days.

She walked to the edge of the roof, three stories high and towering over the coastal path below and sat down allowing her legs to swing free beneath her.

She didn't feel fear, she knew no harm would come to her, she knew it wasn't her time. Her time would come but before that happened she had a job to do. She would get her daughter back; she would expose Ben and what he had done to the world and she would help to reunite those children with their mothers. That was her only purpose now.

She closed her eyes and felt the warmth of the light of a new day envelop her. Breathing in the salty air and listening to the rhythmical lapping of the waves in time with her own heartbeat.

Iris was out there; Iris was alive and waiting for her and they would one day be reunited. She had to believe that, she had to keep going.

She projected an image in her mind of the two of them walking hand in hand on the beach below. She would make it happen.

'I'm coming for you Iris' she whispered into the breeze, willing her words to be carried across the sea and find their way to her daughter.

'Just hold on, I'm coming.'

Acknowledgements

They say it takes a village to raise a child and it seems the same is true when it comes to writing a novel. Writing The Eye of the Storm has been a privilege but could have very easily stayed in the safety of my own head where no one could touch it.

To that end, I am hugely grateful to my wonderful group of family and friends who have willingly read the many versions of the book over the years and provided me with their wisdom, support and feedback in return. Had it not been for each and every one of you this book would not have made it to print. Your support has meant the world to me.

To the incredibly talented Gemma Cronnie for the gorgeous cover design and for being such a wonderful cheerleader, encouraging me to carry on when I wanted to quit and even getting me out there on social media (no mean feat).

To my family who stand by me through thick and thin, listen to my crazy ideas and support me in so many ways raising my little family, thank you.

Finally, to my two beautiful daughters. You've given me a front row seat to the best show in town. You've made me want to be better, fight harder and love stronger as we muddle our way together through this crazy thing called life. I am so proud of the young women that you are growing up to be and I hope that you both have the courage to put yourself into the arena of life, be bold, dream big and if all else fails, fake it 'til you make it.

Printed in Great Britain
by Amazon

51571559R00209